Low Tide,
Lunan Bay

Low Tide, Lunan Bay

Rosalie Warren

ROBERT HALE · LONDON

ISBN 978-0-7090-8753-3

Robert Hale Limited
Clerkenwell House
Clerkenwell Green
London EC1R 0HT

www.halebooks.com

2 4 6 8 10 9 7 5 3 1

To Paul, with love

Typeset in 10½/13½pt Plantin.
Printed in the UK by the MPG Books Group

chapter one

'So, we finally get to meet Keith Brinnett, creator of *The Great Green Wizard*. How does it feel, Keith, to be a world-famous author?'

Though Keith's smile and the hint of a frown that accompanied it were clearly intended to convey modesty, Abbie could see the relish just below.

'It feels pretty good,' he said. 'Though "world-famous" may be a bit of an exaggeration.'

The middle-aged female interviewer gave her characteristic simper. 'But you *are* world-famous. Children all over the world are clamouring to know when your next book is coming out. Children as young as five – even ones who can't read yet.'

Keith leaned forward to catch the eye of his partner, Fiona. 'That's why the illustrations play such an important part.'

Fiona beamed at him. Abbie had noted from the start the way that her tight emerald green sweater-dress revealed an unflattering bulge in her tummy. Surely not a pregnancy bulge? That was impossible, since Keith had undergone a vasectomy a couple of years after the twins were born. No, Fiona's bulge was merely a small imperfection in a woman who was otherwise, by all accounts, perfect.

Seated on either side of Keith and Fiona were the twins, Lizzie and Sarah, aged eleven. As the camera swung round to them, Abbie beamed with pride. They were her daughters, no matter what.

She was glad to be watching the interview on her own, since it was possible she would start to cry at some stage – or even throw a vase at the wall.

She had come home from work early to watch it live. Lizzie and Sarah had gone straight from school to a friend's house, excited at the prospect of seeing themselves on television.

The twins were almost identical in appearance, with Abbie's fine, straight blond hair and grey eyes. Lizzie was leaning slightly forward, a smile not far off. Sarah, on the other hand, slouched, biting her lip as she always did when nervous, arms folded across her body.

'Now let's move on to your daughters, who, I think you said in your *Times* article, were the main source of inspiration for your books.' The presenter smiled at the twins.

They grinned back, Lizzie more broadly than Sarah. Sarah began crossing and uncrossing her legs in the way she always did when bored.

'Lizzie and Sarah, I understand that your daddy's books came out of the bedtime stories he used to tell you when you were tiny. Is that right?'

Sarah and Lizzie both flinched at 'daddy', and possibly at 'tiny' as well.

'Yes, that's right,' said Lizzie. 'We used to like stories about animals and magic so Dad made up a wizard who was a crocodile.'

'How wonderful. So you two were his very first audience? Tell me, Sarah, did either of you ever suggest improvements to the stories? You know, ways to make them better?'

At least she had correctly identified which twin was which.

'No,' said Sarah. 'We always liked the wizard just as he was.'

'Ah,' said the interviewer. 'So you were an appreciative audience right from the start. Did your daddy—?'

Lizzie interrupted. 'But we told Fiona when she got the drawings wrong. She did the wizard the wrong colour of green to start with. We told her to make him darker. And not so scary in case it frightened the little ones.'

'Really?' The interviewer's face was all smiles now. 'And what did Fiona think of that?'

Fiona's voice came out unnaturally high. It gave her an air of girlishness that Abbie found somehow creepy. That had been her impression of Fiona the first time they met – something strange and not quite right about her. She'd mentioned it to Keith but he'd dismissed it as jealousy. Perhaps that was all it was.

'I was only too pleased to take Sarah's and Lizzie's opinions into account, given how closely associated they were with the stories right from the start.'

Such formal diction – another sign of nerves?

Keith intervened at this point, perhaps wanting to get back into the limelight. 'And, of course, Fiona's suggestions have been invaluable to me as well. My work got a real boost when Fiona first read it and came up with her exciting ideas.'

What about *my* suggestions and all the help I gave you with the proofreading? Abbie wondered whether she would get a mention, too, but knew better than to expect it.

'So *The Great Green Wizard* has been very much a family effort, right from the start?' said the interviewer.

'Mum helped a lot with Dad's books,' said Sarah in a low voice.

At first it seemed that the interviewer had not heard her and was going to sweep on regardless. Then she raised her eyebrows. 'Mum? Oh, your mother, of course. That would be your first wife, Keith?'

Keith's chin went up in annoyance and he folded his arms. 'Yes, my ex-wife.' The last word had an upward inflection, as though to ask, What about her? What has she to do with any of us? Then his neck and face reddened as Sarah spoke again.

'Mum used to help Dad type his stories. When he got fed up he used to bring him his favourite bacon and cheese sandwiches.'

Something gave way inside Abbie and she didn't know whether to smile or cry.

'That was nice,' said the interviewer, glancing at Fiona, who had folded her own arms across her tummy bulge.

Keith pursed his lips and said nothing. Abbie felt a surge of pleasure and was glad she had remembered to switch on the video recorder. She would be able to replay Keith's discomfort again and again, whenever she needed to.

Fiona gave a big false smile which gave Abbie almost as much pleasure as Keith's blush.

The interviewer paused for a moment and then said, 'Well, Keith and Fiona, let's hear about the new book that is coming out on Tuesday. Number three in *The Great Green Wizard* series?'

'Yes, that's right,' said Keith, turning to smile at Fiona, perhaps to comfort her after the disconcerting mention of his former wife.

'And I, for one, will be rushing out to my local bookshop to buy it,' said the interviewer. 'Even if I have to queue all night. Keith and Fiona, and, of course, Lizzie and Sarah – thank you very much for joining us today and may I wish you every success.'

When the four of them were gone, the interviewer said, 'That was the incredible family who created between them *The Great Green Wizard*.'

Abbie clicked off the TV and pulled herself up from the sofa. Her palms were sore from digging her fingernails in.

It was time to make herself some supper. The girls were staying overnight with their friend, so for once she was on her own.

Where was her eyebrow pencil? Abbie didn't wear much make-up most days, but after the interview she felt the need to prove something. She smudged navy kohl pencil into the corners of her eyes, as recommended by the magazines to make them look bigger.

Kate, Abbie's office mate in the Department of Physics, had persuaded her to invite her colleagues and friends for an evening in the pub to celebrate her divorce.

'A celebration's the last thing I feel like,' Abbie replied. 'I need to put it all behind me and move on. I'm trying to forget about Keith as much as I can and make a new life of my own.'

'Exactly,' said Kate. 'And this is the way to do it – go out with your new friends, enjoy yourself, get pissed and wake up next day ready to go forward.'

'Going out and getting pissed isn't my style.'

Kate was single. Although, at thirty-four, she was only four years younger than Abbie, the difference in their ages often seemed more like a decade.

'Time you changed your style, then,' she said. 'If you ever want to meet anyone new you'll have to start getting out a bit. You're not going to find a queue of men outside the office or knocking at the door of your bungalow.'

'I don't want a new man,' Abbie said. 'Not now and probably never.'

But she had agreed to a low-key celebration, and was in front of the mirror now, regretting her decision. What was the point, she wondered, of meeting the colleagues she saw at work every day, plus a few neighbours? None of them was a potential partner, that was clear. Even if she'd been looking for love, which she wasn't.

In spite of her efforts with the eyebrow pencil, Abbie's eyes continued to nestle unassumingly in their sockets. Applying mascara never worked, either, since her lashes were as fine and fair as her hair and almost invisible until she reached the point of over-load where the mascara formed sticky lumps.

She'd been a stone or so overweight for several years, but the stress of the marriage break-up had got rid of that. She liked her new figure and the extra energy she'd gained, but expected to put the weight back on again now that the divorce was over – especially if she kept accepting the chocolate bars that Kate stored in her desk drawer.

The celebration was to be held at a pub called the Mouse and Man – something to do with best-laid plans and Robbie Burns, Abbie supposed. The place was shabby and sepia-coloured, reeking of stale beer and rank, mouldy carpets. The lighting had a greenish tinge which was far from flattering. She could only imagine what colour it made her skin.

The pub's advantage was being close to the Physics Department, which made it a convenient venue for the common round of cele-bratory and consolatory events.

Abbie left her middle-aged Fiesta in her workday parking space outside the physics building, deciding that if she drank more than her customary half-lager she could abandon it overnight and take a taxi home. But she couldn't see that being necessary. She was quite prepared for no one other than herself and Kate to turn up.

A surprising number of people did appear, however. Most of Abbie's departmental colleagues were present, including Professor Fred Steadman, the head of department, who greeted her with an enthusiastic whoop and a splashing of his beer over the table. It looked as though he had been there for some time – had perhaps even gone straight from work.

Once Abbie was settled with her drink, he asked, 'So, my dear, now you are free from marital constraints, what do you plan to do with the rest of your life? Are you brimming over with interesting ideas?'

'*This* is what I'm doing with it,' she said, taking a first sip of the full pint of lager he'd insisted on buying her. 'I don't mean drinking …' (this caused a splutter from Fred and more beer on the table). 'I mean working here at Invercarse University. Living on my own – without Keith, that is. Making a home for the twins.' Abbie felt stupid, as though she had said too much.

'Laudable,' said Fred. 'Self-sufficiency – a very worthy aim. And indeed, why should you have any need of us menfolk at all? We are only good for one thing.' He smiled, revealing stained yellow teeth, picked up his tankard and downed half his bitter ale in a mouthful.

Abbie gave an uncertain smile. She assumed that Fred was joking but it was sometimes difficult to tell and he had a slight edge to his voice.

Kate, sitting down beside her, butted in. 'Well said, Professor Steadman.'

They were all on first-name terms in the Physics Department, but Kate liked to use titles when it suited her.

Kate continued, 'Though I don't know how long Abbie will be able to keep up her nunlike existence. Men may only be good for one thing but there comes a time when every woman needs a bit of the old one-thing.'

Fred grinned with delight and leaned over to plant a kiss on Kate's bare shoulder. She pretended to squirm away in disgust, at the same time giving a girlish giggle. Abbie felt her usual rush of awkwardness when Kate flirted with the male staff. It's only banter, she told herself, a bit of harmless fun. But she never knew how to respond.

'Come on, Abbie, admit it – you must be missing the old one-thing,' said Kate. 'No one can be a nun for ever. Or have you got a secret source of pleasure you haven't told us about?'

Abbie's cheeks burned. Any minute now, Kate would start to talk about vibrators. Better say something quickly.

'Och, I've given up on sex.' She tried to sound casual. 'I don't miss it anywhere near as much as I'd have expected.'

Kate gave a laugh that was half-snort and half-sneeze, choking on her drink so that Fred was obliged to thump her on the back. Her pink, low-cut, sparkly top slipped down further, showing a tan line.

'Oops.' Kate rearranged her clothes with rather more of a fuss than necessary, while Fred looked on with interest. 'I didn't intend to reveal my assets quite so early in the evening.'

Fred gave an appreciative gurgle. Feeling a sudden rush of stomach acid in her gullet, Abbie found an excuse to move away. The neighbours who had helped her move into her bungalow just after Christmas had arrived, and she needed to welcome them.

Later, Kate was well on the way to being drunk. She left the bar where she'd been chatting to Pam, the departmental secretary, and sat down at Abbie's table.

The conversation there had fallen into a pleasant, sleepy lull. Steve, one of the computer technicians, renowned for his shyness, had been telling Abbie about his twin brothers. She'd been interested, comparing them with her own twins, and had enjoyed seeing Steve relaxed for the first time. He pulled himself upright, she noticed, when Kate appeared, and his brow crinkled into a furrow.

Kate plunged into the silence. 'Abbie – it's time you started looking for a new man. You can't spend the rest of your life on your own, can you now, let's face it?'

'I don't see why not,' Abbie said, hoping her words were not too slurred. 'And I'm not on my own, anyway. I've got my daughters, and my friends and....' she looked at the faces around the table, 'nice people to work with and a good job. I'm not looking for anything else. Not yet.'

Kate put her glass down, spilling only a little of the lurid blue liquor that almost matched her eyes. 'The best way to get over a bad relationship is to start a new one. A better one. The thing is, you need to go into the next one on your own terms. Make it clear from the start what you want. What you'll stand for and what you won't. You need clear ground lines. Ground rules. Guidelines. That sort of thing.'

Had Kate ever had a proper relationship, Abbie wondered, a serious one? She had a boyfriend called Salvador, who flew in every few weeks from some distant part of the world where, he claimed, his job took him. He was an IT consultant, highly paid and much in demand. Abbie worried that most of the feelings were on Kate's side.

Kate was getting into her stride. Steve and a number of others were listening and she warmed to her audience.

'If I were single, I think I'd try online dating,' she said. 'It's the best way to go about it these days. Though you have to be careful, of course – you don't want some of these guys who lurk around in chat-rooms. I think if I were Abbie I'd go on one of those websites where you can display your attributes ...' she giggled, '... to anyone who is interested.'

Fred Steadman had just joined the group. He leaned towards Abbie and winked.

'Perhaps Abbie doesn't want to display her attributes to all and sundry,' he said, his voice thick with alcohol and possibly lust. 'Perhaps she wants to reserve them for a select few.'

'Now see, you've embarrassed the lassie,' Kate scolded him. 'Hush with your lewd comments, Fred. She's blushed as pink as a hydrangea. Abbie, just ignore him. Back to what I was saying – you need to find yourself a good online dating agency. The sort where they vet people first, to make sure they're not predatory bastards after a good time. You'll need to get your details registered, get a decent picture taken....'

She surveyed Abbie with a frown, head on one side. 'Of course, you'll have to get your hair done. A proper cut. Then ask someone to take a flattering photo. Steve will oblige, I'm sure, with his swishy new camera.'

Steve started to nod then stopped, his cheeks reddening. Abbie gave him a quick smile to show him she hadn't taken offence – not at him, anyway. Kate was a different matter. How long had she known Kate? Four months. It was far too soon, Abbie thought, for Kate to make such personal comments, especially in company.

Abbie wished she were at home, alone in the double bed that almost filled the bedroom of her bungalow. She'd reflected, after buying it, that a single would have made more sense.

'Don't worry,' she said, 'I'm not about to try online dating. I don't want a man just now. Perhaps it's you who should be having a go at it, Kate.'

To Abbie's horror, Kate blushed deep pink and her eyes filled up. Could she be going to cry?

'Now, that's not a nice thing to say, is it?' said Steve. 'We all know that Kate already has her man.'

Then why is she so sensitive? Abbie wanted to ask. But she kept quiet, afraid of making things worse.

Kate mopped her eyes with a tissue and rooted in her handbag for a mirror to inspect her smudged mascara. Abbie noticed that Kate's silver-sequinned bag, which she had admired earlier, was rather cheap and aimed at the teenage market. Then she felt ashamed.

'I'm sorry,' she muttered, not sure why she was saying it.

'It's OK,' said Kate. 'Don't worry. It's just that … well, I can't help it if I don't see Salvador very often. He's always so busy with his work.'

'Of course.' Abbie was feeling guilty now. 'I didn't mean to suggest there was anything wrong with your relationship.' She had the feeling she was making things worse, but in her semi-inebriated state she seemed to have lost her powers of tact.

'Good.' Kate sniffed. 'Because let me tell you – my Salvador more than makes up for it when I do see him. He's a wonderful lover.'

'I'm sure he is.' Abbie felt silly saying this, especially when Fred Steadman gave a little snigger.

'Och, well, no one is perfect,' said Pam, who had just pulled her stool up to their table.

Abbie was always pleased to see Pam. She was tall and graceful, with flawless skin and a sophisticated haircut that made the most of her fifty-something grey. She gave Abbie hope for her future. If Pam could look as good as that in her fifties, Abbie had plenty of time.

Pam continued: 'It sounds good to me to have a partner who'll give you a bit of peace when you want it. I wish Steph would leave me to myself once in a while. She's lovely but she can be very possessive.'

They lingered over their drinks for some time after that, but no one offered to buy another round. Since Abbie's *faux pas*, if that was what it was, the heart seemed to have gone out of the discussion. Abbie was exhausted and longed, once more, to be home. It would have to be a taxi now, of course.

'It's time I was on my way,' said Kate after a few more minutes. 'I need my beauty sleep.'

None of them dared to agree or disagree with that.

As they emerged from the pub into the chill of the early May night, Fred whispered. 'You're a lovely woman, Abbie. If you ever want a bit of company, just give me a ring.' He tapped his chunky, old-fashioned mobile phone as though it might be a source of future phallic delight.

'No, it's OK,' Abbie said. 'I'm quite happy on my own.'

Getting ready for bed, she wondered if she had imagined what Fred had said. Part of her – most of her – hoped so. Having Fred trying to flirt with her would add unnecessary complications at work.

On the other hand, she could not help feeling a little flattered. Flattered – by the attentions of a sixty-two-year-old with yellow teeth and a propensity to chat up young female colleagues? That told her more about her current state than she wished to know.

Perhaps it *was* time to look for someone new?

No. Peace and stability, the chance to recover, was what she and the twins needed now. Perhaps in two or three years' time, depending on how things went, she might be ready to move on.

She had her depression to consider, too. Though she was free of it now, the doctor had warned her to be on guard because it might come back. Although she kept reminding herself it was nothing to be ashamed of, she hadn't been able to talk about it yet, not even to Kate. How could she tell a new boyfriend that she had such a condition, one that might be with her, on and off at least, for the rest of her life?

If only she could get Keith's smug grin out of her head. He and Fiona, laughing with the twins on the TV show, with Fiona's dark shiny hair swinging and dancing for the camera. Even Fiona's tummy bulge had, by now, lost its ability to comfort.

At ten to three Abbie was still awake in her enormous, hard-mattressed, half-empty bed. She would have to be at work in good time tomorrow to compile the staff-hours spreadsheet for Fred. She must try to stop thinking and go to sleep.

But instead she began to muse on Kate's attitude and behaviour. She had begun to think of Kate as a friend, but tonight she had been almost unbearably pushy about the online dating idea. What was she trying to do – force Abbie into trying something she didn't have the courage to try for herself? Salvador appeared to be a far from satisfactory boyfriend, however much Kate sang his praises.

Yet she couldn't dislike Kate – there was something warm and appealing about her – the suggestion of something deeper and worthy of friendship, if one could only get below that superficial glitz. And her advice, in spite of the unfortunate way she presented it, could well be sound. Perhaps looking for a new relationship was not something to be ruled out altogether.

chapter two

'So when are you going to log on to that dating agency?' Kate asked. She had only just arrived at the office and was taking off her outdoor shoes.

'Hang on a minute....' Abbie saved the spreadsheet she'd been working on since her arrival at five to nine. Struggling with the weariness that weighed on her eyelids after a poor night's sleep, she watched Kate changing into one of the pairs of high-heeled sandals she kept in the bottom of her filing cabinet. 'Sorry, what did you say?'

'The internet dating we were talking about last night. You said you might give it a go.'

'I'm sure I said no such thing,' Abbie protested. 'And if I did, it was under the influence of alcohol. I've no plans to do anything about dating for the time being. Perhaps I'll give it a try in about ten years, when I've got over my divorce.'

'I hate to say this,' said Kate, looking as though she was enjoying it. 'But if you're not careful you'll be left on the shelf. In ten years' time you'll be, how old – forty-eight? Do you really think there are any men out there looking for a forty-eight-year-old woman?'

'I'm sure there are plenty.' Abbie glanced back at her spreadsheet. It wasn't at all interesting, but it was better than talking about online dating. Also, she was aware of a deadline looming for a departmental meeting at two. 'What about forty-eight-year-old men, for example?'

Kate snorted. 'They'll all be looking for women in their twenties.'

'Well, fifty-eight-year-olds, then? Surely, however old I get, there'll be men the same age or older looking for women? Or why shouldn't a younger man be interested, come to that?'

'Because they're not.'

'Anyway, I'm not forty-eight. And perhaps I'll choose to stay single, anyway. For ever. It would make life simpler.'

Abbie cast her eyes down at her screen again. The figures there were the teaching allocations for next year – the lists of which lecturers would teach which classes, for how many hours and at what times of day. The issuing of this document always caused hackles to rise. Any mistakes made in the office at this stage would only make things worse.

Kate was making no attempt to work, even though she, too, had material to prepare for the afternoon meeting. Abbie could see part of Kate's screen from where she sat, and Salvador's beach photo was visible, every pore and individual chest hair on display.

'You're a hopeless case.' Kate fiddled with her cuticles, peeling off bits of skin and dropping them on her desk in a way that set Abbie's teeth on edge. 'I think the only way you'll get a man is if I take you in hand and oganize it all for you.'

'No thanks. As I told you last night, I don't want a man – not now, or in the near future. If you don't mind, Kate, I need to get these figures done, before Pam comes in screaming for them.'

Kate grunted. 'Why don't you just invent the numbers? The lecturers will only complain, anyway. They're like little kids. "It's not fair, I've got two hours more teaching per week than him! She's got a smaller class! Why have I got a nine o'clock lecture every morning? Why've I been given the first years again?" '

But Abbie refused to be drawn into further conversation and Kate, with a sigh, turned her eyes back to Salvador's glistening torso.

A few minutes later there was a knock on the door, which turned out to be Steve, the IT technician. His face turned crimson as he said, 'Hi. Kate, can I have a quick word?'

It had been obvious to Abbie for some time that Steve was keen on Kate, and that Kate was aware of his feelings, though she gave him no encouragement. Steve knew about Salvador and no doubt thought he didn't stand a chance with Kate. As he manoeuvred himself to Kate's side to take a look at a problem with her keyboard, his blush intensified, until the part of his face Abbie could see was deep puce.

'Excuse my desktop,' Kate giggled, as Steve's eyes fell on Salvador's naked chest. 'I like to keep my boyfriend before my eyes at all times. Stops me from straying, you know.'

'Ah,' said Steve. 'Right. Of course. Yes, ha ha.'

Abbie could have blushed with him. Kate flirted with every man and Steve knew that, but he couldn't handle it any better than Abbie had dealt with Fred's feeble attempts to flirt with her.

'Nice, isn't he?' asked Kate, as Steve fiddled with her keyboard connection. She meant Salvador.

'Er, yes, I suppose so. Not much of a judge, myself, of men.'

'No, of course not,' said Kate. 'I wasn't suggesting for a minute that you were. I hope my intuitions are a bit more reliable than that.'

Steve coughed and said, 'OK, you need a new keyboard. I'll get Michael to bring you one up from the store later on.'

'You're an angel,' said Kate, giving him her full-on brilliant smile. Her teeth were not as white as Abbie's but she used them to better effect. 'What would we do without you?'

Steve gave another strained laugh and made his exit.

'You're mean, Kate,' Abbie said when he had gone. 'You know how much he likes you.'

'Well then, let him tell me.'

'You know he'll never do that.'

'He's too young for me. And anyway, I've got Salvador.'

'Wouldn't you rather have someone sensible and reliable like Steve?' Abbie knew she should be working, but couldn't resist the opportunity to nag Kate – not after her behaviour over the dating agency.

'Sensible and reliable? God – what a thought. When I'm ninety, perhaps. Or even sixty. In the meantime I'd rather have a bit of fun. And Salvador – let me tell you, Abbie – is fun. Serious fun.'

'Fun?'

Kate rolled her eyes. 'Yes – fun! Have you forgotten what the word means? It's time you started to live a little. I'll help you, if you like.'

'No, Kate. It's very good of you, but—'

The irony was wasted on Kate. 'Not at all,' she replied, 'I'd enjoy it. Perhaps at the weekend, I could come round to your house and we'll set you up with an online identity.'

'No, it's OK, thanks.'

'Think about it.'

Kate fell silent, her attention grabbed by an incoming email or something similar, probably not work-related. Abbie marvelled once again at how Kate ever managed to get any work done.

'No one else in our class goes to bed before ten!' Lizzie stayed where she was, slouched on the sofa, gazing at the TV.

'And what makes you so sure of that?'

'Because they all talk about the programmes they watch,' said Sarah. 'We're the only ones who haven't seen them. It's the most horrible feeling in the world.'

'Dad and Fiona let us stay up as late as we like,' added Lizzie.

The argument was a well-rehearsed one. Abbie pointed out, as always, that they stayed with Keith only on nights when they didn't have school next day. But the twins countered by saying that they always got up early when they were at Dad's, anyway, because of all the exciting things there were to do. At this point, Abbie was, as usual, too weary to pursue the discussion any further.

The ongoing dispute over bedtimes was one of the many ways in which she felt her relationship with the twins was being under-mined by Keith and Fiona. She should speak to Keith about it. She would do so, on a day she was feeling strong.

Lizzie and Sarah had just left the room in a huff when the door-bell rang. This was unusual so late in the evening, and Abbie peered through the spy-hole before releasing the safety chain.

There, to her surprise, stood Kate, holding a bottle and a cake.

'Sorry to disturb you. I know it's a bit late. Do you mind?'

'Of course not. Come in. You look....' She couldn't quite put into words how Kate looked. Dispirited, perhaps. Flat. She had certainly lost her usual bounce.

'I'm a bit fed up,' said Kate. 'Felt like a blether. Is that OK?'

'Of course it's OK. I was just trying to persuade these two to go to bed.'

The twins had reappeared and were gazing with interest at Kate and her cake.

'These are my daughters, Lizzie and Sarah,' said Abbie. 'Twins – this is Kate, my friend from work.'

Kate grinned at them. 'Maybe your mum will let you stay up a wee while longer to have some birthday cake?'

'It's your birthday? Why didn't you say? We could have had a celebration at work.'

'It's not today, it's tomorrow. But I thought I might as well start it now. I just got a call from Salvador. He can't make it tomorrow evening. We were supposed to be going out.'

'Oh Kate – what a shame,' said Abbie.

'Who's Salvador?' asked Sarah.

'My boyfriend,' said Kate. 'My horrible, mean boyfriend who booked to go to Frankfurt for my birthday weekend and completely forgot to tell me.'

'You mean on his own?' Abbie asked.

'Oh yes. A work trip. No plans to take me.'

'That *is* horrible,' said Lizzie. 'I'd dump him, if I were you.'

Kate laughed. 'Maybe I should.'

'Lizzie – that's not a very nice thing to say,' said Abbie. 'Kate – come and sit down.' Abbie took the cake from her and then the bottle, which turned out to be champagne. 'Yes, all right, girls, you can stay up an extra fifteen minutes, but that's all.'

Kate took off the lid of the cake box and pulled out a knife, with which she cut four enormous slices and passed them round.

'I'll get some plates,' said Abbie, watching the crumbs fall all over her furniture and carpet.

'If you insist,' said Kate, her mouth already full.

Once the twins were in bed Kate said, 'They're lovely girls.'

'I suppose they are. I wish I had the energy to appreciate them a bit more. By this time of night I can't wait for them to go to sleep.'

'Sorry – I've interrupted your down-time, haven't I?'

'No, of course not. It's nice to have some adult company. But I'm sorry about Salvador. What he did sounds very thoughtless.'

Kate refilled Abbie's glass and her own. 'That's what he's like,

I'm afraid. Or he can be. At other times, he's lovely. I never know where I am with him.'

'Sometimes I'm thankful to be on my own.' Abbie took a sip of her champagne.

'Do you miss Keith, ever?'

'I miss the family life we had. But it all ended so badly that I'm thankful to put it behind me.'

'Did you have some good times, before it all went wrong?'

Abbie swallowed a big chunk of cake and had to follow it up with a swig of champagne to wash it down.

'Sorry,' said Kate. 'It's none of my business.'

Part of Abbie agreed, but she was none the less interested to explore this unfamiliar side of Kate. 'No, it's OK. I'm just not used to talking about it.'

'You can trust me. I won't blab what you tell me to anyone at work.'

'I know you won't.'

'Have some more cake. I can't take all this home.'

'I couldn't manage another crumb. But don't let me stop you.'

'No, I've had too much already.' Kate licked the icing off the knife, then said, 'Sorry. Bad manners. I'm used to living on my own.'

Abbie smiled.

'So – tell me a bit more about Keith,' said Kate. 'Did he take you for granted?'

'I suppose he did, in some ways. He never did much around the house, even though we both worked full-time. He'd make a meal once a month or so, with a big fuss, expecting lots of praise. He used to say he was at the mercy of his muse – once inspiration struck, he had to follow, even if it meant abandoning the chores.'

'Sounds like he was on to a good thing.'

'Perhaps. But I suppose I encouraged it. When he was a struggling unpublished writer, I kind of enjoyed my role. It was like nursing an invalid. He was irritating sometimes, but I felt I had a purpose. When he got a rejection letter I would comfort him, tell him to try again, that he'd make it one day.'

'And he did.'

'Yes – to my surprise, he did. I suppose it's bad that I was surprised.'

'Do you like his books?'

Abbie nodded. 'Have you read them? You should. And I must admit Fiona's illustrations are pretty good, too.'

'But you spent years supporting him and now she reaps all the rewards. It's so unfair.'

'It does feel a bit like that. I wouldn't mind so much if Fiona was a nicer person.'

'What's she like, then? I didn't like the look of her at the interview.'

Abbie put down her plate and took another sip of champagne. 'I suppose it would be expecting a lot, for me to like her. But it's more than just jealousy. There's something about her I can't stand. I want to use the word "creepy", though it sounds childish.'

'You know, that's exactly the word that came into my head. Something about the way she looked at the camera. What do the twins think of her?'

'They seem to like her.'

'Hmm.'

'I'm glad they do, of course. I wouldn't want it any other way.'

'I don't think I'd feel like that.'

'Oh, you would, if you were a mother.'

Kate bit her lip. 'I don't suppose I'll ever find out.'

'Come on, Kate. Even if Salvador doesn't work out – there'll be someone else. You're only thirty-four.'

'Thirty-five tomorrow.'

'You've plenty of time.'

'I'd be a terrible mother, anyway. But let's not talk about me. You were saying about Keith's writing – how you felt when he got published.'

'My main regret is that if I'd handled it better, perhaps the marriage would have survived.'

'How could you have done that?'

Abbie took another swig of champagne. Kate reached over and topped up her glass.

'Just been more genuinely delighted, I suppose. Not resented all the attention Keith got. Not complained at him for never mentioning me in his interviews.'

'He never mentioned you?' Kate's eyes widened.

'Well, not often. He talked all the time about the twins. "My girls", he would say, and go on about how they'd been such an inspiration. Which they were, of course. It was their demands for stories that got him started in the first place. But I think it was the "my" that got me. Why couldn't he say "our girls" and include my name sometimes?'

'I remember that bit in the interview, where one of the twins said you used to make him sandwiches.'

'Yes – good old Sarah.' Abbie grinned. 'That really threw him – I can still see his face.'

'You're better off without him.'

Abbie gazed at the pattern on the living room curtains – subdued swirls of green and gold – and almost forgot Kate's presence for a minute or so.

Kate interrupted her reverie. 'You mustn't blame yourself. If you want my opinion, Keith was a complete bastard.'

'Maybe. But it's not fair on the twins. They've coped well, but it's not been easy for them. That's why I feel so guilty.'

'Why should you?'

'I sometimes wonder whether the real reason the marriage failed was my depression. OK, I suppose it was brought on by the strain of Keith's success, but I should have coped. Anyone else would have been pleased for him and managed to shrug off the jealousy, not been made ill by it.'

'Don't be silly, Abbie. No one can help depression.'

'Of course, it wasn't helped by the way Fiona was suddenly everywhere.'

'When did their affair begin?'

'I'm not sure. I don't even know if it was while we were still together. Keith always insisted it didn't get started until after we split up – but I don't know whether to believe him.'

'Tell me about the depression,' said Kate.

'It began around the time Keith started to give interviews to the press. His first book shot up into the bestseller charts just before Christmas and he was suddenly in demand – doing book-signings and interviews and promotions all over the place.'

'Without you?'

'I couldn't go to most of the things because of the twins. He was travelling all over the country. I had my work, too – and we ended up hardly seeing each other for weeks on end. I wouldn't have minded so much if he'd tried to get me involved. If he'd given me the occasional mention in his interviews....'

'Didn't you tell him how you felt?'

'I tried to. He said the interviewers weren't interested in me. Then he took up exercise, had a makeover and started to look ten years younger. I felt overweight and frumpy next to him. So I didn't want to appear in photos, even if I was asked. It came to a head when a silly female journalist expressed surprise when she met me. Couldn't believe I was his wife.'

'What, you mean...?'

'She thought I looked too old and ugly. Not glamorous enough to be married to the man she described as "the hunky creator of the Great Green Wizard". It was all downhill from there. I started to hate the way I looked but there was nothing I could do. The worse I felt the more I comfort-ate.'

'Ah.'

'And then Fiona started to appear in the pictures too. As his illustrator – but everyone assumed they were a couple. That made much more sense – she was young and slim and lovely.'

'Bloody hell, Abbie. I'm not surprised you got depressed.'

'I started to hate my appearance. More than that – to really hate myself – with a kind of disgust. I'll never forget that feeling. It was so bad I wanted to die.'

Kate shook her head. 'That's awful. But surely Keith, when he saw how bad you were...?'

'It took a while for it to be diagnosed as depression. I refused to see a doctor for ages. But then I got to the stage where I couldn't work. I was called into see the head a couple of times, over stupid mistakes that weren't like me at all. Or not like the old me. I couldn't even handle the twins. I went to the doctor in the end with awful stomach pains and she told me I was depressed. Gave me pills, which I wouldn't take, at first.'

'Why not?'

'Oh, you know. I didn't believe it was depression. I tried to talk myself out of it.'

'Did Keith realize you were ill?'

'I don't think so. He knew something was wrong, of course, but he saw it as jealousy and it made him angry. When I asked him outright if anything was going on with Fiona, he hit the roof. Maybe up to that point he'd held off starting an affair with her. He admits now that he was attracted to her from the start and it slowly developed into love. Who knows? If I'd not been the way I was, that might never have happened.'

'You don't know that.'

Abbie sighed, got up and turned on an extra lamp. 'I was pretty bad. Must have been awful to live with. When the depression was at its worst, I used to stand front of the mirror, digging my nails into my cheeks, running them down until I drew blood. Watching the red streaks appear. Banging my fists against the side of my head. Then, for some reason, I tried taking my tablets. They didn't work at first – in fact I don't know why I kept on with them. They made me dizzy and every colour looked several shades too dark. It was like wandering about in brown fog.'

'That sounds vile.'

'It was, at first. But then, after three or four weeks, I woke up one morning and for the first time in months I wasn't socked in the stomach by a great lump of self-disgust. I could bear to be me again. I started noticing things – a flower in the garden or something tasting good. It felt like a hole in the prison wall, with fresh air blowing through. No need to climb out just yet, but I knew that I'd be able to when I was ready.'

'And?'

'Well, I came out of my depression, bit by bit, to discover that the marriage was over. Keith told me he didn't love me, didn't want to stay. He was in love with Fiona and that was that.'

'Did that make you worse again?'

'No, surprisingly enough, it didn't. Perhaps the medication held it off. I was upset, of course, but I coped, somehow. I suppose I mainly had to focus on how to tell the twins.'

'Can't have been easy.'

'It wasn't. I tried hard not to present Keith as the bad guy. Or Fiona as the cause of it all. Though I was tempted. As it was, we told them that Daddy and Mummy had decided to live apart. I didn't want to set them off on a bad footing with Fiona from the start.'

'You're too nice for your own good,' said Kate. 'Are you sure you don't want more cake? More champagne?'

'No, thanks. You finish it.'

Kate looked with longing at what was left. 'Better not. I've got to drive home. I'll have a bit more cake, though. Sure you won't?'

Abbie shook her head, and Kate munched in silence for a few minutes. Then she said, 'Perhaps I shouldn't ask, but what about money? Keith must be pretty well off now. It seems unfair that you missed out on all the rewards, when you'd helped him so much.'

'He gave me half of what he earned for the first book, the one I helped with. He got a lot more for the second one, of course, a big advance because the first one sold so well. He offered me some of that, too.'

'Did you accept it?'

'I couldn't – it wasn't mine to take.'

'You must be mad. I'd have grabbed as much as I could.'

'I wanted to be independent. I needed to show I could do it on my own, get a job, a house, make a new home for myself and the twins. So as soon as I was well enough I started applying for jobs. Dundee seemed about the right distance from Edinburgh – sixty-four miles. Close enough for the girls to see plenty of their father but far enough away for me not to keep bumping into him.'

'You didn't want to stay in teaching?'

'I'd had enough of it. I wanted a job I could leave behind at the end of the day and still have some energy left for Sarah and Lizzie.'

'I see what you mean.'

'I fancied somewhere on the coast, within walking distance of a school. Carleith was perfect. We got a bit more than we expected for the Edinburgh house and property is cheaper up here, so I managed to put down a good deposit on this place.'

'You did well.'

'Yes, I love it here. I'm lucky, I know. My friend Heather ended up in deep financial trouble after her divorce.'

'Are the twins OK about only seeing Keith at weekends?'

'They seem to be. It was their choice to live with me. Mind you, they could never have lived with him, anyway, because he travels around so much. Especially now he's got Fiona.'

Kate mopped the crumbs from her plate with her finger. 'It

seems to me, you're just at the right stage to look for someone new.'

'Please don't start going on about online dating again!'

'All right, I won't. I'd better go, anyway. I forgot my mobile and you never know – Salvador might be trying to phone me at home.'

When Kate had left, Abbie sat for a while with the plates and glasses, reflecting on how much she felt able to confide in her. Perhaps Kate had the potential to be a good friend after all, as opposed to a congenial but slightly annoying colleague.

Or perhaps it was the champagne and cake that had improved her mood. She felt as though she might sleep well for once.

The phone rang as she was brushing her teeth. As soon as she heard Keith's voice she suspected that her mood of optimism was about to be vanquished. Keith just wanted to tell her, he said, that he was being considered for another literary prize.

'That's great, Keith. Well done.' But why, why, ring at eleven thirty-five?

'I thought you'd want to know. Hope you weren't in bed?'

'Oh, no. I'd just said goodbye to a friend.'

'A friend?'

'That's right.' She wasn't going to reveal the sex of the friend, which was presumably what Keith wanted to know. Let him guess. Let him speculate about whether she had a boyfriend.

'Are the twins all right?' he asked.

'They're fine. Fast asleep. They had some cake with us earlier on.'

'Oh. Right.' After a moment he said, 'Well, I'd better go.'

'OK. 'Bye then.'

'Just before I go, what did you think of the interview?'

'The interview? Oh, right, the TV thing.' Abbie paused as though she hadn't given it a moment's thought. 'It seemed to go all right.'

'I watched the recording with Fiona. I thought we all came out quite well.'

'The twins seem to have enjoyed it.'

'Yes. They were good, weren't they? Quite forthcoming, about all those stories I used to tell them.'

'Fiona's not pregnant, is she?'

'Fiona pregnant? Of course not. Why do you ask?'

Abbie enjoyed the note of alarm in his voice. 'Oh, no particular reason. She just had a certain look.'

'Nerves, I expect. It was a scary business, going in front of the cameras. Knowing we would appear in all those living rooms all over the country.'

'It must have been. Perhaps, now I come to think of it, it was the dress.'

'What dress?'

'That green thing she was wearing. Sort of wool, jersey material. They say the TV cameras add on at least a stone, don't they?'

'A stone – what do you mean? I thought Fiona looked lovely.'

'Oh, of course. As she always does.'

'Right. Well, Abbie, I'd better go.'

'OK. Thanks for letting me know, about the book award thing.'

'Keep your fingers crossed for me.'

'I will.' Did she mean it? She didn't know.

chapter three

'Sarah was crying in her sleep last night,' said Lizzie, making hollows with the spoon in her milk-sodden Weetabix.

'No, I wasn't.'

'Yes, you were. You woke me up. You started making funny hiccuping noises and then it turned into crying. I was going to get Mum but then you stopped, thank God.'

'Lizzie....' Abbie was spreading a layer of peanut butter on bread for the twins' packed lunches. Lizzie liked a slice of cheese with hers, while Sarah took it neat.

'What's wrong with that, Mum?' Lizzie asked.

'You know I don't like you saying, "Thank God."'

'Why not? Everyone says it, even the teachers.'

'Well they shouldn't.'

'Mum believes in God,' said Sarah. 'That's why she doesn't like you saying, "Thank God". It's unrespectful.'

'Disrespectful,' corrected Abbie. 'And I don't believe in God. At least, I don't think I do. But I don't like the expression.'

'You're old-fashioned,' said Lizzie, her mouth full. 'Isn't she, Sarah?'

'No I'm not. Anyway, what does it matter if I am? What's this about you crying in your sleep, Sarah? Did you have a bad dream?'

'I don't think so. I didn't cry, anyway. Lizzie's making it up.'

'No, I'm not. She did cry, Mum, for ages.'

'I bet you dreamt it, Lizzie,' said Sarah.

'I didn't. You woke me up with the noise.'

'Well, I expect it's just one of those things,' said Abbie. 'Nothing's worrying you, is it, Sarah? Is everything all right at school?'

'Apart from hating Mrs Atkins, yes.'

'You don't hate her.'

'Yes I do.'

The policy at the girls' new school was to put twins in different classes, something Lizzie and Sarah had never experienced before. Lizzie seemed to be enjoying the experience but Sarah was taking some time to adjust.

'I wish I could be in Mrs Brown's class with Lizzie.'

'Well you can't,' said Lizzie. 'Remember, Mrs Strachan explained it to us. They want twins to develop their own identities.'

'That's stupid. We do have our own identities. We're not the same person, are we? We're completely different.'

'You always want to be like me,' said Lizzie.

'I do not!'

'You even want the same clothes as me.'

'I saw those purple jeans first, that's why I wanted them.'

'Girls, stop it. Time to go in a minute. Are your bags packed?'

The school was only five minutes down the road, but it was on the way to Abbie's work so she dropped them off there most mornings.

Having deposited the twins, Abbie tried to turn her mind away from them, to focus on work. But Sarah's crying in her sleep nagged at her. It probably meant nothing, but it was worrying, given that she had not yet fully settled in her new school. She would speak about it to Sarah on her own, later.

The traffic slowed down, forming a long snarl as she drove into Broughty Ferry, on the edge of the city. Abbie wished she could abandon her car and take a walk along the beach, picking through her thoughts in solitude. Apart from Sarah's crying, there was Keith's annoying phone call of last night to be dissected. She was glad she had managed to get in a snide comment about Fiona, though a tiny seed of self-disgust had taken root. Was she really becoming the kind of person who criticized other women's figures?

Let it go, she told herself. Don't think about either of them. Keith has nothing to do with you any more.

Except, of course, that he was the twins' father and always would be. And he and Fiona and the twins had formed a new family, on display to the whole nation, or at least to those who watched afternoon TV.

I'm the one the girls live with, Abbie reminded herself. They come home from school to me every day. I make their meals, I listen to their tales, their daily achievements and disappointments.

No one else knew that, though. Or only a few people knew it. Anyone watching on TV would have thought Lizzie and Sarah lived with Keith and Fiona, the rich, good-looking, artistic-literary couple who were giving them everything a pair of eleven-year-olds could possibly need. True, the presenter had said something at the beginning about Fiona and Keith having met only a couple of years before, but that could easily have been missed. Probably most people watching had thought that Fiona was the twins' mother, while marvelling that she looked so young. Abbie shuddered at the thought and tried, once again, to turn her mind to work.

Winding slowly around the various roundabouts on the way into the city centre, Abbie wondered once again why she chosen to live several miles out of town, requiring a twenty-five minute drive to work every day. It might have been better to get a flat near the centre – perhaps in the West End like Kate. Abbie and the twins could have walked to school and work and avoided this horrible car journey. She had been swayed, she supposed, by the appeal of a seaside village. Carleith was a delightful place to live, with its dark bungalows lining the coast and its long beach and promenade, frequented only by dog-walkers for most of the year. But she was not sure it was worth it.

Think positive, she told herself, turning off the mini-roundabout on to the university campus. The most important thing was that the girls were healthy, happy and settling well into their new home. She had seen no signs that either of them was reacting badly to the divorce.

Abbie was making a chicken and broccoli stir-fry for herself and the twins that evening when the phone rang.

'Answer it, one of you, please,' she called.

Sarah ran into the kitchen, waving the phone. 'Mum, it's Heather.'

Heather, from Edinburgh, a fellow divorcee and faithful confidante during her marriage break-up, was coming to stay for the weekend. The twins were going to Keith's first thing next morning, Saturday, and Abbie was looking forward to a good catching-up session with her old friend. She turned down the heat and with a sense of impending disappointment took the phone from her daughter.

'I'm sorry, Abbie,' Heather began. 'But I've had another offer. I know you'll understand.'

Why, Abbie wondered, did people always expect her to understand?

'What kind of offer?'

'Let me explain.' Heather's voice had risen a tone or two and Abbie could hear the tension in her throat. Is she lying to me, she wondered.

'I have been asked out,' Heather said. 'By a very nice gentleman. Someone I met at my evening class.'

'Not the bloke with the red beard?'

'No, no. Not him. Another one. The bearded one was a bit too old, I decided. This one is younger and actually quite good-looking. He has warm brown eyes and a much nicer nose.'

'Well – congratulations.' Abbie was pleased for Heather, though she couldn't help feeling hurt at seeing her friend's priorities made so plain. Then again, perhaps she would do the same in Heather's position? Would she?

Heather continued, 'I wondered if I could perhaps come the following weekend instead? Then I can tell you all about it. You won't be doing anything, will you?'

Abbie was about to say, 'Well, the twins will be here. You might prefer to leave it for another week or so,' when she found herself saying, instead, 'To be honest, I'm not sure. I've got quite a full schedule over the next few weeks.'

'Oh!' Heather's voice went up high again. 'Oh, that's nice. Anything you want to tell me about?'

'No, not really. When I next see you, perhaps.' Why on earth had she said that? Now Heather would think she had met a man herself, and Abbie would have to make up some explanation the next time she saw her.

But still, it was a satisfying feeling, not to have allowed Heather the last word.

After dinner was cleared away, homework was done and the twins were playing a board game that for some reason involved a lot of shouting, Abbie retreated to her small garden and spent half an hour giving it a pre-season tidy. The evenings suddenly seemed much lighter and the buds were opening. A clump of fine pink tulips had appeared in the corner by the decaying shed. It was exciting, waiting to see what would pop through the ground this first spring in her new home.

Thrusting her trowel under the roots of an enormous dandelion, Abbie thought of precise, manicured Heather with her panstick make-up and her tailored wardrobe. Heather would have no trouble finding a new man, she reflected. And she had obviously decided to start looking. Evening classes in small business management indeed! Heather had gone there, Abbie guessed, in search of a partner of the non-business type, and it looked as though she might be successful.

She tugged out the dandelion, scattering a spray of fine sandy soil into her face and hair. Blinking it away, she looked over the neat borders and wiped her trowel with the pair of Keith's old underpants she had retained for the purpose. Should she stay out here a bit longer? There would be at least another half-hour before darkness fell, and it was mild and calm. No, she decided, better go in and see what the twins were doing.

Abbie left her wellington boots on the doorstep and wandered indoors. Sarah and Lizzie had finished their game and were now, she was pleased to see, reading library books. The TV was on but they were ignoring it. Abbie switched it off and went to the kitchen to make tea for herself and cocoa for the girls.

She sat down at the computer, which occupied a desk in a corner of the dining room. It was a rather battered old desk that she and Keith had bought when they were first married. It was the one he'd sat at for years to do his writing. Since the twins had started using the computer the desk had acquired a number of new scratches, spills and pen marks. No doubt Keith had a brand-new one of his own, in his and Fiona's enormous house up on Edinburgh's Braid Hills.

Over the top of the monitor, Abbie could see glimpses of her garden, the green of the new spring foliage fading to grey in the pink dusk. Her initial sense of satisfaction subsided into melancholy. She had no messages and she felt much sadder than seemed reasonable.

Two hours later, when the twins were asleep, Abbie returned to the computer and typed 'online dating' into the search engine, adding 'safe' as an afterthought. Within a second or so, nearly 200,000 sites were displayed. She clicked on the first and her screen lit up pink, green and purple. An attractive woman beamed at her and boomed congratulations in a poorly disguised Manchester accent overlaid with an American twang.

'You have found us. Congratulations! Now, the next step is to find your ideal partner.'

The Beatles' *All You Need is Love* started to play. A likely story, Abbie thought, but none the less she continued to click – just out of interest, to see what would happen.

'Now it's time to create your profile,' gushed the beaming woman. 'First, you need a name. We advise you never to use your real name. This is for reasons of security. We have your welfare in mind at all times.

'Instead, think of a pseudonym or nickname. You should choose something that expresses your personality.'

This brought Abbie to a halt. What was her personality? A personality was not something she thought of herself as having. People like Kate had personalities – were interesting and difficult – while people like Abbie had to put up with them.

I suppose I'm a calm, placid person, she reflected. Or she had been, before Keith's success and the separation. Friends had told her, once, how serene and patient she was with the children, not getting into a panic even when they hurt themselves or got into trouble at school. But she seemed to have lost that placidity since her depression. Even now, she sometimes woke up in the night, heart pounding, with no idea why but with a general sense of danger. And she worried much more about the twins these days. No, she was not calm or placid.

Outgoing? That was also something she had once been, long ago, when things didn't matter so much. These days it was all so much harder. She could be friendly enough when she had to be, but most of the time she would rather hide away than make the effort to socialize. Look at how she had dreaded going to the pub the other night. And look how badly it had gone. No, Abbie concluded, she was no longer an outgoing person.

Kind? That was how people seemed to see her. Kind and tolerant. But she wasn't sure she was, not underneath. And anyway, a man looking for a woman wasn't going to be attracted by 'kind', was he?

What *would* a man be looking for? Sexy? That was something else from another life, long ago.

Romantic? No, that would appeal to a woman, not a man.

Adventurous?

Enjoys wallpapering? Gardening? If she wasn't careful she would end up with one of the eighty-eight-year-olds Kate had been talking about.

Surely there must be something interesting about her, something alluring? What had Keith seen in her all those years ago? Perhaps, whatever it had been, she could find some residue of it and drag it up to the surface? Should she ring Keith to ask? No, he'd laugh at her. Or Fiona would answer the phone.

That was an idea: perhaps she could lay claim to Fiona's attributes, as described to her by Keith. What was it he'd told her, just after the separation? 'I have discovered a perfect gem of womanhood.' Hmm.

Was there nothing interesting she could say about herself? An ordinary woman in her late thirties, washed up on the beach from a previous marriage, worn out from looking after the twins and going to work. Likes nothing better than to read a book in bed with a mug of tea beside her.

At least I'm not hideously ugly, she told herself. But most people weren't, were they? She was intelligent, or had been once. But didn't everyone think of themselves as intelligent, and did men want intelligence anyway? Not, of course, that she would want a man who *didn't* want intelligence.

She didn't go mountaineering or potholing or even hillwalking. Though, she supposed, she could at least go hillwalking if she chose to. Perhaps she should take it up. She enjoyed paddling her feet in the sea. She liked travel, but hadn't been further than Edinburgh or Perth for about three years.

She had a long-standing interest in psychology and language, and read all the books she could get her hands on. But it was only a hobby. If she mentioned it, it would be just her luck to meet an academic with a string of papers to his name who might pour scorn on her amateurish enthusiasm.

Should she mention that she used to be a biology teacher? How interesting was *that*? as her daughters would say.

Without bothering to close down any of the dating site windows, Abbie turned off her computer and felt a surge of relief as the lurid colours disappeared from the screen. She didn't have to do this.

Or perhaps she would ask Kate for some help.

'Let's try a different site,' Kate suggested. 'This one looks a bit tacky.'

She had drawn up her chair next to Abbie's at her computer. It was their lunch hour, the following Monday, and both were munching. Kate had finished her low-fat tuna-with-mayonnaise sandwich and started one of her store of Mars bars. Abbie was spooning up home-made egg salad, wishing she had remembered to bring some slices of brown bread to make it go further. She was ravenous – afraid that Kate would offer her a Mars bar and that she would be unable to resist.

She had told Kate about her failed attempts to register on a dating site over the weekend.

'Of course I'll help,' said Kate with a delighted grin. 'You just need a bit of confidence, that's all. Let's see what we can do.'

Kate scrolled down the list of sites. 'Look – the next one looks more promising. "Online Introductions for the Older Professional Woman." That sounds like you, doesn't it?'

'I'm not an older woman,' said Abbie. 'I'm only thirty-eight.'

'I'm afraid anything over thirty counts as older in the world of online dating.'

Abbie decided to let this pass. 'I'm not sure about the "professional" bit, either. Does working in an university office make me a professional?'

'Of course it does. Anyway, you were a teacher before, weren't you? That must count.'

'Well, yes.' But was she, Abbie wondered, still that same person?

'You'll get a better class of man if you say you're a professional,' said Kate.

Next came the tricky matter of the name and profile. Kate laughed when Abbie told her the trouble she'd had finding anything interesting to say about herself.

'Do you really think all those other women out there are so bloody marvellous? You're just as good as they are. You need to sell yourself, that's all. Make yourself sound exciting. Invent a few things, if necessary.'

'I can't do that.'

'Why not? Everyone else does.'

'Do they? How do you know?'

'Well, it stands to reason. Just take a look at some of them. See, there's a batch of them here in this pink window. "New members." Let's try Lavender Girl.'

Lavender Girl claimed to be forty, though her photo suggested she was older. She wore a mauve top with a low neckline and listed her interests as sky-diving and astrology.

'Now *that* I don't believe,' said Kate. 'She may squash open her tea-bag every now and then and look at the pattern in the cup, but I can't believe she's ever jumped out of a plane.'

'But what happens when someone meets you in person, and they find out you've been lying?'

'Lying? Abbie, you are so naïve! Believe me, there's no such thing as a lie in online dating. A wee distortion of the truth, maybe. A slight exaggeration for PR purposes. It's like advertising – you hide the bad stuff, make the most of the good. The kind of thing you do to your CV when you apply for a job.'

'But I don't. I believe in being straightforward. If they don't like me they can lump me, as my mother would say.'

'Abbie, I'm talking about presentation here. Displaying yourself in the best possible light.'

'But saying you've sky-dived when you haven't is more than presentation.'

'Well, we don't know for sure she made it up. Maybe she once did a parachute jump for charity. But you see my point. A little distortion, a little highlighting of the truth never did any harm. And bear in mind, Abbie, the men you meet will have done the same thing, so they can't complain.'

'You think all the men are lying, too?' Abbie felt suddenly disconsolate.

'Not lying, Abbie, as I just explained. Exaggerating a little bit, possibly. It's all part of the game.'

'But it's not meant to be a game. I thought it was to look for a new partner?'

'Is it, now? You were telling me a few minutes ago that you'd decided to join up just for a bit of fun. Just to see what would happen.'

'Well, yes. I suppose so. I'm certainly not expecting to find my true love.'

'Well, then. Why worry about a touch of creative exaggeration?'

'I don't like to think of people lying. I don't want to do it myself.'

'It's not lying. It's the same thing you do every time you put on your make-up and get dressed up to go out.'

'Is it?' Abbie wondered about this. Had she ever dressed up in order to pretend to be someone else? Perhaps not. Could that be one of her problems?

Kate's eyes flickered from the screen into Abbie's face and she smiled. 'You're a sweetie, Abbie. Any man who gets you will be lucky.'

Abbie's anxiety dispersed and she felt a rush of warmth towards Kate, who, she reflected, was probably lonely, too. Salvador's visits were very far apart.

'OK then. Let's get this done. What do you suggest?'

'How do you mean?'

'What kind of person shall I be?'

Kate giggled. 'Now you're talking. Let's see.' She chewed her nails, today painted navy blue and already beginning to flake. 'We should give you a great sense of humour – that's vital.'

'What do you mean, give me one? Don't I have one already?'

'Of course you have. But humour gets a bit buried, doesn't it, when you're going through a difficult time? You've not had much to laugh about recently. But you will, soon, when you meet some nice men – so it's not so much a lie as a forecast. Let's put "sense of adventure", too. That always goes down well with men. They read sexual undertones into it even if there aren't any.'

'As long I'm not expected to jump from a plane.'

'You could always say you gave up parachuting after a bad experience. Now, let's see what else there is. There's your organizational ability and your cooking skills – we must include them.'

Organizational ability and cooking skills? Was that how Kate saw her?

'Men like women who cook. Salvador is always moaning at me for feeding him from packets.'

'But these men online are hardly going to go for organizational ability, are they?'

'Well, perhaps not. Though you never know. I'm sure Salvador would like me to be a bit more organized. Put something else, then. You could always say you're a belly-dancer. That might be popular and it's something you could take up quickly, if need be.'

'But Kate, seriously, suppose I do this – create a sort of false identity. It might be fun, I can see that, but what's going to happen if I meet someone I like, who I want to meet up with, in the flesh?'

'You are such a worrier, Abbie. You can face that problem when you come to it. He will have the same problem, remember. Just give it a go and see what happens. These things have a way of working out. I told Salvador when I first met him that I was twenty-eight, because I didn't think we'd be going anywhere. He forgave me when it came out that I was thirty-two. At least I think he did.'

'And what will I do about a photo? Everyone here seems to display one. If I don't, they'll think I've got something to hide.'

'Just slap a bit of make-up on and get Steve to take a picture, as I suggested before.'

'But I hardly wear any make-up. I'd rather look like my normal self.'

'Well, if you insist. Maybe define your eyebrows a bit. And just a touch of mascara. You're so fair – you could come across online as a faint blur.'

That's me, thought Abbie, a faint blur – a star only just visible above the horizon. Would anyone detect her, and did she really want them to?

'Now let's think of a name for you,' said Kate.

After much discussion they settled on 'Harmony', but that name turned out to be a popular one and it was necessary to add a suffix, so Abbie became Harmony777.

Harmony was thirty-six, two years younger than Abbie, and had blond hair not unlike Abbie's except that it fell smooth and sleek and full to her neckline. Her eyes were blue rather than Abbie's grey and her skin had a glowing tan.

Harmony had been married once, but no mention was made of any children. Kate had persuaded Abbie not to mention the twins. Abbie protested that she wanted to include them: they were part of her, they were, to a large extent, what she was all about.

'That's one of your problems,' said Kate. 'You let yourself be defined by other people.'

'I'm not sure you quite understand motherhood.'

'Maybe not,' said Kate, with an edge to her voice that made Abbie wish she hadn't said it.

Feeling guilty, she gave in for the time being, but decided to add Sarah and Lizzie to her profile as soon as she got the chance.

Kate wanted Harmony to be a personal assistant to someone important, a captain of industry, perhaps – someone much better-looking and better-dressed than Fred Steadman or any of their other colleagues at Invercarse.

But Abbie insisted on describing her real job. 'Harmony mustn't be too perfect or no one will believe in her,' she said. 'Let me include a few faults. I could mention the scar on my knee I got roller skating when I was ten. And I think I'll admit that I'm not very confident.'

'Mention the scar if you must, though I don't understand why you'd want to. But you mustn't say you lack confidence. That's the last thing you should admit to. The internet is full of weirdoes and if you're not careful, you'll attract a complete nerd – someone who never leaves the house and hasn't spoken to anyone for a year.'

'Don't be silly. I'm just being honest. I want them to like the real me, not someone I've made up.'

'They'll have plenty of time to get to know you when you meet them in the flesh. But don't forget, there'll be lots that you never meet. Don't you want some fun, a bit of escapism? You could try adopting a new personality. Try out some different identities. You might find one you like, one you can carry over into real life.'

Although Abbie dismissed Kate's words, part of her was tempted. Perhaps there was something to be said for experimenting with a new persona?

'No, I'm too old to change now. And what would the twins say if they saw me with a new personality?'

'They might like it, you never know. And I'm not suggesting you change everything about yourself. Just decide you are going to be more confident, for example. More assertive. More adventurous.'

'You make it sound so easy.'

'Well, get into practice. Start with small things. Buy some exciting clothes. There's a lot more under the surface than you're letting show at the moment. You've gone into retreat since your divorce. Don't deny it, you have.'

'I don't know how you can tell. You didn't know me when I was with Keith.'

'I can see there's a part of you hidden away.'

'Well, it's news to me. If there is, then it's been hidden away an awful long time. Perhaps since before I married Keith.'

Abbie was joking, but Kate took this seriously. 'Perhaps that's right – part of you got buried under your marriage. It happens to a lot of women.'

'Even if it's true, which I doubt, I shouldn't think it's possible to dig it out now.'

'Don't say that. Harmony may just surprise you.'

Abbie gave one of Kate's snorts, saved Harmony's profile for later editing, and turned to her afternoon's work.

chapter four

No replies arrived for a week. Kate made it worse by asking every five minutes whether she had received any messages yet.

Abbie had made a number of changes to Harmony before launching her online. She was now Abbie's true age, her hair was no longer quite so sleek and her eyes were the same colour as Abbie's. She hadn't posted a photograph so far, as it seemed to be acceptable on the dating site to wait a few days before doing so. Steve had agreed to take one whenever she wanted, but she needed to get her hair cut first.

She had kept to Kate's advice and not allowed Harmony to lack confidence. She babbled on about her love of travel and all the exciting places she had been to. She didn't make any false claims but she neglected to mention that most of her visits abroad had been years ago, before her marriage to Keith, and that she hadn't been anywhere remotely exciting for the past twelve years.

She put in a brief mention of the twins, but said nothing about her ex-husband being the children's author whose photo was appearing in all the papers. It felt good, leaving Keith out.

On closer inspection, the site revealed that a number of people had examined Harmony's profile, even though no one had left a message. She wondered whether Kate was right and she hadn't made herself sound exciting enough. Maybe she should remove the twins after all, or even mention that she had once been married to Mr Most-Popular-Author-of-All-Time?

Then, after a week, she got a message from a man from Alaska, calling himself GrizzlyBear, who wanted online sex. After a quick glance, she grimaced and deleted him.

But fortunately, Grizzly was not Abbie's only respondent. A few days later she found in her mailbox a message from a man called Bill who lived in Birmingham. Closer than Alaska but still rather distant for a relationship. Not, she reminded herself, that she was looking for anything more than friendship – not yet. But Bill's first message made her laugh out loud and she decided to reply. There was no reason, it seemed, not to use the dating agency as a way of making friends. A male friend or two would be good for her and might help counteract the rather jaundiced view of men that she had acquired through her dealings with Keith.

> I'm a comedy scriptwriter, mainly for Radio 4. But that doesn't mean I'm funny in real life. Not to order, anyway. And I've rather lost my sense of humour at the moment. My wife left me for a young saxophonist-footballer and I'm very down in the dumps. My teenage boys blame me for everything that's wrong with their lives and the world in general – including global warming. But that's enough about me. I need to forget my own troubles for a while, so please tell me all about yourself.

Abbie didn't tell Bill everything in that first email, but she revealed quite a lot, including Keith's success as an author and his affair with Fiona. She admitted, too, that she had lost confidence in herself. She knew Kate wouldn't approve, but she sensed from what Bill had written that he would understand. If he didn't – well, that was too bad. She wouldn't be interested in such a man.

Bill said he was forty-one and Abbie had no reason to disbelieve him, except what Kate had said about the way everyone lied in online dating. His photo showed him looking, if anything, rather younger. He had a broad face, big brown eyes, heavy eyebrows and the beginnings of a receding hairline. Not at all bad looking, but not so handsome, Abbie considered, as to be out of her league. Not that it mattered, she reminded herself, since they were only going to be friends.

In his second message Bill expressed sympathy over her marriage break-up and told Abbie that if he was in her position he'd be bloody furious about the whole thing.

This was comforting, though it made Abbie feel she had to be more honest with Bill about her own part in things. Telling him how badly she had handled it all wasn't easy. Writing it down made it real: she saw herself, all of a sudden, as a stranger might, someone who had only known her a few days. She worried that Bill might decide she was not a person he wished to know – might classify her as an insecure and jealous woman and break off contact, confirming all her worst fears about herself.

Should she just pretend, Abbie wondered, that Keith had met Fiona, they'd had an affair, and that was what had broken up their marriage? It sounded simpler and clearer and placed the blame squarely on Keith.

But did she want Bill's sympathy, based on false pretences? What if, unlikely as it seemed at present, she and Bill met up at some time in the future and the truth came out?

No, if she was going to tell him any more about her divorce she would have to be honest and take the risk of rejection. Better that that should happen now than at some later time when they'd become closer.

She was surprised, however, at how much she already felt there was to lose.

You will probably not like me for this, Bill, but the marriage break-up was partly my fault. I couldn't bear the way Keith's success made me feel so left out and worthless. The way people thought I wasn't glamorous enough to be his wife. Don't think I imagined this, I had plenty of evidence.

Anyway, I won't go on about it any more because it hurts me to write and I'm sure it's not much fun to read.

I just wanted to be honest with you from the start. Perhaps it's a mistake.

I'll understand if I don't hear from you again, now you know what I'm really like.

She didn't mention her depression. That could come later, when she knew him better. If there was a later.

The trouble with email, Abbie reflected, was that you could spend hours on the wording and then, still unsure whether or not you wanted to send it, you could find your finger on the icon and the message was gone, with no conscious moment of decision. All that deliberation and care and then in an instant it was dispatched beyond recall.

She studied the photos Bill had sent in his second message. There was one she particularly liked of him with his two sons. The younger one, Sam, who was just thirteen, was sitting in the lower branches of an oak tree. Below stood Bill and the older boy, Jon, who was fifteen. Jon had similar features to his father – the same dark-brown eyes, broad mouth and square chin. Sam was fairer, with a thinner face and grey eyes. Like his mother, perhaps. All three looked happy and relaxed. She wondered who had taken the picture and found herself imagining them all on a day out – herself, the twins, Bill and his boys. Would Jon and Sam get on with her twins? Would the boys regard Lizzie and Sarah as too young, beneath their notice? Lizzie would, she imagined, try to charm all three of them, while Sarah would be very shy.

Stop it, Abbie told herself – it's pointless to speculate about such things. Especially now she had sent that too-honest message and would not be hearing from Bill again.

She spent an anxious day, by the end of which there was still no reply. Why, she asked herself, had she indulged in that misplaced orgy of honesty? If Kate had known, she would have told Abbie not to be so stupid. Surely even Abbie had the sense to know that there was a time and place for revealing such things, and it wasn't in the first few days of a relationship with a man. Not even if friendship was all you aspired to.

Yet something about Bill's tone, if such a thing could exist in an email, had encouraged her to say the things she'd said, to blurt out that stuff about how the divorce was her fault. What must he think of her now? Well, he couldn't think any worse than she thought of herself. She had learned a lesson, anyway. In future, if there was a future to her internet encounters, she would hold back, be discreet, not cough up her insecurities all over the screen.

Late in the evening, just before she went to bed, a message from Bill arrived. Just a short one: perhaps Bill was politely telling her she wouldn't be hearing from him again.

Hi Abbie,

Good to hear from you. You are so open about yourself. I really admire that. I will try to be the same. My wife had an affair, too. Her new partner is a musician and outstanding footballer. He had trials for God knows what teams when he was younger. The boys adore him.

You think you're insecure?!?

I'll write again after my deadline, which is tomorrow morning at nine. I'll be up all night correcting a script.

Best wishes,
Bill

Reading this created a warm glow, somewhere in her chest that could have been her heart.

Kate arrived at work late next morning. Her eyes were red, as though she might have been crying, but Abbie didn't like to ask. It was probably something to do with Salvador, and Kate would tell her when she was ready.

Kate flung her denim jacket at the peg on the door, missed and swore. Abbie retrieved it and hung it up. Kate didn't say a word as she sat down and began to rummage for her sandals.

After a few minutes she asked, 'Have you heard from Bill again?'

The glow which had entered Abbie the previous night reasserted itself.

'I got a brief message from him last thing. He's busy with a deadline. He said he'd write to me again today.'

'That's good. He sounds keen.'

'I think he's lonely. His boys live with their mother and he works from home most days.'

But Kate's attention had wandered. 'Any chance of some coffee?'

'I'll make some.'

Kate began reading her messages, staring at the screen. When Abbie put the mug of coffee beside her a few minutes later she saw tears in Kate's eyes.

'What's wrong?'

'Nothing.' Kate wrapped her hands round the mug on her desk, entwining her fingers round it. 'I just got a message from Salvador. He can't make it this weekend after all.'

'That's a shame. You were flying out to Dublin, weren't you?'

Kate nodded.

'Does he say why he can't go?'

'He says it's his work. An unexpected call-out to a project.'

Something in Kate's voice made Abbie say, 'Do you believe him?'

'Of course I believe him,' Kate snapped. 'Are you saying he's a liar?'

'No, of course not. It's just that he's let you down before, and you sounded as though you weren't sure yourself....' Abbie tailed off, knowing she had said the wrong thing.

'He can't help being so busy.' Kate's eyes were blazing, the lighter shade of blue they turned when she was angry or upset. 'It's a bit disappointing, that's all. I wish he could have let me know earlier.'

'Have you booked your tickets?'

'Of course. And the hotel deposit.'

'Surely he'll repay you for that?'

'He's not a millionaire, you know, Abbie – in spite of what you and everyone else seem to think.'

'But you're always saying—' Abbie stopped, knowing she was about to put her foot in it again.

Kate sniffed. 'Salvador is very generous with his money, but it's not limitless. And he works very hard, he earns every penny. I don't mind losing my air fare and hotel deposit. I'm just disappointed not to see him.'

Abbie remembered something. 'Oh, Kate, sorry, I forgot to say. Fred popped in at half past nine. He asked where you were. He wants to see you. I told him you were probably stuck in the traffic.'

Kate sniffed. 'That doesn't sound very convincing, at half past nine. Couldn't you have told him I was at the dentist's?'

'I didn't know you were.'

'I wasn't, but it would have been a good excuse.'

'You know I don't like lying.'

'What did Fred want – did he say?'

'He asked whether you'd finished the new prospectus. He said Morag is ready to do the printing and binding. She's put everything else on hold for today.'

'Has she now? Well, she needn't have bothered, because it's not going to be finished before tomorrow. It may even be Monday – I've still got to proofread and correct it.'

'But they need it for the Open Day on Saturday, to give out to the prospective students.'

'Tough,' Kate muttered. Then she said, 'Well, I'll try. Perhaps I can finish it off tomorrow morning. Morag can print her copies in the afternoon.'

'Fred seemed very insistent that you finish it today.'

Abbie could see that Kate was worried, in spite of her assumed nonchalance, by the way she chewed her lower lip. She would offer to help but had a full workload herself.

'Don't suppose you could give me hand?' asked Kate.

She was good at asking favours, the way her huge eyes blinked at you through her dark unruly strands of fringe. But Abbie had learned to resist.

'No, I'm sorry, but I've got to sort out the exam papers. The comments have come back from the external examiners and I need to send them out by the end of today.'

Kate made a last attempt. 'Please, Abbie. I've got to be home early. I'll need to leave about four. There's no way I can get those prospectuses done before then.'

'Why do you have to leave so early?' asked Abbie.

'Something private.'

That was unusual. As far as Abbie knew, Kate told her everything, often with a good deal more detail than she would have liked.

'OK. But listen, if something's wrong and you want to talk....'

By way of reply, Kate banged her coffee mug down on her desk, scraped back her chair, stood up and left the office.

Abbie tried to immerse herself in the exam comments but could not stop worrying about Kate. Leaning over sideways to view her screen, she saw that Salvador's photo had disappeared from the desktop, to be replaced by a pale green screen dotted with icons.

The task of the external examiners, who came from other

universities, was to study the Invercarse lecturers' proposed questions for the summer exams and suggest improvements. Having received this feedback, Abbie now had to send out the comments to the appropriate lecturers in the Physics Department. After a week or so, she would have to nag a number of them to make the requested changes.

After a few minutes there was a tentative knock at the door and a tall male student with a shaven head asked for Kate.

'I'm sorry, she's not here.'

'Do you know when she'll be back?'

'I don't think she'll be long,' said Abbie, hoping this was the case. 'Can I give her a message?'

The young man, whose name was Dave, replied, 'She said she'd help me with a Java problem in my project.'

'Oh, right. Well, I'll tell her you were here.'

Kate often helped the first- and second-year undergraduates with their programming, which said a lot for her abilities as well as for her rapport with the students. She was a keen amateur programmer who had taught herself from scratch.

'Thanks,' said Dave, his eyes cast down. It wasn't just that Kate helped the students with their code: they all loved her. Male and female, they came to her with their personal problems, even though the university provided a welfare and counselling service.

When Dave had gone, Abbie allowed herself a quick look at the dating website to see if there was another message from Bill. It was time, she decided, to give him her personal email address and ask for his. So far all their interaction had been through the dating agency website. It was still too early for phone numbers, however, and she had no intention of revealing her address just yet. Bill sounded trustworthy but you couldn't be too careful.

There was no new message from him, but she re-read his old one and felt the glow renewed.

Then she noticed a further message from someone new who called himself Batman17 and whose photo showed him wearing the appropriate outfit. He claimed to be thirty-two, but it was impossible to tell because of the mask. He lived in Aberdeen and would be happy to drive down to Dundee to meet her, any time she wished. Did she have a Catwoman costume, he wondered?

Abbie dismissed Batman17 with an amused shake of her head. She was getting used to this type of message.

Turning back to her work, she tried to concentrate on the howler that one of the lecturers had made in question three. The external examiner had made a sarcastic comment to the effect that it was not surprising that students failed exams when their teachers made such stupid mistakes.

Kate reappeared after twenty minutes or so, looking pale and tense.

'Was Fred OK about the prospectus?' asked Abbie.

'No – and he had a go at me for being late. Told me I've got to get it finished by the end of today.'

'Oh dear. By the way, a student came to see you. Dave, that guy in second year. Looking for help with his project.

'Bless the wee man. Bet he's got his Java in a twist again. Did he say anything else?'

'No, why?'

'Oh, he's got girlfriend problems, too. The Java is usually easier to sort out than the emotional troubles.'

'Only because you're so good at it.'

'It's just a matter of being logical. And having confidence.'

'You're wasted in this office, Kate, as I've said before.'

'So are you, come to that. You should be teaching.'

'Never again. Not after my breakdown.'

'You had depression, I thought, not a breakdown.'

'I was bad enough, at my worst, for it to be called a breakdown. But I don't usually admit that.'

'I won't tell anyone.'

'I'm not ashamed if it.'

'At least you know that your breakdown or whatever wasn't caused by your work. I bet you'd be fine if you went back to teaching now, in a different school.'

'I like *this* job. It's something I can handle. Oh, I know there's a lot of hassle and Fred drives me mad, but I don't have to deal with disaffected students and discipline problems and angry parents. Or not very often.'

'I suppose.'

'But you, Kate, it's different for you. You should aim for a career.

You could be a high flier in IT, never mind Salvador. Perhaps you could do a degree? Why not apply to the Computing Department?'

'How could I afford that?'

'It wouldn't be easy, I know, but maybe you could keep on your job here part-time?'

'I don't have the entry requirements. I left school before my standard grades.'

'There are courses you can do to catch up. I bet you'd sail through them.'

'I'm too old. I'd feel silly among all the eighteen-year-olds.'

'There are lots of mature students around. And anyway, you're young at heart.'

Kate looked at her for a moment and said, 'Well, it appears I'm too old for Salvador. He thinks so, anyway. I just got a text from him. He's met a twenty-three-year-old in Frankfurt and they're serious.'

'Kate! That's awful. I'm so sorry.'

'He's done it before,' Kate said. 'I mean, there've been others. Other women. A man, too, I think.'

'Really?'

'Don't looked so shocked. I told you he was bisexual.'

'Did you?'

'Well, never mind that now. The point is, the others weren't serious. I knew about them and I didn't mind. I tried not to, anyway. But he says this one's different – so much so that there's no point him and me going on.'

'That's a lot to say in one text message.'

'I phoned him when I got it. It'll have cost me a fortune. Not that I care.'

'Oh, Kate – I'm so sorry.' Abbie, already hugging Kate, gave her a further squeeze.

'Things haven't been right for a while. He was always complaining that I'm too possessive.'

'The bastard.'

'I knew it would happen one day.'

'Then why did you stay with him?'

'I don't know. Hope, I suppose.' Kate backed away and started ripping down the pictures of Salvador from around her desk.

Having done that, she picked up a framed photo of him and hurled it at the door, where it smashed, leaving a green scrape mark on the crimson paintwork.

'I'll clear it up,' said Abbie. 'Someone might hurt themselves.'

'I don't care.' Kate's sobs were beginning to subside. 'Have you heard from Bill again?'

'Not yet. But I got a message from a Batman. Do you want to see it?'

When Abbie checked the website, she saw that Batman17 had sent another message, this time offering to send her a selection of further photos depicting various stages in the removal of his costume.

She was pleased to see that this made Kate smile.

chapter five

'Abbie, you're obsessed with a man you've never met.'

Kate and Abbie were walking at low tide across Carleith beach on the first warm Saturday of the year. The sun kept dipping behind a cloud and out again, casting patterns across the sand. A light breeze carried the tang of seaweed to their nostrils.

'You talk about nothing else,' Kate added.

Abbie bit back her denial. It was, after all, true.

'Well?' said Kate. 'Aren't you going to defend yourself?'

Abbie watched a pair of seagulls chasing each other above their heads. 'I suppose you're right. Though preoccupied is probably a better word. But what's wrong with that?'

'Because you don't know him.'

One of the seagulls gave an angry-sounding squawk.

'We've been writing to each other every day – twice some days – for the past four weeks.'

'You can't go on like this. You should at least phone him. Find out if he's as nice as you think he is.'

'What will I find out by phone that I can't discover by email?'

'Whether he's genuine or not. You'll get a better idea, at least. He might be completely made up. I mean, all the stuff about his family and his ex-wife might be a pack of lies. He could be planning to murder you.'

'Well, he can't do that by email, can he? And if he is a potential murderer, surely that's a good reason not to give him my phone number?'

'I wish you'd take me seriously, Abbie. I'm worried about you.'

'Kate, it was you who got me started on this internet dating thing. I'd have thought you could be pleased for me.'

'I really am pleased for you,' said Kate. 'Or I would be, if I thought this was going somewhere.'

Abbie knew that Kate was right, and yet at this stage it didn't seem to matter. Her correspondence with Bill was doing wonders for her self-image. Here was someone who spent hours a day composing messages just for her, who sent her jokes and cartoons and photos of himself, often funny ones, who told her how her messages were brightening his days and keeping him afloat during a painful divorce. Reading his latest message was, in a way, pure escapism – it provided relief from the demands of the twins and their endless chatter about their father, Fiona and all the places the four of them planned to go that summer.

She knew they couldn't go on like this for ever. But it was much too early to disturb things.

'Has Bill actually seen your photo?' Kate asked.

'Of course he has. I've sent him a few – ones of myself and the twins in the garden, that kind of thing.'

'I'd be careful, sending photos of the twins.'

'Oh Kate, don't be silly. He's not some kind of pervert.'

'You can't be too careful.'

'I know. I *am* being careful.'

'Let's sit down for a few minutes.'

They'd speeded up to warm themselves in the gathering wind and Kate was out of breath. They found a more sheltered spot on a dry patch of sand and Kate sat down on a rock, rummaged in her bag and found a Mars bar, which she broke in two.

'No thanks,' said Abbie. 'I'm cooking a meal for us when we get back, remember.'

'This won't hurt. I'm starving.'

'I'd rather save my appetite.'

'Don't you ever get fed up with being such a goody-goody?'

Abbie could sense her usual self stung with indignation, ready to spring to the defence. But the feeling was buried below her happiness over Bill, her sense of all being right with the world, and she couldn't summon up the effort to respond.

'That's part of your problem, I think,' Kate added.

'Kate, what are you talking about?' The sun had reappeared and Abbie unwound her scarf, enjoying the warmth on her neck.

Kate's voice was muffled by the Mars bar. 'You being so good. Always doing the right thing.'

'As if!' This time the youth-speak – possibly last year's youth-speak – came out before she could stop it. That was what happened when most of your conversations were with eleven-year-olds. 'If I'd done the right thing with Keith I might still be married.'

'He'd still have had an affair with that creepy Fiona.'

'Not necessarily.'

'I bet he would.'

Kate was silent for a minute or two, sifting sand through her fingers. 'I just don't want you to be let down by Bill.'

'I know.' Abbie watched the sunlight play on Kate's hair. She's beautiful, she thought. And she does care about me. I'm lucky to have her as a friend.

'You've been badly hurt once, Abbie. Don't let it happen again. Don't get too attached to Bill. He might suddenly stop writing.'

'He won't.'

'He might. If he meets someone else. In real life – or even, I suppose, on the internet.'

'No. I don't think so.'

'Have you considered that he might be writing to a number of people, not just you? He might even be sending them the same letter. How would you feel about that?'

Abbie pulled herself to her feet, hoisting her bag over her shoulder. 'You're right – I have got rather attached to Bill. I'd find it hard to do without him now. He's become my refuge, against all the stuff with Keith. He and Fiona are taking the twins to France in August and Italy at October half-term. They're so excited, they talk of nothing else. So I escape, whenever I can, and go and read one of Bill's messages.'

Kate got up too. 'I sympathize. But you're setting yourself up to be hurt.'

'I feel as though he's given me *myself* back again. My real self. Or perhaps a self I've never been before. With him I'm funny and clever and real. When Keith and Fiona and the twins are doing things together, I sometimes feel as though I don't exist. Especially when they're in the papers and on TV – the whole world seeing them as a family. I might as well be dead.'

'That's not true and you know it. The twins love you. You're their mother. Fiona is nothing to them by comparison.'

'I know that, in theory. But it never feels that way. They don't mean to hurt me, Lizzie and Sarah. They're too young to understand.'

'Perhaps they're not. Have you tried telling them how you feel?'

'I couldn't. It would upset them. I should be thankful they've taken it all so well – the separation, the divorce, Keith being with Fiona, us moving up here. They've coped brilliantly – it'd be cruel to make things even harder. No, I've just got to sit it out. And knowing Bill *helps*.'

'I'm your friend, too.'

'Of course you are. But the fact he's a man, it's different. You understand, don't you?'

'Only too well. That's why I'm worried about you.'

'He's a decent man, I'm sure.'

'Well, you must meet him. Face up to some reality before things go any further. Speak to him on the phone, at least.'

They were walking now across the dunes, heading for the road that would take them uphill to Abbie's bungalow. A light rain was falling and the sky inland was a dull uniform grey. Over the sea there were still a few breaks in the cloud and a long line of golden light just above the horizon.

'Perhaps I'll phone him soon,' said Abbie.

'When? Tonight? It's a good opportunity, while the twins are with Keith.'

'I'll see. He may not want to.'

'Of course he will. Send him your number. Or better still, ask for his.'

'Maybe.'

'Why are you so afraid?'

'I suppose I'm afraid of being found out. He'll discover I'm not as funny as I pretended, not as witty and lively. He may not like the sound of my voice.'

'Come on, Abbie. It's you that's been writing to him, not someone else.'

'It doesn't feel like that. Not quite.'

'Maybe he'll feel the same, maybe he's scared, too. There's only one way to find out.'

'OK. I'll do it – soon.' They were going uphill now, and Abbie slowed her pace for Kate, whose face was flushed with exertion.

As they turned the corner into Abbie's road, the circle of neat nineteen-seventies bungalows, Abbie said, 'We've talked a lot about me. I've been meaning to ask – have you thought any more about Steve?'

'No. Should I have?'

'You know he's crazy about you. He's found an excuse to drop into our office every day for the past week.'

'I had noticed. He's sweet and I'm flattered, but I'm not interested.'

'But he's so nice.'

'Well, you pursue him then. I'm sure he'd be better off with someone like you, respectable and clean-living. He goes to church, doesn't he? He'd be shocked if he knew some of the stuff I've done.'

'It's you he likes, Kate.'

'Well, he's got me wrong. Anyway, I'm not over Salvador yet.'

'You're not still hoping Salvador will change his mind?'

'Of course not. But it still hurts.'

'You told *me* to move on.' Abbie opened the gate on to her drive, pausing to admire her orange azalea bush in bloom by the gate.

'I'm beginning to wish I hadn't.'

'Come in, make yourself at home. What would you like – coffee?'

'Please. Then you can show me some pictures of Bill.'

'Oh. Well, I suppose ...'

'Nothing indecent. I'll settle for the fully clothed version.'

'Kate! He hasn't sent any like that.'

'I'm teasing you.'

'Hello?'

'Hello, who's that?'

'It's Abbie. From Dundee. Is that Bill?'

She had finally plucked up the courage to phone him, the following Tuesday evening when the twins were out at Guides. She had discovered, rooting among her saved collection of Bill's messages, that he had included his phone number in a very early one.

Had he been hoping she would call him, all this time? He had never asked for her number. She appreciated the fact that he didn't want to put pressure on her or invade her privacy.

But how difficult it was to ring him. What would she say if one of the boys answered? That was unlikely, since he'd told her they visited him only at weekends, but you could never be sure.

Even worse – what if he had a female visitor? Kate had been right to suggest that he might have other woman friends. Or more than friends. Nothing had ever been said between them about exclusivity. Indeed, it would have been silly – who ever heard of having an exclusive relationship that existed only online?

I've been assuming far too much, thought Abbie – that I'm as special to him as he has become to me. And now my dream is about to be shattered.

Could she bring herself to make this call? But what was the point of continuing with their emails if she didn't? Since her conversation with Kate, she had found herself analyzing his messages for subtle nuances suggesting he was losing interest, that he was looking for a way to let her down gently. Perhaps he had realized that she was taking this far too seriously – that she was trying to make it into something he didn't want at all?

All she could do now was get it over with. After the call she would have an hour, almost, to cry as much as she needed before setting out to pick up the twins. Having to go out would ensure she didn't indulge in her misery for too long. She could always resume it later once the girls were asleep. She could speak to Kate, tell her what had happened, and get some sympathy. Kate would think 'I told you so' but might be kind enough not to say it.

'Abbie! How wonderful to hear your voice.'

'Is it?'

'Of course it is. And I was just thinking about you. Just about to write you a message, in fact. Now I don't need to.'

'You still can, if you like. Write the message, I mean. If you'd rather.'

'No, I'd much rather speak to you in person. Is everything OK?'

'Oh. Yes, fine. I just thought I'd call you. I found your number in an old message.'

'Well....' he paused.

He can't think of anything to say, thought Abbie. This feels all wrong. Where do we start?

'How was your day?' he asked, just as she had opened her mouth to say, 'How are your boys?'

'Not too bad. Pretty much as usual. You know, busy. Lots to do at work. Exam results to collate. Boring stuff.'

'Better than doing them, I suppose.'

'Doing what?'

'The exams.'

'Oh, yes. I see what you mean. Yes, I suppose so.' How could she be so stupid? The quick-witted woman Bill had been corresponding with didn't exist.

'Well, I've had a busy day, too. Working on a new script. Progress was slow.'

Ask something intelligent, she told herself. 'Do you write on your own?'

'Sometimes. Sometimes with a partner. But even if we're co-writing, I usually work on my own right at the beginning. Then we meet up to discuss ideas.'

'That sounds fun.'

'It can be. Except when my co-writer doesn't like my stuff. Or I don't like his.'

'Right.' Abbie's mind went blank again. Later, she would think of good questions to ask, things she genuinely wanted to know. For the moment, her brain produced nothing.

But Bill's voice was warm as he said, 'I can't believe I'm speaking to you, Abbie. After all this time....'

'I know. I can't believe it either.'

'I feel a bit shy. It's like starting all over again, in some ways.'

That made her feel better. 'And me. It wasn't easy, picking up the phone.'

'I can imagine. But I'm so glad you did. I've been wondering whether I should call you. But I didn't have your number.'

'I know. I'm sorry. I should have given you it.'

'No, not at all. Not until you were ready. I've enjoyed the emails. Not a bad way to get to know someone.'

'I agree.'

'So, where do we go from here?'

'How do you mean?' Her heart was thumping.

'I mean what do you want to do next? Speak on the phone instead of sending messages? Or do both?'

'I'd like to do both.'

'Good. Me too. The great thing about emails is you can re-read them.'

'Yes.' So he re-read her messages, did he? Abbie's heart beat even faster, while she felt her body relax. She'd been standing, she realized, for the whole conversation. It was possible she had been shouting. Keith always used to complain that she shouted on the phone.

'Abbie – you've made such a difference to me. I'm so much happier since we've been writing.'

'Really?'

'Of course. Don't sound so surprised. I kind of hoped you'd say the same thing.'

'Oh yes! I'm just a bit taken aback – in a good way. I was expecting this call to wreck everything.'

'Why?'

'Well, you know. That you'd find out I wasn't the person you thought.'

'Abbie, you silly thing. I like your name, by the way. It slips easily off the tongue. Is it short for something?'

'Abigail, but only my mother calls me that. Kate sometimes calls me Abbs.'

'I love "Abbie".'

She liked the sound of that. 'Thank you.'

'Anyway … what I was going to say? Yes, I know it's early days, and we've only just spoken for the first time – but would you like to meet up sometime?'

'I think so.'

'You don't sound too sure. Maybe you'd rather not? We're so far away, after all.'

'Three hundred and sixty miles.'

'You've looked it up?'

This embarrassed her. She had looked it up, of course. 'No, not really. I just sort of knew.'

'OK. Anyway, if you don't want to meet, I understand. We can stick to email and phone if that's what you prefer.'

'Actually – I would like to meet.'

'That's great. Shall I come up to Scotland? I've never been to Dundee.'

'Yes, come and stay. No, I mean … you can stay if you like. Or I could book you in a hotel. That might be better....' She tailed off, embarrassed.

'We can sort out the details later. Maybe a room in a guest house. I mean, I'd love to stay with you, but we should probably stick to the guidelines. Meet up somewhere neutral to start with and all that.'

'Yes. OK.' The excitement was too much. Abbie wanted to run, leap in the air, vent some adrenaline. 'I've got to go. Sorry. My twins need picking up from Guides.'

They didn't, not for another twenty minutes at least, but she needed time alone first – time to relive their conversation and analyse every word.

He said, 'We'll speak again soon. And please keep sending the emails.'

'I will. Goodbye, Bill.'

And he was gone, gone but still there, still hers. And he wanted to meet her.

That would be terrifying, of course, when it happened, but for the moment all she wanted to do was whoop with joy.

chapter six

'Mum, I don't want to go to Dad's this weekend.'

It was the first time either twin had said anything like this, and Abbie found it difficult to take Sarah seriously at first.

'Why ever not? Have you and Lizzie had an argument?'

'It's nothing to do with Lizzie. Can I stay here with you instead?'

It was early Friday evening, ten days after Abbie's first phone conversation with Bill. Since then, they had been ringing each other on alternate days and sending emails on the days between. Three days ago, it had been decided that Bill would visit Abbie that weekend. He planned to set off Friday lunchtime, which should get him to Dundee by early evening. Keith was due to pick up the girls on Friday just before six – so, traffic permitting, everything would dovetail together.

She hadn't yet told the twins about Bill. It was difficult to explain things at this stage, especially when she didn't understand what was happening herself. There was no need to subject them to anxiety which might turn out to be needless if her relationship with Bill never got off the ground. And she didn't want them telling Keith and Fiona about him, and having them all gossiping together about her new relationship.

So when Abbie realized that Sarah genuinely didn't want to go to her father's, she felt punctured – she could feel the excitement hissing out of her.

'Sarah – I need a weekend to myself every now and then.'

This sounded selfish, Abbie realized as she said it. As well as being untrue, since she wasn't planning to spend the time alone. But she ploughed on. 'It's inconvenient for me to change my plans at the last minute. And I don't understand – you love going to Dad and Fiona's.'

'I just don't want to go today.' Sarah's voice was flat. She had, Abbie realized, already accepted defeat.

Abbie persisted. 'Are you feeling ill?'

'Not really. A bit.' Sarah was not a good liar. 'No. I just don't want to go.'

Abbie thought quickly. Bill would be leaving Sunday, mid-morning. 'I tell you what. Why don't we ask Daddy if you can come back early this weekend? If he can bring you back here for Sunday lunch or early afternoon, instead of staying till the evening?'

Sarah's face brightened. 'Can we?'

'Well, we'll need to ask Daddy, to check he hasn't got anything planned. But if it's OK with him, I'll do a home-made pizza for Sunday tea. And make a chocolate cake.'

'Mmm.' Sarah's face broke into a smile.

Abbie felt guilty, bribing her daughter with pizza and cake. But Sarah seemed pleased at the prospect, as though she had forgotten whatever it was that was troubling her about going to Keith's. Abbie crossed her fingers hard. Don't, she begged, let Keith and Fiona have made plans for the twins on Sunday afternoon.

She glanced at the kitchen clock: 5.30. Keith should be here in half an hour to pick up the girls. They'd be away for 6.15, giving her a good thirty-five minutes to get ready. The plan was for her to drive round to Kate's, where Kate would have a meal prepared. It was all part of being careful, of not meeting Bill for the first time alone in her own home. The precaution seemed laughable, since she felt she knew him so well, but Kate had suggested it. When Abbie had put it to Bill he'd thought it was a good idea, joking that he needed to be wary of Abbie as well as she of him.

She didn't feel entirely happy about meeting Bill for the first time in the presence of Kate. But Kate had promised to fade into the background if and when Abbie gave her the signal.

Abbie had booked Bill into a guest house just along the road from Kate's, for two nights, Friday and Saturday. That way, they could see what developed.

Keith arrived on time, rumbling up in a new, shiny four-wheel-drive Abbie hadn't seen before. The twins squealed in response, Sarah's qualms apparently forgotten. Keith stayed in the car and the girls raced out, carrying half-zipped and overflowing holdalls. Abbie followed them and Keith looked at her in surprise, since she usually stayed indoors when he came.

'I just wanted to ask if you'd mind bringing them back early on Sunday? Mid-afternoon, perhaps?'

Keith looked solemn, as though consulting an internal schedule. 'Yes, that should be OK. Any particular reason?'

'Not really. Just fancied having the girls back here early for once. Making pizza for them, perhaps.'

'Well they may not be very hungry. Fiona and I are planning on taking them for a pancake brunch Sunday morning after quad-biking. How does that sound, girls?'

'Fabulastic,' cried Lizzie, using an old family word.

'Don't worry, Mum,' added Sarah. 'We'll be hungry again by teatime.'

Abbie quailed at the thought of the quad-biking. They'd done it before and come to no harm, but still.... She tried to push it out of her mind. Time was getting on and she hadn't even decided what to wear that evening.

'Have a lovely weekend,' she called as Keith revved the engine. The windows were down, the girls waving and calling. 'Take care,' she added.

'We'll look after them,' called Keith, thrumming the accelerator again. It was pure showing-off – he knew he'd need to brake as they approached the junction. Well, she told herself, she didn't care. Bill would be arriving in less than an hour.

Abbie was unusually satisfied with her appearance. Earlier in the week, she had found the time to have her hair cut at a stylist's in Broughty Ferry recommend by Kate. It was expensive but she didn't regret it. The hairdresser had worked some magic that rendered Abbie's hair, even after several days and a couple of washes, smooth and shiny. The cut had a touch of style and she couldn't help returning to the mirror to admire it.

She'd had a hasty shower as soon as Keith and the twins left, and spent fifteen minutes with the hairdryer, turning the ends under. Her make-up was minimal – little more than a touch of mascara to emphasize her eyes. In spite of what Kate might think, she didn't want to pretend to be anything she wasn't, and anyway, Bill had seen the photos of her in her normal state.

She'd gone for a casual look: new jeans a size smaller than her old ones and an emerald silky top that dipped at the front to reveal a hint of cleavage. The jeans were tight and would no doubt be even more so after whatever meal Kate was planning to serve up. Especially as, knowing Kate, there would be a rich pudding to follow, lavished with cream. But she wasn't going to worry about that now. Giving her hair a flick with the brush and adding a little gel to keep it in place, Abbie reflected that she felt unexpectedly calm – that there was a strange sense of inevitability about all of this. Did that mean, she wondered, that the two of them were meant to be together, that fate had decreed this meeting?

She knew she was thinking like a sixteen-year-old, but she didn't care. All that mattered now was to get to Kate's and meet Bill.

It was five to seven when Abbie turned into Kate's road and saw what must be Bill's car, already parked outside. Nothing fancy – a black Volkswagen Golf, several years old.

Her hand on Kate's doorbell, Abbie was struck by the realization that she didn't know this man at all. After all those emails and, by now, a fair number of phone calls, it was easy to believe she'd encountered the real person. But in several senses they knew nothing about each other. The usual cues, clues – whatever you wanted to call them – were lacking. Subtle movements – those bits of body language that gave people away no matter how much they might try to hide. And the even more subliminal messages you received from smell and sometimes touch. All that was missing; all she had to go on came from static visual images and sound. She didn't know how Bill's face changed when he spoke. She had no idea how he moved or took up space, how the air currents disturbed by his body would have an effect on hers. This man she'd thought she knew so well was no more than a stranger.

Her hand froze on the doorbell and she wanted to turn and run, to leave Bill and Kate together. Perhaps they would fall in love and

Abbie would watch from a distance, happy for them both – relieved to be out of it and safe, with only a glimmer of regret over what she had lost.

But she pressed the doorbell and heard footsteps in the hall, followed by a peal of laughter from Kate. Then she was face to face with Bill.

Her first impression was that he was enormous. He took up all the space in the doorway, leaving her no room to step inside. She was whisked back to childhood, to the experience of meeting a huge, terrifying uncle who smiled and hugged her and tried to throw her on to his shoulders while she, the only child of undemonstrative parents, wanted to run away and hide.

This wasn't Bill – a mistake had been made. But she didn't get the chance to explain because the man, whoever he was, hugged her and pulled her into the house, while Kate was yelling something about her being late and could she help with the sauce because it was burning?

And now he was saying, 'Lovely to meet you at last,' and adding, 'Come through, Abbie, sit down. Kate's got some sort of culinary crisis but I'm sure it can wait a minute.'

She couldn't turn her back on him and follow Kate to the kitchen, no matter how much she wanted to. Simple good manners meant she had to stay and speak to him, however much she longed to escape.

She sank on to Kate's sofa and Bill settled himself in the armchair opposite. By doing so he became much smaller and less threatening. He wasn't enormous, after all – probably no more than six foot. Nor was he overweight – just chunkily built, like a rugby player. His face was thinner than it looked on the photos and rather more lined. His smile did odd things to his eyes, making the skin around them crinkle so they almost disappeared. The effect was pleasing rather than grotesque. Would you call this man handsome, she wondered? Perhaps not quite, but his appearance was appealing. So was his laugh, which had a gurgling quality that made her think of a giant baby.

Was he looking at her the same way, she wondered? Did he wonder what had led him to this strange woman in Dundee?

If he thought any of that, he didn't betray it. He seemed excited, like a child on a day out. 'I can't believe we're in the same room at last.'

Abbie realized that she had been sitting in silence for long enough to have a number of thoughts. Bill must think she'd been struck dumb. Or perhaps it was like drowning, and time slowed down to accommodate a thousand thoughts in a millisecond. She hoped, if that was the case, that Bill shared the illusion.

'I know.' Having opened her mouth, the words wouldn't stop. 'It doesn't seem real, does it? All those weeks of emails and phone calls. And now we're finally—' She stopped, brought up short by self-consciousness, the ridiculous sound of her own words in her ears.

'Together,' Bill finished.

'I feel silly,' she said.

He smiled. 'Why?'

'I can't think of anything to say.'

'I feel the same. I got more and more scared, driving here.'

'Did you?'

'Petrified. I almost turned back at Stirling.'

'Why Stirling?'

'No particular reason. It just occurred to me that you might hate me, in the flesh.'

'I don't.'

'That's good.'

'How about you?'

'What do you mean?'

'I was worried you might hate me. Or be disappointed, at least.'

He shook his head, his eyes fixed on her face. 'You're even more beautiful than your photos.'

She jumped at this. But he was joking, of course. 'Liar.'

'I mean it. But listen – I think Kate may need some help, before she burns the house down.'

Abbie registered that Kate was calling. The living room door opened and her flushed face appeared. 'Abbie, please come! Is there anything you can do with this sauce?'

Abbie got up, feeling or imagining Bill's eyes on her as she left the room. She was glad of her new jeans but embarrassed, too – did the close fit make her look tarty?

Kate was stirring the contents of an enormous casserole pan. The smell, which had been rather pleasant and spicy from the living room, was now one of burnt onions and scorched flour.

'I did stir it, honestly,' she said. 'I just left it for a minute while I went to the loo.'

Dark matter from the bottom of the pan swirled in streaks into the pale sauce as Abbie took over the stirring. 'Have you got another pan? If I pour it off I might be able to leave the burnt stuff behind.'

Kate clattered in a cupboard, produced a second pan. Abbie decanted the upper layer of sauce into it. 'Put some cold water on the burnt stuff,' she told Kate.

'You're a genius,' said Kate. 'I told Bill you'd save the day. I should have let you cook this meal from scratch.'

Together they got the rice under way, and when it was simmering, Kate asked, 'So – tell me what you think of him.'

Abbie had not, she realized, thought about Bill for at least five minutes. It had calmed her, sorting out the dinner. She would have liked to stay in the kitchen with Kate, not to have to go back to Bill or even to think about him any more. Not for a while, anyway.

'You look uncertain,' said Kate.

'Oh, no. I like him. It's just all a bit too much, that's all.'

'Well, if you need my opinion, he's fantastic,' said Kate. 'If you don't want him, feel free to pass him on. He's gorgeous and kind and funny. What more could you ask?'

'I knew those things already.'

'Not for certain, you didn't.'

'But he's scary, in the flesh. Too real.'

'He's been your fantasy figure for so long. I warned you.'

'I suppose you did. It's like meeting your favourite pop star, someone you've idolized.'

'Is it? I've never met anyone like that.'

'Well, it's how I imagine it would be. But no, not quite. It's more like the boy you fancied on the school bus, suddenly kissing you out of the blue.'

'Sounds good.'

'No, it's terrifying. Not that Bill has kissed me yet, or anything.'

'Do you want me to go away, leave you together, the two of you?

I could serve up the meal and disappear. I could sleep at your house and leave you here to get on with it.'

'No! No, please don't leave me. I need you here to dilute things a bit. You know what I mean. To make it less intense.'

'Well, if you're sure? I'll leave after dinner, anyway.'

'There's no need. Stay. Bill and I can go for a walk tomorrow. I thought of taking him to Lunan Bay. We can get to know each other there.'

'What about tonight?'

'He's booked into the Tay Prospect guest house, as I told you.'

'What if you decide to spend the night together?'

'We won't.'

'You might.'

'We both want to take things slowly.'

'Did he say that?'

'Well, not in so many words. But I want to, and he knows that.'

'Don't let him go, Abbie. He's a catch, in my opinion.'

'That's only your first impression.'

'My first impressions are usually right.'

Abbie felt uncomfortable, aware of Bill sitting alone in Kate's living room while they talked about him like a couple of school-girls.

'Are you all right now, Kate? Would you like a hand with the serving up?' she asked.

'No, no. You go back to Bill. I'll call you when it's ready.'

'Delicious curry,' Bill commented as they sat at Kate's dining table consuming their meal.

'Saved from the bin by Abbie,' said Kate. 'As you'll soon discover, she's a wonderful cook. Unlike me – I live on carry-outs.'

'Well, this is great. Any chance I could have a bit more?'

Kate refilled Bill's plate. Abbie wished she was hungry herself, since eating would give her something to do, would stop her looking from Bill's face to Kate's and back again.

Kate was exerting her charm. Bill gazed at her, laughing into her turquoise eyes, twice as often as he looked at Abbie. Perhaps he was being polite: he was Kate's guest, after all. But it was disconcerting, the way everything Kate said seemed to amuse him. Come on,

Abbie, she told herself. This is not the time to get paranoid. You'll have a whole day with Bill tomorrow, just the two of you.

But what if it was too late – what if he'd already fallen for Kate, in the way that every man she met was captivated by her? It was not clear why. Kate was overweight and moved with no particular grace. Her features were not beautiful in the classical sense: her nose was a little too large and her teeth not quite even. Perhaps it was her eyes, with their peculiar warm turquoise colour, like shallow sunlit water?

Kate was telling a story about an embroidered tablecloth of her grandmother's, passed down to her as a family heirloom. She had intended to put it on the table until she discovered it was sticky with red candlewax. Not, perhaps, a hilarious tale, except that from Kate's lips it worked magic and Bill was giggling like a schoolboy, in danger of spewing curry sauce over the plain white cloth she had used instead.

Abbie smiled, too. Neither of them had any idea of her discomfort. Kate was not intending to flirt – indeed, she wasn't really flirting at all, she was just being her usual funny, generous, mocking self. She would have been astonished to think she was upsetting Abbie.

And Bill – well, he was enjoying the company of two women who liked him and laughed at all his jokes, while being well fed and offered regular refills to his wine glass. Not giving a thought to which of the two women he preferred, just relaxing in congenial female company after a long drive.

Abbie knew all this, but it didn't comfort her as much as it should have done.

Kate may not have been a great cook but she knew how to do puddings and the dessert was, as Abbie had predicted, sensational. Bill professed not to have a sweet tooth and, after admiring the concoction, asked for only a small portion. After the first bite, however, he declared it to be delicious, and Kate piled more of it into his bowl.

Abbie threw caution to the winds. If Kate was going to lay claim to Bill then it didn't matter if she piled the weight on. She might as well enjoy the gooey calories while the two of them made eyes at each other over the creamy landscape.

But to Abbie's surprise, when they were satiated with meringue, strawberry sponge, fudge, hazelnuts and chocolate sauce, Bill looked at her as he wiped his mouth on his paper napkin and said, 'Abbie, this is a dream come true.'

'Kate made it,' she began, but Kate was getting up, piling up plates to take into the kitchen.

'No, not the dessert – though that was very nice. I mean *you*. You and me, together at last.'

Abbie wanted to cry. It was all too much. Bill reached out a huge hand to hers and clasped it, squeezing her fingers, a question in his eyes – was this allowed? She clutched his thumb in assent and their eyes met for the longest time yet, dipping below the surface of each other's like seabirds, eager and curious.

Kate was gone a long time, and when she came back she carried a jug of coffee. To Abbie's relief, she made no comment on the fact that Abbie and Bill were still touching fingers, their hands resting on the white tablecloth.

'Do you do much cooking?' Kate asked Bill as she poured his coffee.

'A fair bit. I enjoy it when I'm not too busy. When I'm up to my eyes in a script I live on lumps of cheese with the occasional slice of toast and marmalade. That and bananas, vitamin C tablets and whole-nut chocolate. How's that for a healthy diet?'

'I've heard worse,' said Abbie. 'When Keith was writing he often used to eat nothing but salted peanuts all day.'

It felt good, bringing Keith into the conversation over a matter as trivial as food. It put him in his place.

'The temptation is always there for us writers,' Bill said. 'To sit at one's desk, munching. The only way to avoid it is to make sure there's nothing edible in the house before you begin.'

That was good to hear, too: Bill positioning himself alongside Keith as a fellow writer. Two people who, by coincidence, were of almost the same profession. It brought Keith down to earth, made him mortal again.

'What do you write?' Kate asked Bill. 'Anything for TV?'

'No, it's mainly radio comedies,' said Bill. 'None of mine, so far, have made it to the TV screens, though I live in hope.'

How would she feel, Abbie wondered, if one of Bill's series did make the breakthrough to television or did especially well on the radio? Would history repeat itself, would she be unable to bear his success? No, this was different – partly because of Bill's attitude. He was self-effacing, self-mocking; he would take any kind of recognition, she was sure, with a healthy pinch of salty cynicism. Unlike Keith, he didn't take himself too seriously.

The other difference, of course, was that she had not done the chores around Bill for years and years while he struggled with his manuscripts.

'You seem fated to get involved with writers,' Kate was saying to her.

Bill chuckled, apparently taking the 'get involved' in his stride. Abbie didn't quite know what to say.

He stayed another hour or so, having offered to help with the washing up and been turned down by Kate. At 9.30, he said he would make his way to the guest house.

'You sure?' asked Kate. She was being, Abbie realized, deliberately ambiguous.

'Yes. I'm sorry, I'd love to stay longer but I'm exhausted after the drive and everything. Is it OK to leave my car outside your house?'

'Of course.' A minute or two later Kate withdrew, leaving Abbie and Bill in the living room to say their goodbyes and make arrangements for tomorrow.

'She's nice, your friend Kate,' said Bill as the door shut behind her.

A tiny sliver of fear caught in Abbie's throat as though she'd swallowed a piece of metal foil from a chocolate wrapper. She swallowed hard to make it go down. It left a sore place, nothing more. Bill was looking at her, expecting a reply.

'Yes, she's great.'

'I've enjoyed this evening, meeting you both.'

'Me too. It's been wonderful, seeing you at last. I hope you didn't mind Kate being here.'

'Of course not. It made perfect sense. I'd have felt awkward, coming to your house. And we'd have broken all the dating agency guidelines.'

'So we would. Whereas now, you can murder me tomorrow with a clear conscience.'

Bill laughed, but he added, 'Seriously though, Abbie, I hope you do feel you can trust me.'

'Of course I do. I always did.'

'You can't be too careful. If you were to meet anyone else, later, I'd like to think you weren't taking any risks.'

'I know how to look after myself.' Did Bill expect her, then, to be using the agency to look for someone else? But I've found you, she wanted to say. We've found each other.

'Not, I hope, that either of us will need to look any further,' Bill added, on cue. Good.

They touched hands again and Bill planted a light kiss on her cheek.

When he had gone, waving as he went round the corner, she wanted to be on her own, to take in the richness of the evening, sift the memories and throw out the chaff, the twinges of jealousy that could, if not dealt with, spoil the mix. But she felt obliged to help Kate with the washing up and it was clear that Kate wanted to talk.

'You're perfect for each other,' she said. 'And it's obvious he fancies you. Did you see the way he kept looking at you?'

'Not really,' said Abbie, lifting the pan with the burnt sauce from the sink and examining its contents. 'He kept smiling at both of us. He's just a nice, friendly guy. Don't read too much into it.'

'Are you not sure about him, then?'

'I like him. But it's too soon.'

'You don't want to build up your hopes, is that it, in case you're disappointed?'

'Maybe. I don't know. I'm not used to all this, remember. It's years and years since I had a boyfriend. I've forgotten the rules.'

'There aren't any rules.'

'Well, the signals, then. How to play the game.'

'You were doing pretty well tonight.'

'Was I?' Abbie scraped hard at the pan but the burnt skin of sauce still refused to budge. She refilled the pan with water and set it on the side.

'That'll have to wait till morning.' It would sit on the work surface for weeks, knowing Kate, she thought. Well, it wasn't her problem.

'So you're taking him to Lunan Bay tomorrow? A romantic stroll across the sands?'

'That's the idea. Unless it rains.'

'It won't. And then you'll take him home and make passionate love on your living room floor.'

'Kate!'

'Why not?'

'Because it's too soon. And he may not want to. And I may not want to.'

'If there are any rules in the dating game,' said Kate, 'The most important one is "strike while the iron's hot". So, if you want my advice....'

'Thanks.' Abbie was washing glasses now, not quite trusting her manual co-ordination after the wine. 'But I'd rather take things slowly.'

Kate tutted and shook her head.

Later, Abbie took a taxi home, leaving her car outside Kate's, tucked just behind Bill's.

chapter seven

Bill gasped when he saw Lunan Bay curling in a wide arc of white beach, high sand dunes and glittering sea. It was a spectacle he would not have suspected lay only fifteen miles up the coast from brown, post-industrial Dundee.

'This is fantastic,' he said, taking deep breaths of salty air. There was a light wind, just enough to stir their hair, mild and benign. The sun was fitful, diving in and out of clouds that were dark, but too small to be threatening.

'Good, isn't it?' Abbie had discovered this treasure in the first week after her move to Dundee and, having found it herself, felt a sense of ownership. One of the things she loved about Lunan was its emptiness. There were nearly always a few people walking their dogs there, but the beach stretched so far, especially at low tide, that you never felt crowded. It gave you space to feel lonely in the positive sense of the word – alone by choice, part of something big and natural, yet with the freedom to do as you pleased.

Taking Bill to Lunan was, Abbie acknowledged to herself, a bit of a test. If he liked it, she would be more certain than ever that she had found her new love. If he didn't – well, it would be a stumbling block that their relationship would need to overcome. He would need to be worked on and converted.

The drive took just over twenty minutes, the coast road being almost empty on a Saturday morning. Abbie had called at the guest house to pick up Bill, who looked relaxed and happy, with no trace of the lines of tiredness his face had displayed the evening before.

Bill grabbed her hand as they scrambled up the dunes behind the car park, It was a steep climb, at the top of which they saw the sea. Their hands were clasped now, somewhat awkwardly.

The tide being out, there was a mile or more to walk across the bay. 'We don't have to go the whole way,' said Abbie. 'Tell me if you get tired.'

'Oh, I won't get tired,' said Bill. 'I like walking. I'll leave it to you how far we go.'

The double meaning was not lost on her. There was something almost Victorian, or perhaps Austenian, about their courtship so far. Nothing was rushed, yet everything was falling into place. All she needed to do was place one foot after the other as they crossed the shining wet sand to the accompaniment of the squawking seagulls punctuated by the fainter, whinier cry of some other bird.

'You're very lucky, living so close to a place like this.'

'If it was England they'd have built on it,' Abbie replied. 'Beach shops and amusements, bed and breakfasts. Jet-skiing, even.'

'Yes, I suppose so. Though crossing the dunes might put people off. It's a bit of a trek.'

'They'd build a road. But the dunes don't stop people, anyway. It's the weather that stops it being a tourist trap. On the two or three days a year when the weather's good enough to sit on the beach, a lot of families come. Or so I've been told – I've never seen it.'

'Of course, you've only lived here a few months, haven't you? I keep forgetting. I think of you as a native.'

'We moved in last January, just after Christmas.'

'I haven't seen your house yet.'

'You will. I'm going to take you there after our walk. If you like.'

'Of course I'd like to. But I don't want to presume on you. You may want some time to yourself.'

'But you're leaving tomorrow! I don't want to waste any of your visit.'

Bill grinned. 'Well, if you're sure. Thanks.'

'Look there, out at sea! Way out on the horizon....'

He followed her gaze, spotting two silvery arcs entwined, leaping and cavorting.

'Are they dolphins?'

'I'm not sure. We get seals around here but I'm not sure about dolphins.'

'Do seals do that?'

'I don't know. Let's say they're dolphins.'

'Dolphins in love.' Bill kissed her again, this time just above the ear.

Later, she would remember that moment of perfection, with the sand damp and silver underfoot, the half-hidden sun casting long swaths of light across the ridges left by the tide, and a light wind blowing the tang of salt and seaweed into their faces.

Bill said, 'Birmingham isn't a bad place to live. It's got nothing like this, of course. But my flat is down by the canal, close to the water. It's all been restored round there and it's quite pleasant.'

'It sounds lovely. Perhaps I can come and see it sometime?'

'Of course. You must meet my boys, too. I'm sure they'll like you.'

'Are you? Well, I hope so. You must meet my daughters, next time you come.'

'I'd like that.'

A single seagull wheeled above them, squealing.

'I haven't felt as happy as this in a very long time,' said Bill. 'Possibly not since I was first married.'

Abbie squeezed his hand, wishing he had said he had *never* been as happy as this, not even in the early days with his wife. But that was unreasonable, she knew. Only Keith said things like that, about Fiona.

'How about you?' Bill asked.

'The same. I mean, I can't remember when I was last so happy.' She paused. 'Tell me, when did things start to go wrong, between you and Deb?'

He pondered this. 'It's hard to say. I didn't know anything *was* wrong, not really. I suppose we must have slipped into taking each other for granted. It came as quite a shock when she told me about Curtis.'

'Curtis?'

'Deb booked him to give me saxophone lessons for my birthday. Remember, I told you in my emails? I always said I'd like to play. She bought me the saxophone and the lessons, too.'

'Quite a present.'

'Yes. Deb was always generous. Curtis was a nice bloke or so I thought. We got on well. I used to try out my sketches on him. Good sense of humour.'

'He liked your jokes?'

'Well, yes. Or perhaps he was just pretending. Because then *I* became the joke. He and Deb ... well, there's no point going into detail. They found ways to spend time together. It went on for months and I had no idea.'

'How awful. And he was giving you lessons, all this time?'

'Oh yes. I was getting quite good. Could play a few recognizable tunes, anyway.'

Bill fell silent at that point and Abbie didn't feel able to ask any more. He was clearly still upset about what had happened.

The sun had vanished and the sky was darkening, the air colder.

'Do you still want to go right across the bay?' she asked. 'If you like, we can turn back. It's looking like rain.'

'Oh yes, it has clouded over, hasn't it? OK, let's turn back. I'm getting hungry.'

'I should have thought to bring some biscuits. Or apples.'

'Don't worry. We've got sandwiches, haven't we, back at the car? Something to look forward to.'

As they reached the dunes, Abbie, damp and weary, was for some reason overtaken by a need to run. 'Come on,' she cried. 'Race you back to the car.'

Laughing uncontrollably, fighting for breath and footholds, they scrambled uphill, struggling for purchase on the shifting sand and trying to pull each other over. As they reached the top and looked down on the muddy, puddled parking space, they were light-headed, almost drunk.

In the car, munching sandwiches, Bill said, 'You know, Abbie, you're fun. Underneath all the serious stuff and the hurt you've suffered, you're playful, like a child. That's the biggest surprise about you. One of the things I like best.'

Having taken the edge off their appetites and warmed their insides with coffee, they kissed as the rain clattered on the windows and the car filled up with steam.

★

Bill admired the Abbie's bungalow, especially the living-room with its montage almost covering one wall, constructed from drawings, paintings and other artwork done by the twins, going back to their earliest efforts.

'What a marvellous idea.'

'I'm afraid the twins will insist on it being taken down in the not-so-distant future. They're getting to the age of being embarrassed by such things, so I'm making the most of it before it has to be relegated to the loft.'

She made tea and cut Bill a thick slice of fruit cake.

'Hope you didn't go to all this trouble just for me.'

'Not at all. I do a lot of home baking. It's cheaper than the bought stuff and I like to think it's better for the girls.'

Bill had settled himself in the rocking-chair opposite the sofa. He looked as though he belonged there. But Abbie couldn't rid herself of the nagging thought that he still loved Deb. She was considering asking him for some details about Deb's appearance when she heard a car pull up outside the house.

'Good grief – it's Keith and the twins.'

'Ah. So I'm going to get to meet them sooner than I thought.' Bill's face was calm, but Abbie was filled with fury. How could Keith do this to her, wreck all her plans? Of course he didn't know Bill was coming, but still…. He had never brought Sarah and Lizzie back a day early before.

Then she started to worry that something was wrong – perhaps one of the twins was ill. But they were running down the drive, complete with holdalls, looking cheerful and lively.

'I'm sorry,' she said. 'I don't know what's happened.'

'Not to worry.'

Keith didn't come to the door to explain – he simply drove off. She was annoyed but also relieved – at least she wouldn't have to introduce the two men to each other. It was going to be awkward enough with the girls.

At the door, she hugged Sarah and Lizzie in turn. 'You both OK?'

'Yes, we came back early as a nice surprise,' said Lizzie.

'I see – well, it is a surprise. Was everything all right at Daddy's?'

'Of course it was,' said Sarah. 'We had a wicked time. But Fiona and Dad are going to have a special night out. It's two years exactly since they met each other.'

'Is it really?' Abbie and the twins were still in the hall. Bill had remained in the living-room.

Lizzie took over. 'Yes, and Fiona was cross with Dad because he forgot. So she made him take her out for a meal. They had a bit of a row.'

'Quite a big row,' said Sarah. 'I thought she was going to hit him.'

'That's not very nice.'

'She stopped when he said he'd take her out. So he brought us back here. But I didn't mind. Have you made the chocolate cake?'

'Not yet,' said Abbie. 'As a matter of fact, I've got a visitor. Remember I told you a few days ago that I've been sending emails to a man called Bill?'

'No,' said Lizzie.

'I do,' said Sarah. 'Is he your boyfriend, Mum?'

'No – we're just friends. Would you like to come and meet him?'

Lizzie insisted on rushing first to her bedroom to comb her hair, but Sarah went straight through to the living-room where she gave Bill, who was standing up, a shy smile.

He gave her a broad grin and held out his hand.

'Go on, shake hands,' said Abbie.

Giggling, Sarah did so.

'How old are you – eleven?' said Bill. 'You're taller than I expected.'

This pleased Sarah, who was half an inch shorter than her twin. 'Have you got any children?' she asked.

'Two boys – Jon and Sam.'

'How old are they?'

'Fifteen and thirteen.'

At this point Lizzie appeared, with an air of confidence, her hair brushed out of its ponytail. 'Hello.'

'And you must be Lizzie. Very pleased to meet you. I'm Bill.'

'You have to shake hands,' said Sarah.

'Are you two getting married?' asked Lizzie.

Half an hour later, when the twins had told Abbie about their morning's quad-biking (Bill had looked impressed) and then retreated to their bedroom to unpack their bags, Bill said, 'I'll head back to the guest house soon.'

'No, you mustn't do that.' Abbie couldn't decide whether she wanted him to stay or not. 'The twins came back early, without letting me know. They'll have to share me for a while. And they seem quite happy about your being here – it's obvious they like you.'

'Is it? Well, I'm glad. I like them, too. But it's simpler if I go. I can get a meal somewhere and have an early night. I've got a long drive back tomorrow.'

'I feel so bad about this. Why couldn't Keith have rung me, at least?'

'Sounds as though he was being nagged by Fiona.'

'He could still have phoned. That's what he's like. Shows no consideration.'

'Never mind. There'll be another time.'

'Will there?'

'I hope so. If you'll have me back, that is? Or if you'd like to come and stay in Birmingham?'

'That would be great.'

'Look, Abbie – I just want you to know....'

Her heart started thumping. 'To know what?'

'That I like you very much.'

'So do I. Like you, I mean.'

'I was hoping that later on, if you'd wanted to, we could have taken things a bit further. Though you may think it's too soon.'

'Oh. Well. No – I'd like that. If the twins hadn't come....'

'Never mind. Another time. I just wanted to be sure you knew how much I fancied you.'

Her heart did a somersault.

Abbie tried to focus on the twins that Sunday, but it wasn't easy.

Keith rang just after the girls' bedtime.

'Have a good weekend?' he asked.

'I did, actually. Though it was a bit of a shock, the twins coming back early. You might have let me know.'

'Sorry.' He didn't sound it. 'A last-minute thing. Turned out I'd forgotten an important day.'

'Second anniversary of your meeting Fiona. The twins told me.'

'Yes....' He had the grace to sound a little awkward. 'Anyway – there's something we need to talk about. It's Sarah.'

'What about her?'

'Something happened. I don't suppose it's anything to worry about, but I thought I'd better tell you.'

'What happened?'

'She had a bad dream on Friday night. Started screaming in her sleep. Lizzie came to tell me.'

'You mean you didn't hear her yourself?'

'It's a well sound-proofed flat.' Unlike your tiny bungalow with the hardboard walls, she guessed he was thinking but didn't say.

'But Lizzie doesn't normally wake up for anything. Sarah must have been making an awful lot of noise.'

'Oh, she was. Screaming, as I said.'

Keith, she remembered, had always been a good sleeper, had never woken to the sound of babies crying in the night. Or, if he had, he had never let on, but had burrowed under the bedclothes and let Abbie attend to the twins. It seemed that not much had changed.

'She was bright red and sweating but she wouldn't wake up. She stopped screaming after a while and went into a kind of shudder. Quite frightening – I thought it was a fit. Fiona said we should get the doctor.'

'And did you?'

'No, we held her until she calmed down. She did eventually, though it took ten minutes or more. Lizzie was frightened, too, seeing Sarah like that.'

'I'm not surprised. It sounds awful. So did Sarah wake up?'

'No, she went back to sleep, a normal sleep. She was fine after that. Next day she claimed she couldn't remember anything about it.'

'She had an episode of crying in her sleep a while back. Lizzie told me next morning. Sarah didn't remember it.'

'What do you think we should do?' said Keith.

'Perhaps I should speak to Sarah's teacher at school. Find out if there's anything wrong.'

'Good idea. Let me know what they say.'

'Of course. You could come along with me – why don't you drive up one afternoon?'

'No time for that at the moment, I'm afraid. I've got a busy few weeks ahead. Lots of promotions for the new book.'

'Surely Sarah is more important than your book?'

'Of course she is. But you're on hand and I'm not. You can easily go and see the teacher on your own. You've had plenty of experience of schools.'

'That's not the point.' She was beginning to tense up again, the way she often did when speaking to Keith.

'Listen – I've got to go. Fiona's calling. Let me know how you get on at the school.'

chapter eight

The next morning, Monday, Kate arrived at the office twenty minutes late. A glance at her face told Abbie something was wrong. Kate sat down at her desk, slid her feet into her work shoes and logged on to her computer with an enormous sigh. Yes – she did want to be asked.

'What's the matter?'

'Nothing, really.'

'Are you feeling upset about Salvador?' With a prick of guilt, Abbie realized that she had not given a moment's thought to Kate's broken relationship for at least a fortnight. Nor had Kate mentioned Salvador – but perhaps Abbie should have asked.

Kate snorted. 'Not him! I'm not going to let him upset me any more. He's history. No, I'm a bit down because of a silly argument with my mother last night. She was being her usual horrible self. I should be used to it by now.'

'In what way is she horrible?' Abbie already knew that Kate and her mother had a difficult relationship, but she had not seen Kate reduced to tears by it before.

'In every way. She wants me to go and live with her and Dad.'

'What, up in Aberdeen?'

'Of course. They're hardly likely to move down here.'

'But why? Why should you leave your job and everything to go and live with them?'

'Because Mum thinks she and Dad are both at death's door. OK, he has mild angina, but she is perfectly capable of looking after him. She's in good health – she just thinks she has a new ailment every day of the week.'

'Ah.'

'She's been looking for "wee jobs" for me close to where she and Dad stay. Assistant in the village shop – part-time. Bookshelver in the library. That sort of thing. She just wants me on hand – they both do – to take them to their various hospital appointments, make meals for them, do the shopping.'

'But that's ridiculous. Can't you just say no?'

'I have said it. Lots of times – but Mum won't take no for an answer. She told me last night that if Dad dies of a heart attack, I'll have it on my conscience for the rest of my life.'

'That's nonsense – you know it is. Come on, Kate, you're usually an assertive person. Tell her she's being unreasonable. Make it clear what you're prepared to do for them and stick to it.'

Kate lifted her keyboard an inch above the desk and let it bang down again. 'You haven't met my mother.'

'What about your Dad – does he want you to live with them, too?'

'Anything to keep my mother happy, where he's concerned. He just wants to be left in peace with his stamp albums. He knows nothing about my life – neither of them does.'

'You'll have to find a way to tell your mother you can't do it.'

'Impossible. Do you feel like coffee?'

'I should do a bit more work first.'

'Any developments with Bill?'

'Not since yesterday. But I got a phone call last night from Keith. Sarah had a nightmare on Friday night. A really bad one.'

'Poor Sarah. Wonder what's upset her?'

'I can't help thinking it's somehow my fault.'

'How would it be your fault?'

'It might have something to do with Bill.'

'But the twins have only met him once. And they got on well, you said.'

'Perhaps they sensed something different in my attitude. They're very good at knowing when I'm hiding things. Maybe they've picked up that I'm less focused on them, that my attention has moved on to Bill.'

'But it hasn't! You're always talking about the twins. You spend half your life thinking about them. And I don't see any change in that, since you met Bill.'

'Don't you?'

'Of course not. You're worrying far too much. And you're doing that mother thing of trying to blame yourself. Mind you, I wish my mother would blame herself a bit more instead of always blaming me. Tell you what, Abbie – why don't I come round this evening? I've not seen Sarah and Lizzie for a while.'

'That's a great idea. Come round for dinner. The girls would love to see you. Stay the night if you like, then we can have some wine.'

'Great idea. Now I suppose we'd better start work, or we'll have Pam on our backs. She peered in the window a few minute ago and gave me a funny look.'

'Right, that's me finished for the day,' Kate announced at just after 5 p.m. But as she was packing her bag, Steve appeared in the doorway, carrying a computer keyboard. He looked, Abbie reflected, as young as any of the students, though he must be at least thirty. The pinkness of his cheeks was unlikely to be caused by carrying a keyboard along the corridor – it was much more likely to be a reflection of his feelings for Kate.

'Hey, is that my new keyboard?' asked Kate. 'Better late than never.'

'Sorry. I had to order it. Can you manage or do you want me to plug it in for you?'

'I'm just away home. I'll fix it up myself tomorrow.'

'OK.' Steve swayed in the doorway, reluctant to leave. 'Well, if you have any problems with it, let me know.'

'I will. Right – where's my bag? See you tomorrow, Abbie.'

'Er, have you got a minute?' asked Steve. His face was even redder now, like a shy adolescent.

'Not really – can't it wait?' Kate was at the door, trying to edge past him.

'I just wondered it you'd like to come for a drink with me, some-time. Tonight? Or perhaps tomorrow?'

Kate frowned at him, with rather unnecessary unkindness, Abbie thought. 'No, I don't think so. I'm very busy. I'm out tonight. And

I've got my parents coming at the weekend – I'll have to do some tidying up.'

'Oh. Well, perhaps another time.'

'Perhaps,' said Kate, pushing past him into the corridor.

When she had gone, Steve remained in the doorway, gazing at Abbie with bleak disappointment in his eyes. She felt a rush of sympathy but couldn't think of anything useful to say.

'Do you think I should give up on her?' he asked.

Abbie shook her head. 'I don't know. She's finding it hard to get over Salvador. Perhaps it's better to leave it for a while.'

'That's what I keep telling myself. But if I leave it too long, she might find someone else. That's happened to me before.'

'Has it?'

'Not with anyone here. A girl I met in my previous job in Arbroath. I waited and waited, thinking she needed time to get over someone else, and then she got engaged to one of the lecturers.'

'That's tough.'

'I told myself I wouldn't let it happen again.'

'Well, as far as I know, Kate's not interested in anyone else, at the moment. But if I see any signs of romantic activity on her part, I'll let you know.'

Steve grinned. 'That's good of you, Abbie. I appreciate it.'

Abbie felt rather mean, offering to spy on Kate for Steve, but told herself that it was in both their best interests. She liked Steve a lot and thought he would be good for Kate, if only Kate would have the sense to appreciate him.

When Steve left, Abbie checked her mail again, just to see if there was a message from Bill. They'd only spoken last night, but she still longed for the sight of his name on a new message in her mailbox.

There was nothing new except a reminder about the next departmental meeting, sent out by Kate just before she left.

Abbie turned to her work. There was time to file some papers before leaving to pick up the twins. They'd be delighted that Kate was coming to stay the night.

'We're going on holiday in two weeks with Daddy and Fiona,' Lizzie told Kate as they sat at the table over the remains of a shepherd's pie.

'That sounds exciting. When does school break up?'

'This Friday. I can't wait! Then no more Mrs Brown, for ever and ever.'

'Mrs Brown is nice,' said Sarah. 'I wish I was in her class. She's better than my teacher, Mrs Atkins, who looks like a witch.'

'So you two are in different classes?' said Kate.

'It's the school's policy to separate twins,' Abbie explained.

'It's so we get the chance to make our own friends,' said Lizzie. 'So we don't get confused and think we're the same person.'

Sarah snorted, a perfect copy of one of Kate's. 'As if that's going to happen. I'm not likely to think I'm *her*.'

Lizzie put her tongue out at her sister and Sarah pulled a face back. Then both giggled, remembering they had an audience – their mother's friend, the exciting and colourful Kate.

'Would you rather be in the same class?' asked Kate.

Lizzie said 'yes' and Sarah said 'no' simultaneously, then they exchanged glances and each said the opposite.

'I don't think they mind, really, do you?' said Abbie.

'I just wish I had a nicer teacher,' said Sarah. 'But there's only four days to go.'

'And the year after that they'll be off to high school,' said Abbie.

'But not in Edinburgh,' said Sarah.

'What's this about Edinburgh?' asked Kate. 'That's an awful long way to go to school.'

'It's not going to happen,' said Abbie. 'It was a suggestion of Keith's a while back, that the twins become weekly boarders at Fiona's old school. It costs a fortune, apart from anything else.'

'That doesn't matter, because Daddy and Fiona are rich,' Lizzie reminded her. 'But we don't want to go, anyway. We'd be away from all our friends.'

'And we'd miss Mum,' said Sarah.

'Of course you would.' Kate looked at Abbie, eyebrows raised.

'None of us wants it to happen,' said Abbie. 'It was just a silly idea of Fiona's.'

Kate was taking her task seriously. Abbie sat back as her friend asked the twins, 'Do you two like Fiona?'

'Yes, she's nice,' said Lizzie.

'She's OK,' said Sarah. 'Most of the time.'

'What do you mean by that?' asked Abbie. 'I thought you liked her.'

'I do like her – most of the time. When she's not being scary.'

'Scary?' said Abbie.

'Fiona's not scary,' said Lizzie. 'You're just a scaredy-cat.'

'No, I'm not.'

Lizzie glanced at her mother and said, 'She's like a sort of big sister. She doesn't boss us around. She teases Daddy and it's funny.'

'Does it feel strange, sometimes, having two homes?' asked Kate.

Kate was perhaps beginning to lay on the interrogation rather thick, Abbie reflected. But the twins didn't seem to mind.

Lizzie replied, 'No, it's fun. At first we had to remember to take all our stuff from one house to the other. But now Daddy has bought us a new one of everything so it's easy.'

'Sometimes I miss my friends,' said Sarah, 'when we're at Dad's. But not usually. We have a brilliant time when we go there specially when we visit Granny Margaret and Grandad Ryan. They live near the sea and they've got lots of animals.'

'That's Fiona's parents,' said Abbie. 'They live at Burntisland, in an enormous house overlooking the Firth of Forth. Or so I've heard. They've really taken to the twins.'

'And what do you think of Bill?' Kate asked the girls.

'Mummy's boyfriend Bill?'

'He's not my boyfriend,' said Abbie. 'I've only met him once.'

'He seemed OK,' said Lizzie. 'He's got two boys, called Jon and Sam. I've seen their pictures. Jon is quite a looker.'

Sarah giggled. 'He's way too old for you.'

'So you're both enjoying life?' asked Kate.

Sarah and Lizzie looked at each other – perhaps seeking a unanimous reply to an unfamiliar kind of question.

'Except for homework,' said Lizzie, making Sarah giggle again.

'They both seem OK to me,' said Kate later, when the twins had gone to bed and she and Abbie were in the living room sharing a bottle of white wine. 'Not that I'm an expert with children.'

'But they like you, and they love it when you ask them things. It makes them feel grown up. Perhaps that's Fiona's secret, too. As Lizzie said, she's more like a big sister.'

'Well, having two families doesn't seem to be doing them any harm. I think you're the one who's finding it hard going.'

'Well, it *is* hard. But all I really want is for them to be happy. And they do seem it, don't they?'

'As I said, they seem fine. Though I was surprised to hear about the Edinburgh school thing.'

'Oh, that was ages ago. Neither of them liked the idea so it was dropped. Thank heavens. No, I don't think that's bothering them at all.'

'Something must be causing Sarah's nightmares.'

Abbie shook her head. 'Well, I've no idea what. Perhaps the holiday in France will put things right. The girls have had to cope with a lot of changes this year.'

'There was that thing Sarah said about Fiona being scary. What could that mean, do you think?'

Abbie took a sip of wine. 'I don't think it meant anything. She's never mentioned it before. She probably just meant that the situation was a bit overwhelming at first – getting used to her dad having a new partner.'

Kate reached for the bottle and poured more wine for Abbie and herself.

'That's enough,' said Abbie. 'Work tomorrow.'

'Who cares?' said Kate, topping up her own glass further. 'A slight hangover makes work more bearable, I find.'

'Not in my experience.'

'Are you taking the twins on holiday yourself this summer?' asked Kate.

'We'll probably stay with my mother for a few days, down near Peebles.'

'And what about Birmingham? Any plans to take them to see Bill?'

'Not yet. Not until I've been there on my own. If I do.'

'I wouldn't mind a bit of a holiday myself.' Kate stretched out her legs on the sofa, examining a hole in the toe of her black tights. 'You know, over the summer is when I used to see most of Salvador. I'm going to miss him this year.'

'Of course.' Abbie felt another pang of guilt. 'Maybe you and I should go somewhere for a few days. A trip to Oban, perhaps?'

'Maybe. Or you could come with me to Aberdeen. Help me deal with my mother.'

'If you think it would help.'

'Just a joke. My mother is beyond help.'

'Has she always been like that with you?'

Kate sighed. 'As long as I can remember – or just about. She and Dad have always disapproved of everything I do. A mixture of being over-protective and over-dependent. They want to keep an eye on me and they want me to look after them. They hated Salvador....'

'Well....'

'Oh, I know, they turned out to be right. But it wasn't just him. Anyone I went out with, they hated. Anyone I made friends with. They'd probably even manage to hate you.'

Abbie wasn't sure how to take this.

'Oh, you know what I mean,' said Kate. 'Even someone harmless and nice, they'd manage to object to. If they met you they'd think I was mixing outside my class. Getting above myself, my Dad would say.'

'Me, outside your class? Are you joking?'

'You know what I mean. You, with your respectable middle-class Edinburgh background. Brought up in Morningside. I mean, I know you're not snobbish, but they'd assume you were.'

'But I've no reason to be a snob. My background's no different from yours. Not really.'

'That's not true. You didn't leave school at fifteen, did you?'

'Well, no. I didn't think you *could* leave before sixteen. How did you manage that?'

'It's not too difficult, if you get yourself pregnant. Or it wasn't in those days. The school didn't exactly plead with me to go back. Not that my mother would have let me even if they had.'

'Are you saying you were pregnant?' Abbie tried not to sound shocked.

'There you are. It's a whole other world to you, isn't it? At fifteen I bet you were still drooling over ponies.'

'Ponies? I never had a pony. We weren't rich – anything but.'

'Well, reading pony books, then.'

'Not much. I preferred *Ramona and her Sister*. And *Finn Family Moomintroll*.'

'Well, whatever. At least you weren't shoved up against the bikesheds with Dougie Balfour, your fanny stuffed with face cream because someone told you it worked and it was all you had.'

'Face cream?'

'It was supposed to be a contraceptive, if you pushed enough in. I'm not sure whether it was meant to scare off the sperm with its smell, or just trap them in the goo. It didn't work, anyway.'

'So you got pregnant, with a boy from your school?'

'Yep. Now, do you see why you and I are different? That would never have happened to you, would it?'

'It did happen – not to me, but to other girls at my school. Of course it did. Maybe not quite the way you describe. I don't know – I was too scared of boys to go anywhere near them.'

'Or too nicely brought up?'

'No! Not in the way you think. As I keep telling you, we weren't well off at all. We lived in a tenement flat, not a mansion.'

'I bet you never even slept with anyone before you got married.'

Abbie bit her lip and felt herself blush. 'Keith and I did.'

'Was he your first boyfriend, then?'

'Not quite. I went out with a couple of blokes at university. Nothing serious, though. But Kate, what's all this about? Stop attacking me.'

'I'm not. Just pointing out how different we are.'

'OK – maybe we are, in some ways. But what does it matter? Tell me about your pregnancy – what happened?'

'Can't you guess? I had an abortion, of course.'

Abbie tried to read Kate's expression but it was impossible. 'That can't have been easy.'

'It wasn't. I suppose you disapprove.'

'Why do you think that? Stop putting words in my mouth.'

'If *you'd* got pregnant – unlikely, I know, but suppose you had – you'd have been allowed to keep your baby. Your mother would have looked after it while you went back to school. And you'd all have lived happily ever after.'

'To be honest, Kate, I can't imagine what would have happened. My mother would have been horrified. I don't know what she and Dad would have done.'

'They'd have supported you, one way or another.'

'I suppose so. Once they'd calmed down, got over the shock. But it would have been a nightmare. As it must have been for you.'

'She was a girl and I'd decided to call her Selinda.'

'Oh, Kate.'

Kate's face was still blank. 'I thought it was a beautiful name. I still do. I don't know where I'd heard it. Anyway, she was Selinda, from the start, not "it" or "the foetus."'

'Did you have a scan?'

'Of course not. They didn't do them in those days, not without good reason.'

'So how did you know she was a girl?'

'I just knew. Do you understand that?'

'Of course I do. I knew I was expecting twins, right from the start – don't ask me how. Mind you, there are twins in Keith's family so it wasn't completely unexpected. But as soon as I got the pregnancy test results, I thought, "Right, there are two of them in here." No one believed me, of course. When it became clear, weeks later, that I was expecting twins, people said things like, "Oh, every first-time mother thinks they're having twins." But I knew, I really did. There were two distinct people right from the beginning and I could tell.'

'That's impressive.'

'No more than you knowing your baby was a girl.'

'Well, I never had any proof. Because she was aborted. Terminated. Unlike your lovely twins.'

'Oh Kate. I'm sorry.'

'You don't need to be sorry.'

'You know what I mean.'

'I love your girls.'

'I know you do. They love you.'

'Good. Well, do you want to hear the rest or not? It's not a nice story.'

'Of course I want to hear.'

'I'll start again, at the beginning, with me and Dougie.' Kate paused.

'What was Dougie like?'

'Just a lad the year above me at school. Pretty ordinary, I suppose, looking back. He told my best friend Carol he fancied me. I was flattered – he wasn't bad-looking. Better than most. We went out a few times in a group. Then I heard he'd been seen with another girl. He and Annie, sitting on the harbour wall, sharing a can and kissing. I made the mistake of challenging him. Asked him what was going on. He said he had lots of girlfriends, all the time. I could be one of them, if I wanted. So I told him I didn't want that. I wanted him all to myself.'

'And?'

'He laughed, thought it was a hilarious idea. But I could see he was taken by it. He liked thinking I'd fallen in love with him. Not that I said so, but he must have seen it in my face. I expect I gave him mooning looks. I must have seemed a complete idiot. Anyway, he said, fine, I'll be your boyfriend, your one-and-only. On one condition.'

'What?'

'He asked me to meet him round the bikesheds at break on Tuesday morning.'

'I see. Hence the face cream.'

'I wasn't stupid. I knew about babies and diseases. But getting hold of a condom was a different matter. And I half-believed the face cream story. It made sense, kind of. And I didn't think we'd go the whole way, the first time. I didn't know you *could* go the whole way, standing up. Especially not when the boy was much taller, as Dougie was. I couldn't picture it, if you know what I mean. I thought it would be a matter of – well, a bit of fondling and kissing, maybe his hand up my skirt.'

'But it went further.'

'Of course it did. He knew what he wanted. But even then, I thought I'd be OK. You know, you never believe you'll become pregnant first time. Then there were more times and I started to wonder. But it was all part of the deal. Until I discovered he was going behind my back, anyway, still seeing other girls, most likely shagging them behind the bikesheds, too, or down by the harbour wall.'

'How awful.'

'I suppose I was stupid to trust him in the first place. A good lesson to learn early in life. At least I knew my baby was Dougie's. There weren't any other boys then. I've always been glad about that – to know he was the one. He wasn't bad at all, Dougie Balfour. He might have made a good father for Selinda.'

'Except that he deceived you.'

'He wouldn't have seen it that way. It was what they all did. There were no rules to break, where they were concerned.'

'Did he know he'd got you pregnant?'

'Of course he didn't.'

Kate looked about fifteen now, Abbie reflected, lying there on the sofa in the dim light. Her hair had escaped its slides and tumbled across her face and down to her shoulders. There was a frown of concentration on her face and her cheeks were flushed.

'So, what happened?'

'To cut a long story short, my parents hit the roof. Hit it and kept going – went right through it. I'd known I was pregnant for a few weeks. I was determined to keep Selinda. I'd made plans, about how my mother would look after her while I was at school. I was sure she would do that – she always cooed over babies in their buggies. She used to tell us how the happiest time of her life was when my brothers and I were small. So I didn't think there'd be a problem once she got over the shock. It was just a matter of finding the right time to tell her.'

'And when you did?'

'I didn't tell her, in the end. She saw how I'd let out my school skirts. She noticed there'd been no sanitary pads in the bin for two or three months. She put a lot of twos together and made a great big four. One evening she and my Dad got me alone in the front room and laid into me. Told me I was a disgrace to the family name. How I'd dragged them down into the mud after they'd struggled for years to improve themselves. A load of guff. But it made me cry.'

'I'm not surprised.'

'Everyone thought I was strong in those days. I was one of the tough girls. You wouldn't have liked me.'

'Who knows? You probably wouldn't have liked me, either.'

'Anyway, Mum didn't want a grandchild, it turned out. She didn't want a daughter, either, not if it meant being lumbered with a baby, too. Her word, "lumbered." She said I could find myself somewhere else to live if didn't get rid of it.'

'Really?'

'Yes, really. I told you you wouldn't understand. Not the sort of thing your nice middle-class parents would have done, is it?'

'They'd have been angry and upset. I'm sure they'd have felt I'd let them down. Perhaps they'd have expressed it in a more subtle way than yours. But still....'

'They'd have let you keep the baby?'

'I don't know. Perhaps they'd have had it adopted. I can't imagine I'd have had much say in the matter. It's difficult to imagine myself with a baby at that age. I wouldn't have had a clue.'

'But surely your mother would have helped look after it?'

'She had a job – she was a teacher, too. They couldn't have managed without her salary. I don't know what we'd have done. Perhaps they would have talked me into having a termination. How I'd have felt about that later, I don't know. I'm not against women being offered terminations, especially not at that age.'

'I wasn't offered one – I was blackmailed. They threatened to throw me out.'

'I know. That's terrible.'

'The worst of it is, when I look back now, I know what I should have done. I should have kept Selinda. Walked out on my parents. I'd have probably got a council house. I wouldn't have been home-less and I'd have still had my baby. She would have been eighteen now.' Kate's voice shook and her eyes brimmed with tears.

They were silent for a moment. Abbie got up from her chair and joined Kate on the sofa, taking her hand. 'Kate, you can't blame yourself.'

'Of course I can. I let them kill her. Do you think that's easy to live with?'

'But you were fifteen and terrified, with your parents threatening to evict you.'

'I should have loved my daughter enough to keep her.'

'That's asking far too much of yourself, as you were then. It's all too easy to judge your old self, now you're an adult.'

'Anyway, my parents never spoke about the baby again. Once it was done. I was never allowed to mention her, either. Not that I tried. I knew she was a banned topic. She has been, ever since.'

'Even now?'

'Oh, we've never spoken about Selinda.'

'I'm beginning to see why you don't get on with your mother.'

'But that doesn't stop her wanting me to go and live with them.'

'You don't owe them anything, by the sound of it.'

Kate sighed. 'It's not quite so simple. Mum loved me in her own way – still does, I suppose. She's helped me out with money and she gave me a place to stay when I split up with Pete. It's not as easy as you might think, saying no to her. She's very determined and she knows how to make me feel guilty.'

'Mothers are good at that.'

'I sometimes think I should just resign and do as Mum suggests, go and live with them. Get a part-time job in a shop or as a cleaner and spend the rest of the time ferrying my parents to their various appointments.'

'Don't be silly. You mustn't think that way.'

'I haven't even got the excuse of Salvador now, for staying here. Not that it made much difference to him where I was. But at least I could tell my mother I had to stay in Dundee because of him.'

'Well, if you were to get together with Steve....'

'Steve?' Kate chuckled. 'There's no way that's going to happen.'

'Why not? He's a nice bloke and he likes you. Can't you give him a chance?'

'Didn't you understand a word of what I said earlier?'

'What do you mean?'

'All the stuff about my past. Do you think Steve would be interested if he knew what had happened to me? He and his parents go to church together, every Sunday. A posh one.'

'What difference does that make? And just because you had a termination years and years ago, why would he hold that against you?'

'He might. Religious people can be funny about these things. But it's the other stuff I was talking about, the class thing. He's like you, he's had a nice upbringing. If he knew half the stuff about my life, the kind of people I've been with, the stuff I've taken.'

'Stuff you've taken?'

'Drugs.'

'But you don't do that now?'

'Of course I don't. Not even Salvador could persuade me to do that again. But there's another thing – I can't have kids. I don't think I can, anyway. Pete and I never conceived in three years. The abortion must have damaged my tubes or ovaries or something.'

'Kate, I'm sorry. But tell me, who's Pete? You mentioned him before.'

'I was married for a few years in my twenties. Pete was OK. We didn't talk much about it, but he knew about Selinda. He was a nice man, worked hard, a good laugh. Kind.'

'So what happened?'

'I'm not sure. Maybe if we'd had a baby, we'd have stayed together. But it didn't happen and we somehow gave up on the whole thing. Our sex life wasn't wonderful, with the stress of trying to get pregnant. We both met other people. He's in Canada now. His new relationship lasted, or I assume it did. Mine didn't.'

'I'm sorry.'

'You keep saying that.' Kate rubbed her eyes with a tissue. 'I'd better clean myself up.' She paused. 'I've told you a lot about myself tonight. Still want to be friends?'

'Of course I do.'

'Don't throw away your chance of happiness, Abbie. Don't let Bill go.'

'I'm not going to, if I can help it. But I didn't tell him about my depression – not properly. I'm worried he'll change his mind about me when he finds out. And now, after this nightmare of Sarah's, I'm afraid that our relationship will upset the twins.'

'I'm sure it won't. They'll handle it, as long as you explain it properly. But you've got to be honest with Bill. Tell him about your depression – and about your worries about the twins. If those things put him off, he's not worth keeping. You've nothing to lose.'

'How can you say that, when you say you could never tell Steve about Selinda?'

'It's different for me.'

'Is it?'

Kate didn't reply and they fell silent for a few minutes. Abbie had begun to feel very tired and Kate looked sleepy, too. 'You ready to go to bed?'

'I suppose. There's no more wine, is there?'

'No.' Abbie held up the empty bottle. 'Sorry.'

'No problem. Thanks for listening to all my stuff.'

'I hope it helped,' said Abbie. 'I'm glad you felt able to tell me about Selinda.' She went to her bedroom to get a sleeping bag and pillows for Kate to make herself a bed on the sofa. After that, she checked her email, but there was nothing from Bill. As she brushed her teeth, she thought about sending him a message, but couldn't work out what she would say.

She peeped in at the twins, who were sleeping soundly. Lizzie was on her back in the bottom bunk, faintly snoring, and Sarah on the top one, curled up like a foetus, thumb in her mouth. Abbie blew them each a kiss, slipped out and went to her own bed.

chapter nine

Something startled Abbie from a dream and within seconds she was in the twins' room, still half-asleep. Sarah and Lizzie were both breathing gently. Had she dreamt the sound? No, she could still hear it – a faint sobbing coming from somewhere else in the house.

She opened the living room door. Kate was no longer on the sofa but sprawled on the floor, wearing blue pyjamas, looking not unlike Sarah, with her thumb in her mouth. She seemed to be sleeping so soundly that Abbie wondered for a second time whether she had imagined the sobs.

She sat in the chair opposite for a few minutes, making sure that Kate was not going to cry again. Then she whispered, 'Sleep well', pulled the cover over Kate and padded to the door.

She was too wide awake now to go back to bed and went to the kitchen to pour herself half a glass of orange juice, which she sat down at the computer to drink. This led to checking her email once more, to see if Bill had sent a late-night message.

There was nothing there but advertising junk, mocking her from her mailbox for being the sad kind of person who checked her email at 3 a.m.

Head in hands, she thought about what Kate had told her that evening, about her parents and Selinda and Pete. For some reason she found herself opening up a message box and typing words to Bill.

Hi Bill,

It's a funny time of night to be writing but I don't feel sleepy and there are a few things I need to say.

First of all it was lovely meeting you though I'm sorry your visit was cut short. Sarah and Lizzie have told me several times how much they like you. I like you too, of course – very much indeed. But I'm worried.

Which brings me to another thing – my depression. I mentioned it to you and you seemed to think it was no big deal, which was good in one way but I wonder if you realize how bad I was. I should have gone into more detail. I was off work for months and have only just come off my anti-depressants after over a year. It could come back at any time so I have to be on guard. I'm not telling you this to get sympathy, but so you under-stand it's serious and know what you are taking on. I'm afraid to say this because it may put you off me, but I don't want to get to know you on false pretences. I don't want you to get hurt, either.

I'm also concerned about the effect of our relationship, should it become one, on the twins. I know you are probably thinking I should have thought this through before joining the dating agency. Well, you are right – but I don't think I really believed I would find anyone. Certainly not anyone as nice as you. The twins have been through a lot and I don't want to make things any worse for them.

Sorry to be so negative. I will understand if you don't want to hear from me again after this.

Love, Abbie

She studied what she had written, corrected a couple of minor errors, then pressed 'send'.

Within five minutes she was back in bed and asleep.

Bill's reply, which she read next morning before 7 a.m., was time-stamped 3:32 a.m. He must have written it, Abbie realized, soon after hers arrived.

Dear Abbie,

What an unexpected treat to get your email just now. I was sitting at my computer, trying to dredge up some inspiration for a script, and suddenly there it was.

I'm very moved at your honesty. Let me reassure you that I understand how serious and long-lasting depression can be (my mother has it) and that it doesn't change my feelings for you at all – why should it? But I understand your fears about getting hurt again and I will do my best not to let that happen.

Only you can decide whether you are ready to move on, and of course we both have children to take into account. If you feel that it's too soon for the twins to get used to your having a man in your life, I will understand. Though I will, of course, be very disappointed. But I understand you have to put Sarah and Lizzie first. (They seem to have accepted Keith's new partner, though....)

Things here are not good. Today was a miserable day. I spoke to Jon on the phone this evening and he told me he doesn't want to see me on Saturdays in future. He has other more important things to do. These, I know, include going to see the football with Curtis. But that's enough of my moaning.

I'll send this now in case you are sitting at your computer, waiting.

Lots of love and all the reassurance I can give.

Bill

Reading this in the morning, Abbie could hear a commotion in the kitchen as the twins helped themselves to cereal and milk. Kate was in there with them. Let them look after each other, she thought. She wanted to stay with her email, reading Bill's words over and over.

He had managed to say exactly what she needed.

'Abbie,' called Kate. 'Do you have any muesli?'

She closed the mail program and shut down the computer. She had arranged to take Sarah straight to the GP's surgery after dropping Lizzie off at school. Abbie had imagined they would all three go together, but Lizzie insisted she didn't need to see a doctor, as she wasn't the one having nightmares. Sarah, too, had seemed to prefer the idea of going there without her sister. Abbie also planned to speak to Sarah's teacher later in the week.

Kate said, 'I wanted to make Sarah and Lizzie my special recipe breakfast mix. I found some dried apricots and nuts but we couldn't find the muesli. And do you have some honey?'

Abbie checked the kitchen clock. 'We're rather short of time. Can't you just have cornflakes as usual, girls?'

But the twins protested and Abbie found she was turning out the contents of a kitchen cupboard before a packet of muesli, three months out of date, was found.

That evening, as Abbie and the twins ate chicken salad on the lawn, enjoying the still air and gentle sunshine, she told Lizzie and Sarah about her plans.

'I'm going to stay with Bill for a weekend while you two are in France.' She tried to sound casual but managed to half-choke mid-sentence on a piece of spring onion.

'Where does he live?' asked Lizzie.

'I told you – Birmingham.'

'That's in England, isn't it?'

'Yes, right in the middle.'

'Does that mean he's your boyfriend now?' asked Sarah, her hand stopping halfway to a slice of bread.

'I wouldn't say that. We're hoping to get to know each other a bit better, that's all.'

'Is he coming to live with us?' asked Sarah.

'No, no. It's much too early to make plans like that.'

'Are we going to live with him?' asked Lizzie.

'No, as I said, it's much too early to think that way. This is just a friendly visit.'

'Does Daddy know?' asked Lizzie.

'Not yet. But I don't mind him knowing. You can tell him and Fiona, if you like, next time you see them.'

Sarah asked unexpectedly, 'Does Bill write stories?'

'No, I don't think so. He's a kind of writer, though. He writes comedy scripts for the radio.'

'Not for TV?'

'I don't think so.'

'Does he do drawings for his radio programmes?' Sarah asked.

'No, I'm pretty sure he doesn't. Why would he? You can't see drawings on the radio.'

'Stupid question,' said Lizzie.

Sarah, to Abbie's surprise, blushed. She was not normally

bothered by insults from her sister: they each gave the other as good as they got.

'I was only asking,' Sarah said.

'Were you wondering if he's a bit like Fiona?' Abbie asked.

'How can he be like Fiona, when he's a man?' said Lizzie.

Sarah snapped, 'You're the stupid one.'

'That's enough',' said Abbie. 'You've met Bill so you already know he's a nice man, who you get on well with. You don't mind me spending a weekend in Birmingham, do you?'

'No, of course we don't,' said Lizzie. 'We are going away so why shouldn't you?'

Sarah nodded in agreement and Abbie felt a wave of relief.

Later, when Sarah and Abbie were finishing the clearing up in the kitchen and Lizzie was in her bedroom, Sarah touched the back of Abbie's soapsuddy hand with her finger and said, 'I hope Bill *doesn't* become your boyfriend, Mum.'

Abbie dried her hands on the tea towel and put her arm round her daughter. 'Why, pet?'

'I just don't want him to.'

A sigh escaped Abbie before she could stop it. 'But you told me you liked Bill.'

'I *do* like him.'

'Then why?'

'Just a funny feeling.'

'But you're all right with Daddy having Fiona. Why is this any different?'

'It just is,' said Sarah. 'It's different because you are our mum. And because one is enough.'

'You mean you can put up with one parent having a man or woman friend, but not both of us?'

'Yes.'

'But Sarah, don't you think that's a bit unfair on me?'

'But you're our mum.'

'Of course I am. And I'm not going to stop being. I won't suddenly start going away all the time, like Daddy.' Abbie felt guilty for saying this. 'Though a lot of it's because of Daddy's work, of course. His books. All I'm planning is to occasionally go to stay with Bill for a weekend, while you're with Daddy and Fiona. And maybe have him here again. You don't mind that, surely?'

Sarah looked doubtful. 'Maybe not.'

'Sarah, I promise you I won't love you any less. Neither of you. I'll always love you and Lizzie more than anyone. I'll always be here.'

Sarah hugged Abbie back, squeezing hard. 'I know. I love you, too, Mummy.'

'Then promise me you won't worry.'

'OK, if you promise you won't ever go to live in Birmingham and leave us with Dad and Fiona.'

'I've no intention of doing that, I promise. If I go anywhere, you'll come too. But I've no plans to move, not for years and years, at least. We're well settled here, aren't we, you and me and Lizzie?'

'I suppose.' Sarah's attention had wandered and she was eyeing the cake tin. 'Is there any of that chocolate cake left?'

Later, Abbie showed the twins some further photos of Bill and his boys. Lizzie asked a number of questions and appeared quite happy. Sarah said little and continued to look, Abbie thought, rather anxious.

'What happened to Jon and Sam's mum?' Sarah asked.

Abbie explained about Bill and Deb's divorce and that Deb now had a new partner.

'It's like musical chairs,' said Sarah. 'Where you rush round to get a chair and one person is left without one.'

'That's why Mum doesn't want the leftover person to be her,' said Lizzie. 'I don't blame you, Mum. I wouldn't either.'

'But there doesn't have to be a leftover person, does there?' said Abbie. 'It's not as though someone's taking a chair away each time, not in real life.'

'But some chairs are comfier than others,' said Sarah.

This made Lizzie laugh. She replied, 'Some chairs are more like sofas,' and the two of them collapsed on the floor, tickling each other in a pile of squeals and giggles.

Abbie congratulated herself that she'd handled it all quite well, that both girls seemed to have begun to accept the idea of her relationship with Bill.

★

'Mummy, I'm not stopping Lizzie. She can still go to France with Daddy and Fiona.'

Abbie was hanging out the washing on the rotary clothes drier at the back of the house. It was a bright morning with a sharp breeze disturbing the bushes, chilly enough to make Abbie envious of those who were about to travel to the south of France.

'But Sarah, she won't want to go without you.'

'She *does* still want to go. I asked her. She says it'll be better without me. She'll get more attention.'

'Darling, what's all this about?'

A week had passed and Sarah and Lizzie were due to be picked up that evening by their father. The plan was to stay overnight in Edinburgh prior to an early flight next morning to France.

'I've changed my mind, that's all. I'd rather stay here with you, Mum. There's a nice beach here in Carleith. I don't need to go all the way to the south of France. We can go on picnics and things together. We can go to Moomin Bay.'

'Lunan Bay.'

'I know. I just like calling it that. Please, Mum – don't make me go.' Sarah paused, then added, 'I might have nightmares if I go to France.'

Abbie dropped a couple of pegs but left them lying on the grass. 'Sarah, you haven't had one for over a week now.'

Was this a genuine worry of Sarah's, Abbie wondered, or was she using her nightmares as an excuse to avoid the holiday? 'I can't understand why you suddenly don't want to go. You've been so excited about it, ever since Dad booked it. What's changed in the last day or two?'

'Nothing. I've just changed my mind. Dad says changing your mind is a woman's per … gorative.'

'Prerogative.'

'Yes, that's it. He said it when Fiona wanted to exchange the lovely dress he bought her for her birthday.'

'I see.'

'So I can change my mind about going to France.'

'But it's all paid for.'

'You can get the money back through insurance. That happened to Josie, when they couldn't go on holiday because her gran died.'

'That's different. There has to be a good reason, like someone dying or being ill. You can't just change your mind.'

'I could be ill.'

'You're not ill. Anyway, it's much too short notice. Daddy and I would still have to pay for you, even if you didn't go.'

'Not Daddy and you, just Daddy.'

'No, both of us. I'm paying a share of it.'

'Why are you, when you're not going?'

'Because you and Lizzie are my daughters. It's only fair.'

'But Daddy has lots of money these days. Much more than you.'

'That's irrelevant.' Abbie bent down to pick up the dropped pegs and took another damp towel from the basket.

'Mummy, I wish you were coming too.'

'To France? Well, yes, it would be nice, to have a holiday somewhere warm. But I can't, can I? It wouldn't make sense. I'd be in the way.'

'No, you wouldn't. Not to me and Lizzie. We could all three of us do things together, and Daddy and Fiona could stay in the hotel room and snog.'

Abbie turned round quickly to face her daughter. 'Is that what they do?'

Sarah pulled a face. 'Sometimes. When we went on that first holiday with them to London they snogged all the time. They don't do it so much now.'

Abbie pegged the towel to the line. 'Sarah, do you know what Lizzie's doing at the moment?'

'She's in the bedroom, packing.'

'Why does she want to go to France and you don't?'

'Why shouldn't she? You always tell us we don't have to be the same.'

'I'm not saying you should be the same. I'm just asking.'

'Lizzie likes Dad and Fiona together, and I don't.'

Abbie felt the first twinge of panic as it dawned on her that Sarah was serious. If she refused to go to France, what would happen to her own trip to Birmingham?

'But you *used* to like Daddy and Fiona together. Only last

weekend you had a lovely time at Burntisland with Granny Margaret and Grandad Ryan.'

'Fiona is better when Granny Margaret is there. She doesn't ...' Sarah stopped, reached down into the basket and picked out a tea towel.

'She doesn't what?'

Sarah used the tea towel to lash at a passing butterfly with such vigour that Abbie jumped.

'Don't do that, Sarah. What harm has that butterfly done to you?'

'Sorry.'

'You were saying about Fiona. What is it she doesn't do as much of when Granny Margaret is there?'

'She doesn't talk as much.'

'She talks a lot, does she?'

Sarah sighed, as though some things were too difficult to explain. 'Mummy, your parents never got divorced so you don't understand.'

'Perhaps not. But I'd like to. Can you tell me a bit more? Please?' Abbie had abandoned the rest of the washing and was sitting on the hammock seat now, looking hard at her daughter. 'Please, Sarah, tell me what's wrong. Something is, isn't it?'

'No!' Sarah cried, jumping on to the hammock beside Abbie, bouncing. 'Nothing. But if you make me go I'll have nightmares every night. I know I will.'

Was it emotional blackmail – an attempt on Sarah's part to stop her going to Birmingham? Maybe Sarah didn't even realize what she was doing. Abbie hated herself for suspecting it, but she couldn't get the thought out of her mind. If Sarah had seemed more upset about the whole thing, she might have been able to find more sympathy. But her daughter's manner was nonchalant, verging on cheeky.

To her horror she found herself saying, 'Sarah, you're being selfish. I was looking forward to going to Birmingham to see Bill. You know I was. You just don't want me to enjoy myself.'

Sarah gasped, deflating before Abbie's eyes. 'Mum, I hate you! You're horrible! You don't care if I have a terrible time in France. You only care about that stupid Bill.'

'No, Sarah, it's not like that. Oh, I'm sorry. Don't cry, sweetheart.'

Sarah nestled against her, just as when she was small, and Abbie rocked the hammock, swinging it too and fro with her foot on the ground, assuring Sarah that she didn't have to go to France if she didn't want to. She felt as though she had broken every rule in the book of motherhood.

'Bill, I'm sorry. I feel so bad. After all the plans we made.'

'Abbie, it's OK. I understand. I know what kids are like. Believe me, I know.'

'I was looking forward to it so much. I'm really disappointed.'

'And me.'

'Can we do it again, another time?'

'You bet we can. Just let me know when you can manage it.'

'Of course.'

'I could come up to Dundee this weekend, instead, I suppose.'

'Sarah will be here.'

'Well, I don't mind. I'd like to meet her again.'

'To be honest, I don't think Sarah would want it, the way she is at the moment. So clingy. She keeps talking about how nice it will be, just her and me. I'm sorry.'

'Could that be it, maybe? She's seen the chance of a bit of time alone with you? It must be a bit like that, when you're a twin, you hardly ever get your parents to yourself.'

'I don't think it's that. They both get time on their own with me. And Sarah's never been like this before. It's completely out of the blue, this wanting to be with me. Normally they can't wait to shoot off to Keith's.'

'Poor things – they can't win, can they?'

'Ouch. It's just the timing that's so bad.'

'I know. I do understand. Please don't worry about it. We'll be together soon, you and me. We'll just have to wait a bit longer.'

'Are you taking the boys on holiday?'

'Possibly, for a few days somewhere. If I can drag them away from Curtis. They're still at school, remember – the holidays in England don't start for another two weeks.'

'Of course. Oh Bill, I'm so fed up.'

'Chin up, Abbie. Think of this as a good time to find out what's wrong with Sarah. If there is something, this is your chance.'

'You're right. But I don't *want* to be a selfless parent at the moment. I was looking forward to a bit of time off.'

Bill laughed. 'I know the feeling. I've got problems with both my boys at the moment. Sam hates school and Jon hates me – he'll barely speak to me any more. I've no idea why. He seems to have decided to let Curtis take my place.'

'That's awful.'

'So be thankful your daughters love you.'

'I don't expect they will, by the time they're Jon's age.'

'Hmm. Well, I don't know. I keep thinking with my boys it must be something I've said or done.'

'It won't be that. You're a great father. It's their age.'

'Hope you're right. Take care, Abbie.'

'You too.'

'I don't care that Sarah's not going to France,' said Lizzie later that day, when the call to Keith had been made and the whole rigma-role of questioning Sarah gone through again.

Keith, Abbie noted, appeared to handle Sarah no better than she had. She was not sure how she felt about this.

When he finally conceded to Sarah's staying behind, Sarah jumped up from the sofa, beaming, and ran into her room to unpack the few things she'd already put in her holdall, including her old Sammy rabbit.

'Samantha's glad that Sammy's not coming on holiday,' said Lizzie. Samantha was Lizzie's rabbit, Sammy's twin. This comment made Abbie wonder if Lizzie did mind about Sarah's defection, after all. Lizzie had a tendency to revert to baby play when things got too much for her.

Sarah ignored her sister and continued to unpack her bag and rearrange her treasures in their places around the room.

'It'll be more fun without you,' said Lizzie, 'We'll be able to do grown-up things.'

'I'm as old as you are.' But Sarah's heart wasn't in the argument. She was too happy to make the effort.

'Not quite,' said Lizzie. 'You're seven and a half minutes

younger. But that's not the point. You don't like grown-up things like drinking wine. Daddy said I could have some on holiday.'

'He said I could, too.'

'But you don't like wine.'

'I know I don't. But he still said I could have some if I wanted.'

Lizzie changed tack. 'I'll have a whole room to myself. Two beds to choose from. I'll sleep in one the first night and the other the second.'

'Then you'll have to go back to the first one again.'

'I know I will, stupid.'

'So what's the point?'

'The point is, it'll be fun. I'll have the whole wardrobe for my clothes. All the coat hangers.'

'I don't care.'

'I'll get more treats because you're not there.'

'No, you won't.'

'Yes, I will, because there'll be more money to go round.'

'There doesn't have to be enough money to go round. Not now, with Daddy's books. He's always got lots of money.'

'But he doesn't want to spoil us.'

'So he won't spend extra money on you, in case you get spoilt.'

'I bet he will.'

'Then you'll get spoilt.'

'No, I won't. I'm grown-up enough to handle it.'

'Girls, stop arguing.' Abbie's head was beginning to ache.

Keith had had 'a quick word' with her on the phone after he'd spoken to Sarah, and it had lasted over an hour. Abbie had ended up feeling it was her fault that Sarah didn't want to go on holiday. 'Couldn't you have persuaded her?' was the gist of his argument. Followed by, 'Fiona will be so hurt.'

'You don't need to tell Fiona that it's because of her that Sarah doesn't want to go,' Abbie said. 'You can make some excuse, surely. Anyway, it's not clear that is the reason. She may be genuinely worried she'll have bad dreams.'

'Well, we'll see,' said Keith. 'Though I think it *is* because of Fiona that Sarah doesn't want to go. She has never got on as well with Fiona as Lizzie does.'

Why put it that way round, thought Abbie. Wasn't it the adult's responsibility to make an effort to get on with the child? But Keith would never be able to see any fault in his beloved Fiona.

'I didn't know that Fiona and Sarah didn't get on.'

'Oh, they get on, of course they do,' said Keith, his voice tetchy even though he'd said almost the same thing. 'It may just be a matter of temperament. I think Fiona and Lizzie are more alike. Fiona was telling me the other day that Lizzie has a real aptitude for drawing.'

'I can't say I've noticed it.'

'Well, sometimes it takes someone outside the family to spot these things. And Fiona is an artist herself, don't forget.'

'I'm hardly likely to.'

'What's that supposed to mean?'

'Just what I said. She's your illustrator, so I'm not likely to forget she's an artist.'

'It wasn't some bitchy reference to the publicity?'

'What publicity?'

'The publicity we've been having recently, Fiona and I.'

'I didn't know you had.'

'You saw us on TV.'

'That was months ago.'

'Only a few weeks.'

'Anyway – this behaviour of Sarah's is inconveniencing me as well as you, Keith. I'm having to give up a trip down south.'

'Can't you take Sarah with you?'

'No, I can't.'

'At least you're not losing money over it.'

'Yes, I am.'

'Oh, don't be silly, Abbie. I'll repay your contribution to the holiday. It wasn't a massive amount.'

'I was quite a lot, to me. But you don't need to refund me.'

'There's no pleasing you, Abbie. You complain about being poor but you never let me help.'

'I don't complain and I *do* let you help, with the girls.'

'I mean you don't let me help *you*.'

'Of course not. Why would I? Why should you help me? I can pay my own way.'

Keith was silent.

To close the conversation, Abbie said, 'Make sure you keep an eye on Lizzie, won't you? I know she seems OK but I can't believe one twin is in trouble and the other isn't affected.'

'In trouble?'

'You know, all this unexpected behaviour. The nightmares and refusing to go to France.'

'I think "in trouble" is overstating it a bit. But of course I'll keep an eye on Lizzie. I am a responsible parent, you know.'

'I'd like to think so.'

'I think this conversation has gone on long enough.'

'I agree.'

'I'll see you when we're back from France.'

'Sarah sends you her love.'

'Does she? Well, you'd better give her mine, I suppose – the infuriating little sod.'

'Keith!'

''Bye, Abbie.'

'It was great,' said Lizzie, her voice flat and tired, her pale face contrasting with tanned limbs and over-bright eyes.

Abbie searched her daughter's face. Something wasn't quite right, that much was clear – but it might be no more than the fact that they had flown through a thunderstorm on the way back from France. That, and the lateness of the hour.

Keith had offered to keep Lizzie overnight in Edinburgh and drive them up to Carleith next day. But Sarah, who had missed her sister a lot, insisted she couldn't bear to spend another night without her, so Abbie had driven down and they had waited nearly two hours in Arrivals for the delayed plane.

'Was the lightning scary?' Sarah asked.

'No – it was exciting,' said Lizzie. 'A few people were frightened but I was really brave. I was better than Fiona, wasn't I, Dad?'

Fiona was not with them – she was waiting in Keith's car to be driven home.

'Yes, you were very brave,' said Keith. 'Not that there was anything to be frightened of. The pilot knew what he was doing.'

After a pause while they manoeuvred Lizzie's luggage into the boot of Abbie's car, Sarah said, 'Mum and I had a brilliant time while you were away, didn't we, Mum?'

'Yes, we did some fun things,' said Abbie.

'So why didn't you enjoy it?' Sarah asked Lizzie.

'I did enjoy it. It was cool. I drank white whine and I tried mussels.'

'Urrggghhhh.'

'They were nice. And I had an oyster. That wasn't so nice but I was glad I'd tried it. Fiona says you have to try things.'

'Lizzie'll become an alcoholic, Mum, won't she, with all that wine?'

'I doubt that she had enough for that, did you, Lizzie?'

'Of course she didn't,' said Keith, who was standing apart from them, ready to bid the twins goodbye.

'Of course I didn't,' echoed Lizzie, with a clipped surliness Abbie hadn't heard from her before. Perhaps that was what you got for separating eleven-year-old twins for a fortnight. But it was what both girls had wanted.

Once Keith was on his way and the twins were in the back of the car, Abbie said, 'It's good to be back together again, we three, isn't it?' Her voice came out far too upbeat and made her cringe as she settled into her seat.

'We Three Kings of Orient are,' said Lizzie, and Abbie gave up trying to improve the atmosphere. But Sarah giggled, at least.

Kate sprayed herself with sun lotion and rubbed it into her bare shoulders and legs. She and Abbie were on Kate's porch on a sunny Saturday afternoon towards the end of the school holidays. 'Tell me more about your plans to see Bill.'

'I'm off to Birmingham this weekend. Second time lucky, I hope. It's boiling hot down there, Bill says. I need to buy myself some skinny T-shirts.'

Sarah and Lizzie were currently with Keith, having departed quite happily for the weekend. Sarah had had no nightmares for some time and Abbie was beginning to hope that the problem was dying away.

Kate surveyed her own bare midriff. 'Get yourself some proper sexy clothes.'

'Maybe I will, you never know.'

'Lucky you.'

'Who knows? I haven't seen him for so long. And we got no further than a kiss when we met before. I'm quite nervous – it's a long time since I got close to a man.'

'It'll all come back to you, like riding a bike.'

'I hope so.'

'Are you planning on the full works, this time?'

'I'll see how it goes.'

'Go for it, babe. Bill is drop-dead gorgeous.'

'Well, perhaps that's an exaggeration. But he does it for me. We've been having some quite intimate talks, on the phone.'

'Have you really? You've made progress, Abbie.'

Kate stretched out her bare legs and examined them. She'd put on some extra weight, Abbie noticed, over the past few weeks. Perhaps it was due to comfort-eating in the absence of Salvador. Kate looked out of condition, too, her face pasty and her hair lacking its usual lustre, with the ends beginning to split.

Abbie said, 'We thought of going away somewhere together for a few days, didn't we? But it's been such a complicated summer, with Sarah's nightmares and her refusing to go on holiday with Keith.'

'She's OK about you going to see Bill?'

'She seems fine about it; they both do. I think they're getting used to the idea of my having a boyfriend. And of course they've already met him, which helps.'

'Do you think you'll see Bill's boys while you're there?'

'Maybe Sam, the younger one. I don't expect Jon will want to see me. He's not speaking to Bill at the moment.'

'Poor Bill.'

'Yes. It's hard on him. He doesn't know what he's supposed to have done.'

'Well, give him a big kiss from me. Bill, I mean, not Jon.'

Abbie grinned. 'Maybe.'

'If you change your mind about him – remember I'm in the queue.'

'Can I have some of that lotion?' Abbie took the bottle and sprayed herself. 'I see Steve's still hanging round, finding every opportunity he can to drop by our office.'

'I've told Steve I'm not interested. I wish he'd back off.'

'I think he's lovely. Perfect for you.'

'We've already had this conversation.' Kate lay back and closed her eyes.

'And I didn't understand what you said. Steve's not posh. He's Dundee born and bred.'

'It is *possible* to be from Dundee and be posh.'

'I know. I'm just saying that he's not.'

'If Steve knew about my past....'

'You're an idiot, Kate.'

An hour or so later Abbie was roused from semi-sleep by Kate's doorbell ringing. Kate, muttering oaths, got up to answer it and returned a few minutes later with an elderly couple who were presumably her parents.

Abbie, still barely awake, pulled herself to her feet and smiled, waiting to be introduced.

'You said you were coming at seven,' said Kate.

'We were going to take our time driving down,' said Kate's mother, 'but your dad didn't feel too well.'

'What's wrong, Dad?'

'I'm fine. A wee touch of angina, that's all. I used my spray and it did the trick as usual. Dinnae make a fuss, Molly.'

'I think your dad should lie down,' said Kate's mother. 'Have you got a bed made up?'

'Not yet – he can lie on mine.'

'There's no need – I told you I'm fine.' Kate's father turned to Abbie, who was beginning to feel awkward. 'And who's yon bonnie lass?'

'This is my friend Abbie,' said Kate. 'Abbie – my parents.'

Abbie held out her hand to each in turn.

'John and Molly Anderson,' said Kate's father.

'Lovely day, isn't it?' said Abbie. 'We were just enjoying a bit of sun.'

Ignoring her, Molly Anderson addressed Kate. 'I wonder if we should get the doctor, just in case.'

'What do you think, Dad?' asked Kate.

John shook his head. 'No need at all. Stop fussing, Molly. Abbie – that's a pretty name.'

'Thanks.'

'Can we go inside?' asked Molly. 'It's too hot for me out here and this sun is bad for your dad's skin.' She turned to Abbie as though registering her presence for the first time and said in a confiding tone, 'He had skin cancer a couple of years back. It was touch and go.'

'Oh dear,' said Abbie, wondering how soon she could make her escape. Would Kate want her to stay or not?

When they were seated in the living-room with the curtains closed against the sun, Molly said, 'I'd like a cup of tea, Kate. And your dad will have his usual, but not too much.'

Kate got to her feet, her face that of a sullen teenager.

'Can I give you a hand?' asked Abbie.

'No, you stay here.'

Abbie's heart sank.

Molly Anderson had Kate's turquoise eyes but on the older woman they had a faded, washed-out look, Her hair was grey, flecked with a few remaining tufts of black. Instead of Kate's wide smile, her mouth was pursed as though she was constantly sucking her lips.

John's hair had once been ginger but was now almost white. He had a harassed, put-upon frown, and Abbie guessed he would rather be at home in his garden or whatever it was he enjoyed.

Neither of them spoke, so she decided she had better make an effort. 'Did you enjoy the drive down from Aberdeen?'

'Not one little bit. It was packed with traffic. Such an effort, coming all this way to see Kate. It would be a lot easier if she lived a bit nearer to us.'

'My eyesight's too poor to drive now,' said John. 'So Molly has to do it, which she doesn't enjoy. It's a pity, since I used to like it.'

'That's a shame,' said Abbie. 'Aberdeen's a lovely city.'

'Tell that to Kate,' said Molly, turning round and running her finger along the windowsill. 'I don't know when that was last given a wipe. All it takes is a damp cloth once a week.'

'Kate does have a full-time job,' said Abbie, trying not to let her dislike of Kate's mother show in her face.

'I had a full-time job for years, with three children to care for and a house to keep clean. You never saw dirt on my windowsill.'

'Give the girl a wee break, Molly,' said her husband.

'So, do you have a family, Abbie?' Molly asked, frowning as though trying to work her out.

'I've got twin daughters of eleven. Lizzie and Sarah.'

'And a husband?'

This woman was downright rude, Abbie decided, but she replied as politely as she could. 'Not any more. I'm divorced.'

Molly's eyebrows went up but she made no comment.

John said, 'Eleven – that's a nice age. Give you the run-around, do they?'

Abbie smiled. 'They can be a bit of handful. But they're not too bad, no. They're great company most of the time.'

John smiled and she warmed to him, while her dislike for Molly grew stronger by the second.

Kate appeared, carrying a tray laden with a teapot, china cups Abbie had never seen before, a milk jug, a sugar bowl and a glass of whisky for John. Molly fussed over the amount of milk she wanted and Kate tried to pour some back into the jug, spilling it.

'Clumsy,' said Molly, mopping it with her tissue. 'I'd prefer brown sugar, Kate.'

'I haven't any,' said Kate. 'Sorry.' She said this as though she didn't mean it at all.

Abbie accepted a cup of tea and a biscuit, though she was longing to leave.

'We've some good news,' said Molly, picking up the first of the three biscuits she had taken. 'There's another job come up. The newsagents on Smart Street – you know, just round the corner. Eight till two daily. It would be perfect.'

'You're thinking of taking a job, Mum?'

'Not for me, silly girl. You know very well what I mean. It's just the kind of thing for you. Good hours and nothing too demanding. You'd be home in plenty of time to take us out and then get the tea.'

'Mum – I've already got a job. I'm quite happy where I am.'

'Kate's very good at her work,' said Abbie. 'She'd be really missed if she left.'

'Is that right?' said John, beaming. 'So you work with her, do you, Abbie?'

'Yes, I do. In the same office. We have a lot of fun.'

'Fun?' Molly's eyebrows went up into her hair.

Abbie wished she hadn't used the word. 'I mean we enjoy each other's company. We work hard, too.'

John gave her a friendly wink. Molly put down her cup and sucked in her lips even harder. 'You hear of such terrible things going on in universities.'

Molly turned to her daughter. 'I've something else to tell you.

There's a lovely wee man just moved into the big house at the bottom of Elm Walk. Quite handsome and with a good job, I hear.'

'Mum, stop trying to pair me off. I'm fine on my own.'

Molly assumed her confiding expression again and said to Abbie. 'I've been trying to find her a nice man for a while, ever since she split up with that awful Salvador. Did you ever meet Salvador?'

'No, I didn't,' said Abbie. She drained her cup and got to her feet. 'Well, it's been nice meeting you, Mr and Mrs Anderson, but I really must be on my way.'

'Don't go,' said Kate, as though she meant it. 'Have some more tea.' She picked up the teapot and refilled Abbie's cup before she had time to protest.

Abbie sat down again, while Molly started to tell Kate about some long-lost acquaintance she had met up with last week in a wool shop. Abbie pricked up her ears when she heard the name "Balfour".

'Minnie Balfour, it was – Dougie's mother. You were at school with Dougie, do you remember, Kate?'

'Of course I remember.' Kate shot Abbie a glance.

Abbie gave her a small grimace of support.

'She was telling me about Dougie. He's doing well for himself – has a business selling computers in Paisley.'

'Good for him,' said Kate.

'Has a big family, too – five or six children.'

Did Molly know, Abbie wondered, that Dougie had been the father of Kate's baby? Was she playing some kind of game, or were her remarks innocent? Kate's face lacked all expression and it was impossible to tell what was going on.

'Nice whisky,' said John. 'Any chance of a wee drop more?'

Kate got to her feet, but Molly said. 'That's enough, John, with your heart in such a poor condition. The doctor told you not to drink at all.'

'It's my only pleasure,' said John, giving Abbie another wink.

When he had another half-inch in his glass, Molly returned to the subject of Dougie Balfour. 'He was always a good-looking lad. Minnie says he still turns the ladies' heads.'

'Is that right?' said Kate.

'Pity you couldn't have settled down with someone like him.'

'Leave her alone, Molly,' said John.

'But as I was saying, the new man seems very nice and not bad-looking at all. In his early forties, I'd say. Next time you come and see us, I'll introduce you.'

'Mum, I told you. I don't want a man. Stop trying to matchmake for me.'

'Have you a boyfriend, Abbie?' asked John.

Abbie felt herself blush. 'Not really. A male friend who lives in Birmingham. That's all.'

'So you'll be moving away soon?' said Molly.

'Oh no – definitely not. We've no plans to get together. It's early days.'

'In my day you stayed together for life,' said Molly. 'None of this bed-hopping the young ones go in for these days.'

'Right – I really must go,' said Abbie, picking up her cup to take to the kitchen. 'Sorry, Kate.'

She held out her hand briefly to Molly, who gave the ends of her fingers a reluctant squeeze. When she tried to do the same to John he gave her a peck on the cheek. 'Nice to meet you, my dear. Take care, now.'

Kate accompanied Abbie to the front door, where she whispered, 'Now you see what she's like.'

'I tried my best with her.'

'There's no point.'

'Your dad's nice.'

'Yes – I think on his own he would be. But he never gets a chance.'

'Kate – you must say no. You can't think of going up there to live. You'd hate it. Just tell her you can't.'

'If only it was as easy as that.'

Driving home, Abbie reflected that she had never seen the normally assertive Kate so timid and cowed. She felt irritated with her friend for not sticking up for herself, but perhaps it wasn't as easy when the people in question were your parents. Abbie thought of her own mother, gentle and supportive, making no demands, and her father, who had died ten years before and was much missed.

Abbie had sometimes wondered whether Kate exaggerated the problems she had with her mother, but if anything, it seemed, she had played them down.

chapter eleven

'So this weekend you'll get Daddy to yourselves, for a change,' Abbie said. 'That'll be good, won't it?'

It was Friday evening and Keith was due at any time to pick up the twins and take them to Edinburgh. Lizzie had mentioned earlier that Fiona was not going to be there: she was away at an illustrators' conference.

'It'll be wicked.' said Sarah. 'Dad's going to take us to North Berwick, where we used to go when we were little. And maybe to the beach at Gullane. We're going to have fish and chips on the sand, and go in the sea if it's not too cold.'

'Well, be careful.'

'We will. I can't wait to swim in the sea.'

'It'll be freezing,' said Abbie.

'You always used to swim, Mum, when we went to Gullane.'

'I know I did. I was tough in those days.'

'I wish it was those days now.'

'Do you?'

'I wish we were all still together, you and Daddy and Lizzie and me. Don't you, Lizzie?'

Lizzie inclined her head. 'Don't know.'

'Well, I do. And Mummy does, don't you, Mummy?'

'I'm not sure. In some ways, perhaps.' She thought of Bill and her planned visit, starting tomorrow. 'No, not really.'

'Mummy's got Bill now,' said Lizzie. 'She doesn't want Daddy back, do you, Mum?'

'No. Not exactly. But, like Sarah, I suppose I sometimes wish things were the way they used to be.'

'Well, they're not,' said Lizzie. 'It's no use crying over spilt milk. That's what Granny Margaret says.'

'That's silly,' said Sarah. 'Spilt milk is different from getting divorced. You can wipe up spilt milk. And I don't like milk, anyway, or only on cereal.'

'What do you think of this top?' Abbie asked her daughters, holding up a sleeveless turquoise blouse.

'It's OK,' said Lizzie.'

'You suit that colour, Mummy,' said Sarah. 'It makes you look beautiful. Try it on now.'

'Daddy will be here in a minute,' said Lizzie.

The doorbell rang a few minutes later and the twins rushed to answer it. But it wasn't their father – it was Kate.

'Hi, you two. I've come to help your mum pack her things for Birmingham.'

Abbie, feeling a little silly, greeted Kate. It had been Kate's idea to help her pack. She had assured her she didn't need any assistance, but Kate had somehow talked her into it.

Kate said to Abbie, 'Sorry I'm a bit earlier than I said. Mum's been on at me again on the phone and I had to get out of the house.'

'Hello, Kate,' said Lizzie. 'You'll be able to see our dad. He's arriving in a minute.'

'Oops,' said Kate. 'Do you want me to hide until he's gone?'

'Of course not – don't be silly,' Abbie replied. 'You've met Keith before, haven't you?'

'Yes, remember, I met both him and Fiona, though only for a minute.'

'That's all you'll see of him this time. He probably won't even come into the house.'

Moments later the doorbell rang again and the twins picked up their bags, gave Abbie a quick kiss each and hurried to the door. There stood Keith and, just behind him, Fiona.

Keith hugged Lizzie, who reached him first. In her rush to appropriate her father she might not even have noticed Fiona. But Sarah had seen her and hung back, her grin collapsing. She was not far from tears.

Keith released Lizzie and turned to Sarah, who dived back into the kitchen.

'Come in. Hi, Fiona, nice to see you.' Abbie put the merest hint of a question into her voice.

Fiona replied with a stiff-jawed smile that looked as though it was an effort, but made no movement to enter the house.

'We won't stay,' said Keith. 'Fiona's mother will have dinner ready for us in an hour. But isn't this a wonderful surprise, Lizzie? Where's Sarah gone? Fiona's conference was cancelled so she's here with us after all.'

'Yes, it's lovely,' said Lizzie, so calmly that Abbie couldn't tell if she meant it or not.

'Keith, it's not exactly lovely for me,' said Fiona, stepping reluctantly inside. 'I've missed the chance to present my new designs to that German publisher.'

'Of course, I'm sorry,' said Keith. 'I just meant it was a nice surprise for the girls. Come on, Sarah. Have you got your bag, Lizzie?'

'Sarah doesn't want to go,' announced Lizzie.'

'What? Of course she does? Sarah!'

'I think she went into her bedroom,' said Kate.

'Hello again, Kate,' said Fiona. 'I think we met before.'

'Yes, we did.' There was an awkward silence as Kate gave Fiona a bland stare.

'I'll go and find Sarah,' said Abbie, something inside her beginning to crumble. 'She must have forgotten something.'

But Sarah was on the bottom bunk, where she had been sleeping since her nightmares began. Before that, she and Lizzie had alternated beds week by week. She was beating the pillow with her fists and making stifled sobbing sounds into the pillow.

'Sarah, whatever's the matter?' Abbie placed her hand on Sarah's hair, then on her hot neck. 'Shh, darling. Tell me what's wrong.'

'I'm not going if *she*'s there.' The words were barely audible. Sarah raised herself up, kicked out with her legs and thumped Abbie on the chest.

'Ouch. Careful, pet. What do you mean, if she's there? You mean Fiona?'

Sarah didn't answer but resumed her sobbing.

'But Sarah, you've always liked Fiona.'

'She's upset because it was supposed to be just Daddy this weekend,' said Lizzie, appearing in the doorway. 'We were looking forward to it. But it can't be helped, Sarah. It's just one of those things. Come on – Daddy and Fiona are in a hurry. Bye-bye, Kate.'

'I'm not going,' said Sarah.

'You have to,' said Lizzie. 'Mum is going to Birmingham on the train tomorrow. You can't stop her again, like last time.'

'I don't care.' Sarah had her head up now, red-faced and dripping tears. 'I'll stay here on my own.'

'You can't do that,' said Lizzie. 'You're too young.'

Abbie wondered for a moment whether there was any possibility of Sarah staying with Kate while she was away? With the neighbours? Or could Abbie's mother be prevailed upon to have her? Perhaps she could drive down to Birmingham instead of taking the train and drop Sarah off in Peebles?

But Sarah was crying hard now, as though she had no intention of stopping, and all Abbie could do was to hold her, nestling the hot head against her chest.

Perhaps Sarah could come with her to Birmingham? It wouldn't be the same, of course, but she would still see Bill. He'd understand.

'Mummy, don't make me go with them.'

How could she resist that appeal? 'No, no, of course I won't.'

Lizzie sniffed. 'Well, *I'm* going,' she said. ''Bye Sarah. 'Bye Mum.' She reached to give Abbie a cheek-peck and scurried out of the room, Abbie heard her cry, 'Daddy and Fiona, Sarah's not coming. Again! Can we go now?'

'Is that right?' Keith had come in, popped his head round the bedroom door. It seemed wrong for him to be there.

'Sorry, Keith, said Abbie, not quite knowing why she was apologizing. 'It looks like she's staying here with me.'

Keith made a sound of annoyance, shook his head and left. Abbie heard Fiona give an exclamation of surprise, then the door slammed and they were gone.

When Abbie turned back to Sarah she had stopped sobbing and was wiping her face on the duvet cover.

'Sarah, why?' Abbie stood beside the bed, her arm round Sarah. 'Tell me.'

'I just don't want to go. I don't like Fiona.'

'Why not?'

'I just don't.'

'Does she get angry with you?'

'No.'

'Does she say things you don't like?'

'No.'

'Sarah.' A dreadful, inadmissible thought had struck Abbie. 'She doesn't try to make you do anything, does she? Anything that you don't want to?'

'Mummy!' This was said with scorn, as though Abbie had said something rude or embarrassing. 'Of course she doesn't. Fiona's not a stranger. And she's not a man.'

'No, but....'

'Mummy, we did all about abuse at school. I'm not a little girl. I'm nearly twelve. Fiona is *not* like that.'

'I just thought I'd better ask.'

'I want to stay here with you. I like you best, Mummy.' Sarah raised a hand to stroke her mother's hair.

'Well, thank you. I'm glad you want to be with me. But you do understand, don't you, that it's a bit awkward this weekend? I was due to go and see Bill.'

'You said you would always love us the most. Me and Lizzie.'

'Of course. I said it and I meant it. I always will. But that doesn't mean that I can't sometimes do fun things, too.'

'You can do fun things with me.'

'But that's different. Darling, I love being with you. But going to Birmingham was a special treat for me. And for Bill. Just one weekend together. Daddy and Fiona are together all the time.'

'Yes and I hate it. Daddy doesn't belong to us any more.'

'Sarah, that's not true. Daddy loves you as much as ever. Just as I do. He really likes having you to stay.'

'He loves Fiona more than me.'

'He doesn't.'

'He does! You don't know, Mummy. When I tell him that Fiona is annoying, he doesn't take any notice.'

'What kind of annoying?'

'Just annoying.'

'You mean, like you said before? Telling you what to do?'

'Yes.'

'Bossing you around?'

'Yes.'

'But that's perhaps her way of getting involved. Being part of things. It can't be easy for her. As I said to you at the beginning, you must try hard to make Fiona feel welcome, a member of the family.'

'I do. We both do. We try really hard.'

'Good. I'm sure you do.'

'But I'm sick of trying. I don't want to see her any more. Ever again.'

'But you're going to Venice with her and Daddy in October. You were really excited about it.'

'I don't want to, now.'

'Oh, Sarah.'

Sarah sat up and slid towards the edge of the bed, ready to jump down. 'Can we go to Moomin Bay? Me and you, now? Kate as well, if she likes?'

'No. Not now.'

'Tomorrow, then?'

'I've got my train ticket for Birmingham. Tell you what, Sarah, why don't you come with me? Bill will be pleased to see you again.'

'No he won't. He wants you to himself. Like Daddy and Fiona.'

'Not all the time. Just occasionally. That's all I meant.'

'I wish I was grown up.'

'Why?'

'So I could have a house of my own and not have to go and stay with people who don't like me and I don't like them.'

'Who doesn't like you?'

'Daddy and Fiona.'

'Of course they like you!'

'Fiona doesn't. And Daddy doesn't when he's with Fiona. Which is all the time.'

'I'll have a word with Daddy. Perhaps we can arrange for you and Lizzie to have some time with him on your own. I'm sure he'd like that. He probably just hasn't thought of it.'

'No, Mummy. Don't say anything to Daddy. He'll be cross.'

'He won't, if we explain it properly.'

'He will.'

'Does Lizzie feel the same as you?'

Sarah sighed and reached for a tissue to mop her eyes. 'No. Not really.'

'Does Lizzie still like Fiona?'

'Yes. Maybe. Sort of. It's different for Lizzie.'

'Why is it different for her?'

'I don't know. Mum, stop asking me questions. It's like being at school.'

'OK. But I need to understand what's going on. We must talk some more about this, later.'

'Can I go on the computer now?'

'All right. I'd better phone Bill.'

'Mummy, say sorry to him for me.'

'Oh, you silly-billy. But yes, I will.'

'Say sorry I spoilt your weekend.'

'OK.'

'I *am* sorry.'

'I know you are.'

'I'll go with them next time, I promise.'

'All right. We'll talk to Daddy before next time. And perhaps to Fiona as well.'

'No!'

'Why not? All right, just to Daddy, at first anyway. Now, let me speak to Kate and then make my phone call.'

'Abbie – I really don't like that woman,' said Kate as Abbie entered the living room.

Abbie sank on to the sofa. 'You mean Fiona?'

'Of course I mean Fiona. I found her worse than creepy today. And shouldn't you be asking yourself – why didn't Sarah want to go with them, once she knew Fiona was there? Doesn't it make you suspicious?'

'Of course not. You're not suggesting Fiona's a paedophile or something?'

'I don't know what to think.'

'I did check with Sarah about that. She laughed at me. Said

they'd done abuse at school and she knew all about it. No – I'm sure it's nothing like that. I think it's just jealousy.'

'It's an awful shame for you. Especially as you've already cancelled once.'

'Don't remind me. I hope Bill understands.'

'He's got kids of his own so he should.'

'But they're much older and he seems to have the opposite problem – they don't want to spend time with him.'

'He'll understand. Tell him how upset you are.'

'That won't be difficult.'

'Here.' Kate passed her a tissue. 'I'll go and let you make your phone call. Unless you want me to stay.'

'No, you go. Pop in and say goodbye to Sarah first. She's on the computer.'

'OK, I will. Chin up, Abbie. You and Bill will get together soon.'

Bill began by being understanding, though Abbie could hear the effort he was making to overcome his disappointment. Was his voice coloured by just the slightest hint of resentment? No, it was probably guilt making her imagine it.

'I'm terribly sorry,' she said.

'And me. Again.'

'I tried to get her to come with me to Birmingham. You wouldn't have minded, would you?'

'No, not at all.'

'But she's set her heart on being here with me this weekend.'

'Not to worry. There's always another time.'

She tried to draw out the usual warmth of his voice, but it wasn't there, not quite.

'Perhaps once the holidays are over she'll be better,' she said. 'When they're back at school and she's settled in her new class. I'll talk to Keith.'

There was a long pause before Bill replied. 'I suppose we could always put things on hold.'

'What do you mean?' Her breath caught cold in her throat and her heart started thudding.

'I mean you and me. Maybe we should cool things off a bit, until things are easier for you and the twins.'

'Cool things off?'

'You know. Put the brakes on. I'm running out of metaphors.'

'I know what you mean. I just can't quite....'

'Don't be hurt, Abbie. I'm not trying to end our relationship. I just think that, seeing as it's so difficult at the moment, we should take a step back. Or stay where we are. Not keep getting closer and then end up being disappointed. It's happened twice now. I get so worked up about your coming, and then....'

'I know. Me too. And I'm so sorry. You know I am, don't you?'

'Of course I know.'

'You believe me, don't you? You don't think it's some kind of excuse?'

'It's not, is it?'

'Of course not! Can't you tell how upset I am?'

'If there *was* anything – you'd tell me, wouldn't you? If you and Keith....'

'If I and Keith what?'

'Nothing.'

'You don't seriously think that Keith and I are getting back together? And that I'm using Sarah as an excuse?'

'No. But I do seem to be rather insecure at the moment.'

'There's no need. There's absolutely no chance of Keith and me getting back together. It's the last thing I'd want. And the last thing he'd want, I'm sure. He's got Fiona, remember? And even if he hadn't....'

'OK. I'm sorry. Nothing in my life is going right at the moment. My sons despise me – especially Jon. Work is horrendous. I won't go into detail, but one of our team has left in a huff because he thinks he didn't get enough credit for a script. That's given the rest of us more work to do. What with that and Jon – I've no energy left for anything else.'

'Including me? Perhaps it's as well I'm not coming, then.' She could feel the tears pricking her eyelids.

'I didn't mean it like that. I was looking forward to it.'

'OK. I'm sorry.'

'But as I said, I think we should perhaps speak a bit less often. Not every day.'

'But Bill....'

'That'll give us both a bit more time. You for Sarah and me for Jon. And for me to try and talk to Deb.'

'To Deb?'

'Talk to her about Jon, that's all I meant.'

'I know you did.'

'So if we phone every three or four days or so....'

'Yes. All right.'

'That's OK, isn't it?'

'Yes, of course.'

'And we'll try to get together when we can.'

His voice was cool – not cold but cool. Abbie had her tears under control now but her legs felt weak and she had broken out in a tingling, shivery sweat, like the ones she'd had when coming off her anti-depressants.

''Bye for now, then, Bill.'

''Bye, Abbie.'

Abbie put the phone down and slid to the hall floor. She stayed there for at least five minutes, unable even to go and check whether Sarah was all right.

Sarah had a nightmare that night. Abbie was woken by a cry and hurried into her daughter's bedroom. Sarah's body was stiff, her eyes open and staring as though wide awake, but she did not register Abbie's voice and was clearly fast asleep. Abbie tried to hold and comfort her but it was impossible – Sarah was in a world of her own. Abbie began to shake with terror as though she had somehow entered into Sarah's dream. After what seemed like an hour but was, according to the clock, only ten minutes, Sarah's limbs relaxed, her eyes closed and she fell back into a normal sleep.

Abbie kissed her and left the room, but she wasn't able to go back to bed for over an hour. When she did, she couldn't go to sleep – every time she began to drop off something like an alarm in her brain woke her, and she jumped out of bed convinced that Sarah was screaming again. Even when she had checked and found her daughter quiet, it was a long time before she drifted back to sleep – at which point her internal alarm sounded again and whole process repeated itself.

Sarah, next day, claimed not to remember a thing and told Abbie to stop fussing.

But the nightmares happened again on Saturday night.

chapter twelve

'Do you think she should see a psychiatrist?' Abbie asked Dr Griffin.

It was Monday morning and she was in the surgery with Sarah. The twins were still on holiday from school and Abbie's neighbour had offered to take Lizzie shopping in Broughty Ferry.

'I think it's a bit too soon to be thinking of that,' Dr Griffin replied. 'Let's see how things go when she's back at school. It may all just settle down on its own.'

'But you said that weeks ago, and it hasn't happened. Instead she's getting worse.'

'I'm fine,' said Sarah. 'It's all a fuss about nothing.' She had made similar comments throughout the consultation. When Abbie had mentioned her refusal to stay with Keith and Fiona, she had said, 'It's just that I don't like Fiona. You don't need to see a doctor just because you don't like someone.'

Dr Griffin, smiled and said, 'That's a good point, Sarah. And it may well be that you don't need my help at all. But we just want to make sure there's nothing for me to do.'

'There's nothing for anybody to do,' said Sarah. 'I'm not ill. Everyone gets nightmares.'

'How do you feel about going back to school?' Dr Griffin asked.

'I can't wait.'

'That's good. Tell me, Sarah, are you having your periods yet?'

'No.'

'OK. That's fine. And are you eating well?' Dr Griffin cast a glance at Abbie.

'I've got a good appetite. Mum says I never stop eating. I'm not anorexic, if that's what you're worried about. I'm just thin.'

'You're a lovely shape. I'm just making sure I cover everything.'

'Do you like being a doctor?'

Dr Griffin, surprised, gave a thoughtful smile. 'On the whole I like it. It's hard work, but it's interesting to meet so many people. Do you have any idea what you'd like to be when you're grown up?'

'I want to be a writer like Daddy and Fiona.'

'Her father writes children's books,' explained Abbie.

'*The Great Green Wizard*,' said Sarah. 'Have you read any of them?'

'Oh, those ones! My children love them. Gosh, is your Daddy Keith Brinnett?'

'Yes. His partner, Fiona, does the illustrations,' said Abbie.

'Goodness. But wait a minute – you said you wanted to be a writer like your Daddy *and* Fiona. Does Fiona write as well as draw?'

'Yes, a bit. But she mainly draws.'

'I see. Well, that's interesting. So you want to be a writer, too?'

'If I can. It's not easy. Daddy had to try for years and years before he got his book published. Lizzie wants to be a vet but she's scared of dogs.'

'Ah. Well, perhaps she should be a doctor instead?'

'Lizzie wouldn't be a good doctor. She's not sympathetic enough.'

'Isn't she?'

'She's not nice to people who are upset.'

'Is that right? Is she not nice to you when you're upset?'

'Sometimes she isn't.'

'I didn't know that,' said Abbie. 'I've not noticed Lizzie being like that. Are you sure, Sarah?'

Sarah ignored her mother and continued her conversation with Dr Griffin. 'She says you have to be strong and brave and deal with things yourself.'

'Does she? Well, it's intriguing that the two of you seem to be quite different. Do you get on well together?'

Sarah hesitated.

'You do, don't you?' Abbie prompted her. 'Most of the time?'

'We don't fight much any more,' said Sarah.

'That's good.'

'So you don't think Sarah needs to see someone?' asked Abbie.

'I won't rule it out, but I'd rather wait until I've spoken to Lizzie as well,' said Dr Griffin. 'Try not to worry. These things usually go away as quickly as they come.'

'Mum worries too much,' said Sarah.

Dr Griffin smiled. 'Mothers always do.'

They left the surgery with Sarah skipping beside Abbie as they approached the car. 'Thank God I don't have to see a psychiatrist,' she said.

'Sarah....'

'I mean thank goodness I don't. Mum, no one says "thank goodness." It makes me sound like Granny Margaret.'

'I don't like swearing.'

'"Thank God" isn't swearing. Everyone says it. Fiona says it. I bet Dr Griffin does.'

'I'm sure she doesn't.'

'Kate says it. I've heard her.'

'That doesn't make it right.'

'I bet Bill says it.'

'I'm sure he doesn't.'

'Mum, are you in love with Bill?'

'No. I don't know. Perhaps a bit. Shall we call at the shop for an ice cream?'

'Yes, OK. I think you *are*, Mum, aren't you?' Sarah climbed into the car.

'I'm what?'

'In love with Bill.'

'Of course not. It's far too soon for that. I've only met him once.'

'That's because of me. I'm sorry.'

Abbie started the engine. 'I know you are. You don't need to keep saying it.'

'I feel guilty.'

'Well, it's good that you understand my feelings. But I don't want you to feel bad. You can't help your nightmares.'

'Why doesn't Lizzie get them?'

'I've no idea.'

'I missed Lizzie at the weekend.'

'Did you?'

'I always miss her. More than she misses me.'

'Are you sure? Perhaps she just doesn't say?'

'I just *know*. I don't really mind. We're different people.'

'Of course you are.'

'It must be funny, Mum, not having a twin. I can't imagine it.'

'Hmm, that's interesting. Because, of course, I can't imagine having one.'

'It's not always good.'

'No, I can see that. But you like it most of the time, don't you?'

'Yes, it's OK. It's just how things are. It's good at night-time when you're going to sleep, to have someone to talk to. I don't like going to sleep on my own.'

They had reached the shop, and Abbie opened her purse to give Sarah the money for two mint-chocolate-chip cones.

When Sarah came out, licking each in turn before handing one to her mother, she continued, 'We talk about everything that's happened in the day, me and Lizzie.'

The two of them sat on a low wall beside the shop to eat their ice creams.

'That must be lovely,' said Abbie. I'd do that with Bill, she thought. She pictured them lying together in bed, and then tried to banish the image.

'But sometimes Lizzie doesn't want to talk. After the stories she just wants to go to sleep.'

'After what stories?'

'The bedtime ones.'

'Oh, you mean when Daddy reads to you?'

'No, he doesn't do that now. He says we're too old.'

'That's a shame. No one is ever too old to be read to.'

'Yes, they are. Eleven-nearly-twelve is too old to be read to. But Fiona sometimes reads to us.'

'Does she? What does she read?'

'Just some stories with pictures, from a book. I always want to talk about them afterwards but Lizzie doesn't.'

'What are they about?'

'All sorts of things. Elves and ghosts and werewolves. Dragons.'

'A bit like Daddy's stuff?'

'Yes, kind of. But for older children. For young people like us.'

'And do you like them?'

'They're wicked.'

'So that's something about Fiona that you like, at least.'

'I suppose.'

'You're not scared by these stories?'

'Of course not.' Sarah took a big bite of very cold ice cream and struggled to keep it in her mouth. When she had swallowed most of it, she said, 'I'm too old to be scared by stuff like that. They're really exciting stories, much better than Daddy's ones.'

At dinner that evening, Sarah announced, 'I don't care if I never see Dad and Fiona again.'

Lizzie ignored her sister. She had been telling Abbie, for at least the third time, what fun she'd had at Fiona's parents' at the weekend.

'I rode one of their horses on the seafront,' she said. 'Granny Margaret says I'm big enough now. You missed it, Sarah. But you might not be tall enough, anyway, so she might not let you.'

Lizzie had grown an inch over the summer and was proud of being so much taller than Sarah, who had stayed the same height.

'See if I care,' said Sarah. 'I don't care if I never see Granny Margaret again, either. Or the horses.'

'Liar,' said Lizzie.

'Stop it,' said Abbie. 'Lizzie, I know you had a good time but you've told us about it three times, now. And don't be rude.'

'I wasn't being rude,' said Sarah. 'I didn't say anything bad about Granny Margaret. I like Granny Margaret and Grandad Ryan. And the horses.' She bowed her head, stricken, perhaps, at the thought of not seeing them again.

'I meant that Lizzie was being rude, calling you a liar,' said Abbie.

'No I wasn't,' said Lizzie. 'I was stating a fact. She is a liar. She's upset because she won't see Granny Margaret and the horses ever again.'

'Of course she will,' said Abbie. 'Perhaps Sarah just needs a bit of a break from the routine.'

'I don't need anything,' said Sarah. 'Stop going on about me as if I'm ill. And when we go back to school, don't you dare tell Mrs Lemmon about my nightmares, Mum. I don't want anybody to know.'

'Stop having them, then,' said Lizzie in a matter-of-fact voice.

'It's not as though she can help it,' said Abbie.

'Of course she can, if she tries,' said Lizzie.

'Lizzie, that's ridiculous. No one would choose to have horrible nightmares like that.'

'I don't mean that. She didn't choose to start having them but she can choose to stop.'

Confronted by this logic, Abbie shook her head but said nothing. She'd had a brief discussion with Keith when he brought Lizzie back on Sunday, but nothing of substance had been said. When Abbie told him about Sarah's most recent nightmares, he said, 'It'll sort itself out soon enough. It's probably just part of growing up. Girls are complicated creatures. You should know.'

She had wanted to phone Bill to bring him up to date, but it was too soon. Three or four days between calls – that was what he'd suggested.

Things would be better, Abbie told herself, when the girls were back at school. They would have plenty to distract them; they'd be more tired and sleep better, which might well solve Sarah's problem. She had already decided, in spite of what Sarah had said, to speak to her new teacher, Mrs Lemmon, as soon as she could.

'Pam, I've just had an urgent call from the school. Lizzie's in some kind of trouble.'

It was eleven in the morning and Abbie was in the office on her own, since Kate was off work with a stomach bug. It was the twins' second day back at school.

Pam looked up from her computer. 'Lizzie? I thought Sarah was the one with the problems?'

'So did I. I don't know what this is about. But I've been told, in no uncertain terms, to go and pick up her as soon as possible.'

'What's wrong – did they say?'

'They assured me she wasn't hurt or ill. It seems to be some kind of misbehaviour. Hard to believe – neither of them has ever been in that kind of trouble before.'

'Maybe Lizzie is the victim?'

'It didn't sound like it. From the tone of Mrs Strachan's voice it sounds as though Lizzie has murdered at least three of her class-mates. She asked me to "remove her from the premises" as soon as possible.'

Pam frowned. 'What on earth can be going on? Well, you must be worried. Off you go – we'll manage here. Though it would be good if you could come back later. Fred's just been in here tearing his hair out about the departmental seminars. We're three people short for this term and he wanted someone do so some ringing round.'

'I'll come back if I can, but I don't know who I'm going to find to look after Lizzie. And anyway, she may not be in a fit state to be left with anyone. And Sarah may be upset about it, too. Whatever it is....'

'It's bad timing, on a day when Kate is off sick.'

'I know. I really am sorry.'

'You can't help it. Give me a ring, later, to let me know when you'll be back.'

It occurred to Abbie as she drove out of the university that she might be able to leave Lizzie with Kate, if Kate was feeling better. That would allow her to come back to work.

But as soon as she saw her daughter she knew there was no hope of leaving her with anyone. Lizzie was sitting in the head's office, her face blotchy and tear-stained, her hair tousled.

'Whatever's happened, pet?' Abbie raced over and enveloped her in a hug. Lizzie seemed undecided at first whether or not to accept the embrace in the presence of Mrs Strachan, but after a moment's hesitation decided she would.

'Mrs Strachan will tell you what I did.' Her voice was low, almost a growl. That sullen note again.

'No, Lizzie, I think you should tell your mother yourself,' said Mrs Strachan. 'Tell her what happened in music this morning.'

Lizzie refused to meet her mother's eye.

'Tell me, Lizzie.' Abbie tried to make her voice sound normal and encouraging.

'It wasn't my fault.'

Mrs Strachan sighed.

'What wasn't your fault?' Abbie asked.

'The fight.'

'Fight? You've been fighting?'

Mrs Strachan gave another, deeper sigh. 'Well, seeing as you don't seem to want to tell your mother, Lizzie, I will.' She paused as though for dramatic effect. 'Lizzie punched another girl on the nose towards the end of their music lesson.'

'Lizzie, no! You didn't?' Abbie could not believe this. To her knowledge, neither of her twins had ever involved themselves in fights or any kind of physical violence. Not, at least, since the days when they were squabbling toddlers.

'It wasn't my fault,' repeated Lizzie. 'She told me I was singing out of tune. Three times. She annoyed me.'

'And you punched her, for that?'

'She was really getting to me. Her name's Clarissa and she's horrible. She was saying nasty things about Dad in the playground at break.'

'About your father? What sort of things?'

Lizzie was silent.

'Lizzie, answer your mother's question,' said Mrs Strachan.

'What did Clarissa say about Daddy in the playground?' Abbie asked.

But Lizzie still said nothing.

'I think we can sort out all that later,' said Mrs Strachan. 'For the time being, I would like Lizzie to go home. She must understand that violent behaviour is not acceptable in this school.'

'Yes, of course. Lizzie, where's your jacket?'

'Hanging up outside the classroom, but I'm not going back there. I might see someone.'

'But it's raining.'

'Mum, I don't care. Let's just go home.'

'I'll see you tomorrow,' said Mrs Strachan, looking at Lizzie. 'Perhaps by that time you'll have accepted responsibility for what you did, and be ready to apologize and make amends.'

Lizzie was silent so Abbie said, 'She will.'

'It's so unlike you, Lizzie, that's what I can't get my head round,' said Abbie, over their lunch of scrambled eggs and baked beans at the kitchen table. Lizzie had requested a grilled bacon accompaniment but Abbie refused, telling her that treat food was not appropriate for the occasion.

'Mum, I've said I'm sorry half a million times.'

Lizzie still sounded cross rather than repentant, but her voice had lost its sullen note and regained some of its energy.

Abbie had phoned Pam to ask if she could take the rest of the day off. Pam had not been pleased, even when Abbie assured her she would make up the time.

Abbie put down her knife and fork. 'Look, darling, it's not enough just to keep saying sorry. It's important to tell me exactly what happened. You told Mrs Strachan you punched Clarissa because she said bad things about Daddy. Was that true?'

'Of course it was true. I don't tell lies.' Lizzie loaded her mouth with a large chunk of scrambled egg.

'So did you punch her in the playground when she said those things?'

'No, it was in music, remember? Mrs Strachan told you,' said Lizzie, her mouth still full. 'Clarissa was being annoying, saying I can't sing in tune. I know I can't sing, but it's not very nice to have someone say it. And it reminded me how horrible she was in the playground and I punched her. Not very hard. She made a big fuss over nothing.' She picked up her glass of orange juice and drained it.

'It must have been pretty hard to give her a nosebleed.'

'She must have a weak nose.'

'What did she say about your father?'

Lizzie looked down at her plate. 'That he's a paedophile.'

'What?' Abbie almost choked on her food.

'I know, it was stupid. I don't know where she got it from. She just made it up. Said she'd read it in the paper.'

'And does Mrs Strachan know about that? And your class teacher – Mrs Mackenzie?'

'I don't know.'

'I shall tell Mrs Strachan tomorrow when I take you to school.'

'Mum! Just let me go back tomorrow without any fuss. It doesn't matter.'

'It certainly does matter. That's a horrible accusation for Clarissa to make. I'm not surprised you were angry. Though it doesn't excuse what you did, of course.'

'Look, Mum. I'll go to school tomorrow and say I'm sorry to everyone. It'll all just blow over. Don't say anything to make it worse.'

'Well, you need to apologize, I'm not arguing with that. But I'd like to see this Clarissa girl taken to task for saying such things about Daddy. What's her surname?'

'I can't remember.'

'Of course you can. Try your hardest.'

'Don't say anything to Mrs Strachan, Mum.'

'You *are* telling me the truth, Lizzie? About what Clarissa said?'

'Mum! I always tell the truth.' Lizzie was close to tears now, her meal abandoned.

'All right. I just wanted to make sure.'

'Clarissa was showing off. She's only just learnt the word "paedophile".'

Abbie realized she didn't want any more of her own lunch and pushed her plate away. 'I'm not having the father of my children slandered in the school playground.'

'Mum, you're being a drama queen. You're as bad as Sarah with her stupid nightmares.'

'At least Sarah and I haven't hit anyone.' Abbie wished immediately that she hadn't said this.

'Not yet,' said Lizzie.

'What do you mean by that?'

'The way Sarah's going, with her loopy nightmares. She's much worse than me. And you're so angry you'll probably hit Mrs Strachan. Then you'll be in prison. God, what did I do to deserve this family?'

Lizzie slid off her kitchen chair and ran outside into the garden, ignoring Abbie's plea of 'Wait, Lizzie.' More than half Lizzie's egg and beans lay untouched on her plate.

Abbie started to clear up, taking a quick glance through the window to see what Lizzie was doing. The rain had stopped and she was on the hammock, her back to Abbie, pushing it back and forth, making it squeak. Abbie, with a sigh, started clearing up.

★

Later, in the car with both girls after picking up Sarah from school, Abbie said, 'I'm wondering whether we should speak to Daddy about this.'

'That's a bit mean, telling on Lizzie to Daddy,' said Sarah, who now knew the story. 'He'll be really mad.'

'Fiona will be even worse. She'll go on about how she was always such a good girl at school,' said Lizzie.

'Does she do that?' asked Abbie.

Sarah ignored her. 'She'll send you into the woods,' she said in a strange, hollow voice.

Lizzie gave a wolf howl and both girls started laughing.

'What do you mean, send you into the woods?' Abbie asked.

'It's just a joke, Mum,' said Lizzie. 'Don't worry about it. It's a joke between me and Sarah.'

The twins continued to giggle and make howling noises the rest of the way home. Abbie's head was aching by the time they got out of the car.

As soon the twins were asleep, Abbie phoned Keith. Lizzie and Sarah were not due to stay with him that weekend and it seemed important to let him know of the day's events as soon as possible.

But her call went unanswered and then clicked on to the answering machine, with Fiona's Fife accent proclaiming that, 'Neither Keith nor Fiona can take your call just now. Please leave a short, clear message after the beep.'

Who else, Abbie wondered, would specify a 'short, clear' message rather than just a message? Was the implication that Keith and Fiona's time was too precious to be wasted listening to anything that was long or unclear?

Or was she becoming hypersensitive?

Abbie then phoned Kate, who said she was still feeling bad and was unlikely to be at work next day. Abbie gave a brief account of her visit to the school, but Kate was clearly too engaged in her stomach troubles to show more than a perfunctory interest.

'You couldn't bring me a couple of yogurts, could you, on your way home from work tomorrow?'

'I'll try, but I'm not sure I'll get the chance to call at the shops.

I've got to go and see Lizzie's teacher. And I'm supposed to be catching up on today's work.'

'Oh Abbie, stop being so bloody conscientious.'

'Someone has to be.' She wished, immediately, that she hadn't said it.

Kate's tone was prickly. 'Are you suggesting I'm skiving?'

'No, of course not. That's not what I meant. I just meant that someone has to do the work.'

But Kate was offended and didn't say much more before signing off, telling Abbie she needed to dash to the loo. Perhaps she meant it. Abbie didn't care any more.

She considered going straight to bed. An early night and a long sleep would better equip her for her conversation with Mrs Lemmon tomorrow. But she suspected that sleep would be slow to come and she wanted to tell someone in detail about the events of the day. Someone who would soothe and sympathize.

Until recently, Bill would have been the obvious person. But they hadn't spoken now for nearly a week and it wasn't easy to make the decision. If he was out – or worse, if he didn't appear to care, how would she feel? Could she risk the chance of disappointment?

She decided to try.

He'd picked up the phone almost immediately, which was, perhaps, a good sign.

'Bill, how are you?'

'I'm doing OK, thanks. Busy as usual.'

Did he sound a little short or was it her imagination? 'How's the script?'

'Oh, you know. Two steps forward and nine back. More trouble in the team.'

'Oh dear. Sorry to hear that.'

'How are you, Abbie? You sound tired.'

'I'm exhausted. I've had a horrible day. Lizzie is in trouble at school. Kate's off sick and I'm overloaded with work.'

'Poor you.' Bill sounded genuinely concerned, but he didn't ask any more about Lizzie. Perhaps he hadn't heard her properly.

Abbie said, 'Lizzie's in trouble for punching a girl in her class.'

'Kids!' Bill exclaimed, his voice warm but showing no real

interest. She got the impression he wasn't quite with her, that he wanted to get back to whatever he'd been doing.

'How's Jon?' she asked.

Bill grunted. 'Impossible. I'm trying not to think about him.'

She waited, but he said no more. 'Oh well. I'd better go. Just thought I'd give you a quick ring.'

'Yes, nice to hear from you, Abbie.'

And that was it. All she could do was say goodbye and click the phone off. There was no point struggling to hold back her tears. She finally had the chance to cry alone, as long as she did it quietly. But habit prevailed and she couldn't manage more than a few drops.

She wondered if Bill had someone with him. Perhaps even Jon? They might be in the middle of an argument. Perhaps Deb was there, too? Or Deb might be there on her own. If so, what were they doing – talking about Jon? Reminiscing about old times? Abbie told herself to stop being silly, not to think that way, but it didn't seem possible. Her headache was back and she felt sick. She had no wine in the house. Not that drinking wine alone in such circumstances was sensible – but tonight might have been an exception.

She sat down at her computer, tempted to look back at Bill's old messages, the ones she'd saved, going right back to early May when their correspondence had begun. But there was no point making herself even more miserable, torturing herself with the gradual warming up of their friendship, the simmering feelings, the boiling over into love. A love that had now evaporated on his part.

Don't be silly, Abbie told herself. Your relationship with Bill isn't over. You agreed to let things cool off for a while, to give you both the chance to deal with your domestic problems, and that's what you're now doing.

But she couldn't get rid of the sense that something had been lost, and after a few moments she was in tears again.

chapter thirteen

'Why won't she come in?' asked Abbie.

'Oh, I don't know. She feels a bit awkward, I think.'

Keith had arrived at six to pick up the twins. It was a Friday evening in mid-October and they were off to Venice for half-term. Fiona was with him, back from her trips abroad, but as usual she had remained in the car.

'Well, she doesn't need to feel awkward. I'm perfectly capable of being pleasant.'

'Of course you are and so is she. But it's difficult, isn't it, for the second wife – the new partner, I mean – finding a way to relate to the first one?'

'Is it? I wouldn't know.'

'Well, use your imagination. Put yourself in Fiona's position.'

Abbie shook her head. 'Can't see it, I'm afraid. All she has to do is step over my threshold and be polite, drink a cup of my coffee, perhaps – surely that's not too taxing?' After a pause, she added, 'She doesn't seem to feel any qualms about relating to the twins.'

'That's different. Where are they, Abbie – are they ready to go?'

'In their bedroom doing some last-minute packing.'

'I hope there's not going to be any trouble this time.'

'There won't be. Sarah's been fine for weeks now, as you know.'

They were standing in the hall. Keith made to step forward to go into the girls' room, but Abbie put a restraining hand on his arm.

'Hang on a minute, Keith. I'm serious about this. I'd like to meet the woman who spends so much time with my daughters.'

'You have met her.'

'I'd like to spend some time together, get to know her a bit.'

'Well, another time, perhaps. But not tonight. We have to be on our way.' He pulled his arm away and eased past her. 'Lizzie, Sarah – are you ready?'

The girls appeared, each carrying a large suitcase and a holdall.

Abbie had thought she detected, that morning at breakfast, a trace of tension in Sarah's face. But it passed quickly and she told herself it was her imagination. Sarah looked happy enough now, if a little subdued.

Lizzie was her usual boisterous self. 'Can't wait to go, can't wait to go,' she chanted, oblivious to Abbie's feelings. 'See you in a week and a bit, Mum.'

Abbie hugged and kissed them both in turn, feeling her tears well up. Her daughters' skins were silky, their limbs wriggling and impatient.

Sarah settled against her, nestled there for longer. There *was* something, Abbie was sure of it now.

'Are you OK, petal?'

'Yes.'

'Really sure?'

'Yes.'

'You don't have to go if you don't want to.' Dangerous words, she knew, but she couldn't help saying them. She had to give Sarah a way out if the girl didn't want to go on this holiday.

'She does have to go, we both have to go.' Lizzie was swinging her bag, chanting the words. 'Come on, tortoise. Fiona's in the car.'

Abbie felt Sarah's muscles tighten for a moment before she let go.

''Bye, Mummy,' she said, kissing Abbie's cheek, and followed Keith and Lizzie from the room.

Abbie stayed at the window for five minutes after the car had driven off.

The evening dragged and she could settle to nothing. As she was getting ready for bed, the phone rang.

'Abbie, is that you?'

'Of course it's me. Are you OK, Bill?'

'No, I'm not so good, to be honest. Have you got a minute?'

'Of course I have. I've got all evening. Tell me what's wrong.'

Her heart had started thumping when she heard Bill's voice. She took long, deep breaths as she listened, trying to be calm. It seemed so long since he had phoned and she was no longer clear whether they still had anything that could be called a relationship.

'More trouble with the boys. I need a second opinion, if you don't mind.'

'Of course I don't.'

'But first, tell me how you are.'

'Me?' she said stupidly. 'I'm fine. Well, you know. OK.'

'Good. How are the twins?'

'They went off with Keith and Fiona earlier this evening. They're going on holiday to Venice.'

'Sounds nice.'

'Yes, doesn't it? I wouldn't mind a holiday myself.'

'How are Sarah's nightmares?' Bill asked.

'She hasn't had one for nearly a month now. And they both seem happy at school. They've got over their bad start to the year.'

'That's great news. I'm so glad.'

'It's quite a relief.'

'Abbie. It seems a long time since we spoke.'

'I've lost count.'

'How do you feel about the girls going away with Keith and Fiona?'

'Oh, you know. The usual. A bit left out and sorry for myself. Mixed with relief that I've got some time on my own. But also worried. Sarah looked sad earlier on today. Kind of wistful.'

'It must be strange for them, leaving you behind.'

'I don't know. They've been for quite a few holidays now with Keith and Fiona. Apart from Sarah's upsets in the summer, they've always seemed quite happy about it. Almost too happy, if you know what I mean.'

'I know exactly what you mean.'

'Anyway, you were supposed to be telling me *your* troubles.'

Bill sighed. 'Perhaps I'm making a fuss over nothing. But both my sons have now decided they don't want to see me at weekends.

Or they want to restrict their visits to once a month at the most, depending on the football.'

'This is the football with Curtis?'

'Yes, it's the real thing – Curtis the Magnificent in action. He plays for an amateur team, I think I told you, and the boys want to go along every Saturday to support him.'

'But can't they come to you after the match – at least spend Saturday evening and Sunday with you?'

'That's what I suggested. But no, it seems that various social events take place after the football, including a visit to a pub and some kind of curry supper.'

'But they're only fifteen and thirteen, aren't they? Isn't that rather young for pubs?'

'Jon's sixteen now. I don't think they drink any alcohol. I hope they don't. Perhaps I should check.'

'What's to stop them spending Sunday with you?'

'On Sunday morning, I'm told, a long lie-in is required to recover from the excitement of Saturday. After which, Deb prepares brunch – muffins and waffles and the like. Then they go for a family walk.'

'I'm getting the picture.'

'And in the afternoon Curtis helps the boys with their home-work. He's a maths teacher, you see, when he's not being a saxophonist or a muscular centre-forward. Both boys struggle with maths and Deb and I are hopeless at it, so it's ideal. I suppose I should be glad they've found someone who can help them.'

'Not good for one's pride, though, is it?'

'Brings out all your most childish feelings, ones you've not had for years.'

'Don't I know it. Look, Bill, can't you just talk to your boys? Be honest – tell them how much you miss them? Surely they can do their maths with Curtis during the week?'

'They're too busy going to watch him play in his band. Or he's cooking amazing meals – apparently he's a whiz at Thai food.'

'He would be.'

Bill giggled.

Abbie continued, 'Bill, you can't let them push you around like that. You're getting hurt and it can't be good for the boys, either, not to see you at all. Goodness, what *is* it about these second marriages?'

'They're not married, Deb and Curtis. Not yet.'

'You know what I mean. Why do our exes have to *prove* things all the time – prove how well they can do without us, show off how much better their new partner is than their old? And why do the children just lap it up?'

'That's not true of your girls.'

'No, I know. Or at least, it's more complicated than that.'

Bill paused, and when his spoke again his voice was full of warmth. 'I tell you something, Abbie. Hearing your voice is doing me the world of good.'

'And me, hearing yours. I've missed you.'

There was another pause, then Bill said, 'I'm glad we can still be friends. I've haven't felt much like talking just lately – not to anyone.'

'You sound very low.'

'I suppose I am. My life feels like unremitting hard work, with everything I do turning sour on me.'

'I suppose I could come down to stay, if you think it would help?' Abbie was surprised to hear herself say this.

Bill's voice brightened in a way that made her heart pound again. 'What, you come here, to see me?'

'Well ... the twins are away till next weekend. I'm due some holiday and things are quieter now we've got into the new term and the students are settling down. If I ask nicely, I might get Friday and Monday off. I could come down on the train for a long weekend. If it's convenient, that is....'

'Abbie, that would be fantastic.'

'OK then. I'll book my tickets – Friday to Monday.'

'You're sure the twins have really gone? That there'll be no last-minute changes of mind?'

'Not this time. I'm sure of it.'

'You've cheered me up no end.'

It was true, she heard it in his voice. A wave of excitement swept through her. 'I'll make the arrangements.'

'I'm hoping you'll live up to your name and bring me some harmony.'

'Harmony – my pseudonym. I'd almost forgotten.'

'I've kept all those emails you sent me early on.'

'Have you?' For some reason she didn't tell him that she had kept all his, too. 'That's nice. Well, I'll see you very soon.'

'Take care, Abbie.'

'And you, Bill. 'Bye.'

She discovered, putting down the phone, that she had spent the conversation scratching away at a sticky label on the back of it, and the remnants were rather painfully embedded under her fingernail.

Sarah's text message arrived while Abbie was on the train, somewhere between Leeds and Doncaster. She had received five texts so far from Lizzie, but this was only Sarah's second.

Miss you Mummy. Home soon, love Sarah xxxx

Of course, these words did not necessarily mean that Sarah was homesick and unhappy, but Abbie suspected that that was exactly what they did mean. Abbie wished she could speak to her, but the arrangement was, as always, that they would rely on texts for communication unless there was an emergency. Abbie remembered agreeing at the time to this suggestion of Keith's, and couldn't understand now why she hadn't protested. But the girls had always seemed contented to text and be texted to, and she had acquiesced.

If she were to phone now (hang the expense) it would, no doubt, cause a disturbance, interrupting some exciting activity or even something embarrassing like a guided tour, where it would turn out that the twins should have switched off their phones and hadn't. It would make trouble, and she, Abbie, would be chided for it later by Keith as well as the girls.

'Mummy, you're such a worry-can. All I said was I miss you. Why do you always make such a fuss?' would be Sarah's reaction.

Abbie gazed out of the window, trying to focus on the grey fields, small farms and occasional cluster of power station cooling towers. She'd eaten her sandwiches long ago and finished her paperback and there was nothing to take up her attention. Her companion opposite, a girl of about fourteen, had got on the train at York and spent all the time since on the phone to one friend after another, laughing widely enough to show a mouthful of pink chewing gum on several occasions. Abbie tried not to look.

A couple of hours, she reminded herself, and she'd be there, with Bill waiting to meet her on New Street station. Then two whole days in Birmingham, with him. It was a bit like visiting one of her female friends, such as Heather, she told herself. You anticipated simple pleasures like a good natter, a few laughs, a pleasant, relaxing break. It was nothing like meeting a lover. She felt completely different from the time Bill had come up to Dundee, when she'd been so excited and nervous.

Of course, there was something a bit different about a male friend – something that might be said to give cross-gender friendship the edge over same-sex ones, at least in some respects. There was that sense of complementing each other, of offering compatible but different perspectives and a kind of appreciation that you didn't always get in female friendships. Men could be a blessed relief from the suffocating quality of female emotion such as she'd had from Kate in the last few weeks. Recent encounters with Kate had left her more than once with the sensation of having a mirror thrust in front of her face – being forced to look closely at her own emotional make-up in magnified, grainy detail.

Yes, seeing Bill and exploring Birmingham would be just what she needed. He had asked if she would come shopping with him on Saturday and help him choose some new things for the flat which, he admitted, was almost bare since Deb had come to reclaim her share of their possessions.

'I'd like your advice on a new colour scheme, too,' he said. 'I've decided to redecorate over Christmas, to give myself something to do.'

She agreed, delighted by the idea. 'Maybe I can help – we could start painting while I'm with you.'

Bill laughed. 'Don't be silly, you're coming for a holiday. As well as to be my adviser, of course.'

The motion of the train had started to make Abbie's stomach feel queasy and she slid out of her seat and made her way to the shop to look for something new to read. Of course, motion sickness and nervous tension could produce very similar symptoms. If she hadn't known better, she might have thought she was feeling sick with excitement at the thought of meeting Bill.

He was waiting on the platform as she opened the door to scramble down, having somehow guessed the exact point at which she would emerge from the train. He took her bag and guided her out into the current of passengers, directing her to the escalator with a firm hand on her shoulder. It was difficult to make themselves heard above the noise of the loudspeaker announcements.

As they came off the escalator and found a quiet place to stand, Abbie found that they were hugging tightly. When they stepped apart, Bill said, 'You're only a few minutes late.'

'I seem to have been on that train for days.'

'Well, it's great to see you.'

'What's the matter?'

'How do you mean? Oh, I look fed up, do I? I had another row with Jon last night, on the phone. I'll tell you more when we get to the flat. Are you OK with a ten-minute walk? Here, let me take your case.'

Once they were out of the station and away from the worst of the crowds, Abbie asked, 'So what was your row with Jon about? The weekend visits again?'

'No, not exactly. It started when I asked him if he'd like to come shopping with us tomorrow. Sam said he wanted to come, so I made the mistake of ringing Jon again, to give him the chance to change his mind. He said, "No, you can't buy me off with new trainers the way you do Sam," which I thought was below the belt. Then I heard Deb shouting something in the background. I gathered that she was quite keen on the idea that Jon and Sam would both come with me because it would give her and Curtis Saturday afternoon to themselves.'

'What about the football?'

'I don't think Deb cares about the football.'

'Right. So what happened?'

'Well, I heard Jon shouting something about how neither of us wanted him. I told him that of course we did. He said something which I won't repeat about Deb and me. I'm afraid I rather lost my temper at that point.'

'What did you say?'

'Oh, a few words to the effect that I didn't care if I never saw him again – that as far as I'm concerned Curtis can be his dad from now on.'

She gasped. 'Oh dear.'

'Yes. I regretted it as soon as I'd said it, of course.'

'Did you tell him that?'

'I didn't get the chance. He shouted, "I hate you, Dad," and banged the phone down. I called back but he wouldn't speak to me. Deb harangued me for an hour over what I'd said. She said Jon was in his room, crashing furniture around. I tried to talk to her about it, to say I was sorry, but she wouldn't listen.'

Abbie reached for Bill's hand, the one that wasn't carrying her suitcase, and squeezed it.

'I feel so bad,' he went on. 'I can't believe I said all that to Jon.'

'He's said some hurtful things to you.'

'Nothing as bad as that. And I'm supposed to be the adult. I more or less disowned him.'

'You didn't disown him. As long as you explain that you said it in anger, that you didn't mean it. Just talk to him, as soon as you can.'

'Easier said than done. No doubt he's pouring out his heart to Curtis now, and that wuss is telling him to hush, hush, don't worry, I'll be your father from now on.'

'I can't imagine that happening. Jon won't want to talk to Curtis about it.'

'You don't think so?'

'I'm sure he won't. I don't expect he'll tell anyone. Why don't you park me at your flat and go straight round to Deb's and see him?'

'Because he won't let me in. Anyway, it's miles away. And I haven't invited you here to abandon you.'

'I invited myself, didn't I? I don't mind. It'll give me time to snoop around and make myself at home.'

Bill managed a laugh and squeezed Abbie's hand, which had somehow remained attached to his.

'Nearly there now,' he said. 'Just down these steps.'

Bill's flat was on the first floor of a block by the side of the renovated canal. It looked new, having perhaps been built only a year or so before. The deep-red-brick construction gave the building a kind of warmth, but the overall effect was rather bland, Abbie thought. It was livened to some extent by the ducks on the water and the geese honking on the bank. A narrow boat was moored a little further along, its occupants, a middle-aged couple with outdoor complexions, enjoying a nap in the fading afternoon sunshine.

'This is fantastic,' Abbie said when she saw it. 'I'd love to live in a place like this.'

'Would you? It's not as good as the sea.'

'Maybe not quite – but the water's so close, it laps under your windows. It must be so soothing at night.'

'I've not sure I've ever noticed,' Bill replied. 'Do come in, anyway. Your long journey is finally over.'

The flat smelt of fresh plaster and paint – a hint of new beginnings that Abbie rather liked. Her own bungalow, when she moved in, had retained the musty odour of its previous occupants until she had replaced the carpets and repainted every room.

The décor was unimaginative, the walls washed in a pale peachy off-white she guessed had been there when Bill moved in. What little furniture there was was minimalist and functional, not so much an aesthetic choice, Bill told her, as a lack of effort on his part. That, and the fact that Deb had taken all the good stuff.

'It's just the place I work and sleep,' he said, opening the door of his bedroom, which was to be Abbie's for the duration of her stay. There was no other bedroom but he was, he assured her, quite happy to sleep on the sofa.

'So what happens when the boys come for the weekend?' she asked.

'One of them has the sofa, the other has an old folding bed,' he said. 'They seemed to like it at first. But it's become another point of contention recently. Jon won't sleep in the same room as Sam – he claims that Sam snores. It's yet another reason Jon gives me for not wanting to stay over. Deb told me at the time I should get somewhere with two bedrooms, or even three, so they could have one each.'

'But could you have afforded that?'

'Only if I'd gone miles out of town. A grotty semi in one of the suburbs. Whereas this place is perfect for work – close to the Mailbox, the BBC place where I go for meetings.'

'So you like it here?'

'As I said, it's convenient and easy to maintain. I have the ducks and geese for company, to say nothing of all the passers-by on their way to the waterside restaurants and pubs. It's fine, just what I need.'

She was sitting on the sofa now, a squat, boxy affair that she could not imagine Bill sleeping on, unless his legs hung over one of the arms, his feet in mid-air. She sipped a gin and orange, telling herself she deserved it after the long journey. Bill had already drunk most of the whisky he'd poured for himself.

'Abbie, you make me feel so much better. I'm very glad you're here.'

'I'm glad, too. It's nice seeing you on your home ground.'

'I don't know what you must think of me. I don't come across as the best of fathers.'

'It's not easy. I understand. But you must speak to Jon as soon as you can.'

'I'll phone him. But first, you must be hungry. We can eat in one of the restaurants near here. There's a whole cluster of them within five minutes' walk along the canal.'

'I am quite hungry. But I'd be just as happy if you cooked something. I'd prefer it, in fact.'

'My cupboards aren't well-stocked. I usually shop on Saturdays. It would only be something like an omelette.'

'That would be fine.'

'You're sure you wouldn't rather go out?'

'Not unless you would.'

'No, if an omelette's what you want, that's what you shall have. I'll make you the Bill Special, which means throwing in a week's worth of leftovers. You prepared to risk that?'

Abbie giggled, overtaken by sudden carefree happiness. 'I'll take a chance.'

Bill finished his drink and got up from his cushion-less wooden rocking-chair, smiling. It was clear to Abbie that he was happy, too, and possibly as unused to the feeling as she was.

'Shall I come and help you?' she asked.

He paused at the door, smiling. 'I'd rather you didn't. You'll disapprove of my kitchen arrangements – any woman would.'

'Of course I won't.'

'No, I'd rather do it on my own. Then you won't see me scraping up the things I drop on the floor.'

'What, back into the omelette?' She grinned back.

'Exactly. Now, you make yourself at home. Put the TV on or read the paper.'

'I'm going to watch the ducks and geese,' she said, getting up and moving to the window. It was dusk now and a row of fairy lights twinkled alongside the canal, its reflection waving in the rippled water.

'There's a couple of swans that sometimes put in an appearance,' he said. 'But not usually on Friday nights – too many people around.'

Abbie left open the heavy, floor length curtains and sipped her remaining gin and orange as she stood at the window looking down. It was as good, she decided, as being in Venice. Well, as good in some ways. She must, at this moment, be at least as happy as Keith and Fiona. Perhaps even more so.

The kitchen door was slightly open and the smell of warming oil, garlic and onions soon wafted through, making Abbie realize how hungry she was. Her sandwich on the train must be five hours ago now. She hoped Bill would be generous with the eggs.

Later, satiated by the omelette, which was thick, creamy, well-filled and highly spiced, the two of them sat together on the sofa, looking out through the open curtains to the towpath below, teeming with young people eager for Friday night.

Neither of them said much – there seemed to be little need. When Abbie had complimented Bill on the meal he'd waved away her praise in his usual self-mocking way, though it was obvious he was pleased. He had opened red wine, which turned out to be a perfect accompaniment to the spicy omelette and crusty bread. Neither wanted dessert and they brought the remaining wine with them into the living room, where it sat on the large upturned earthenware plant pot Bill used as a coffee table.

Gentle jazz that Abbie didn't recognize bled into the soft, cool air around them that moved a little in the draught from the open window. She was, she realized, not so far from sleep. She and Bill were not touching but she was aware of his solid presence, very close. Shutting her eyes, she discovered, made him seem closer still.

He was suddenly real, as real as she was, very much present, complex and colourful both in body and mind. Her eyes still closed, she knew that Bill's head was bending towards hers and that, in a moment, they would kiss. She could open her eyes and see the blur of Bill's face, or she could choose to keep them closed and question nothing.

What followed was not, perhaps, perfect, but it was as near perfect as she could have hoped.

Both giggled, admitting to being out of practice and, before that, having grown used, over the years, to the idiosyncrasies of just one partner. Somehow, these confessions seemed more intimate than the semi-familiar pattern of their bodily movements. It was, Abbie felt, as though she was admitting him into her past, her history, the most private domain of all.

As they lay together afterwards (on the carpet by this time as the sofa had proved too small) Bill whispered, 'Abbie, you are beautiful. I'm so lucky to have found you. I love you very much.'

His words flowed straight to the place that needed healing, the wound made by Keith's declaration that with Fiona he had finally discovered true love.

'Are you sure?'

'Of course I'm sure.'

'I love you, too.'

'You don't need to say that. Wait until *you're* sure.'

'I am sure, Bill. I really am.'

'Take your time. I can wait.'

'You don't need to wait. I love you.'

'I wasn't quite expecting this.' His voice was muffled, his mouth buried in her neck.

'Me neither.'

'I hope you don't feel rushed.'

'Rushed?'

He sat up a little. 'I didn't invite you here for this, Abbie, believe me. I mean it wasn't my intention to lure you here and seduce you.'

She gave a little laugh.

'I hope you believe me. I'd hate you to think....'

'Don't be silly. I invited myself. And I was a willing participant. You didn't exactly rape me.'

'Of course not. But I gave you the wine and the omelette....'

Now she couldn't stop laughing; it bubbled up into her gullet like champagne. 'Do you really think it was the omelette that seduced me? What did you put in it, hash?'

'No – honest to God.'

'Have we both been denying something?' she asked.

'I think so. For quite a while.'

'And you're OK with it?' The air blowing in had turned colder. Bill pulled himself away from Abbie and got up to click the window shut.

'I'm more than OK.'

He sat down again, not beside her but on the chair opposite. She missed the warmth of his body.

'But what about the stuff you said?' he asked. 'About putting your twins first and all that?'

'I've moved on a bit since then. For one thing, the twins are much better. And I've been missing you a lot.'

'Have you?'

'An awful lot.'

'And me you. But I really thought you didn't want me – that you were so preoccupied with your daughters....'

Abbie stuck out her foot to stroke his leg. 'Let's not talk about it any more. We're together now – that's what matters.'

Hours later, when they were lying together in Bill's bed, he said, 'I forgot to phone Jon.'

'You'd better do it tomorrow. First thing.'

'Will you help me? Tell me what to say?'

'You need to say sorry. Tell him you love him. Start with that and see what happens.'

'I don't know if I can.'

'Of course you can. It's the truth, isn't it?' She stroked his forehead, ran her fingers up into his thick hair.

'That can make it harder to say.'

'Just say it. It'll be easier in the morning.' Abbie was over-whelmed, all of a sudden, by the need to sleep.

chapter fourteen

'Keith, what is it? What's happened?'

Abbie's mobile phone, placed the previous night on the box of books beside Bill's bed, rang at ten past seven on Saturday morning, rousing her from a deep sleep. It took a few moments to remember where she was and to locate her phone. When she saw Keith's name on the display she clicked to answer it, heart thumping.

'What's the matter, Keith? Are the twins all right?'

'Abbie, where are you? I tried to ring you at home but there was no answer.'

She had told Keith she was going away for the weekend; he must have forgotten. He didn't know she was at Bill's, as there hadn't been time to explain. What had she told him, she tried to remember – that she was staying with a friend? Not that it mattered now. Something must be wrong, for him to phone at this time.

'I'm away down south. Keith, what's happened? Are the girls all right?'

Bill stirred beside her, his sleep-swollen face taking on a puzzled frown. 'What is it?'

Abbie moved the phone away from him.

'Nothing to worry about,' Keith was saying. There was tension in his voice. 'It's just there's a bit of a problem. I'm bringing the twins home early.'

'Why, what's going on? Is one of them ill? Has there been an accident?'

'No, nothing like that. They're both fine.'

'Can I speak to them?'

'No, they're still asleep. It's only eight-fifteen here.'

'I know, it's only seven-fifteen here. That's why you frightened me, ringing so early. You woke me up. What's going on?'

'Nothing. Abbie, was that another voice I heard?'

'No!' She didn't want to deceive Keith, but there'd be time to correct the fib later. 'Look, Keith, you can't ring me at this time and expect me not to worry. Either something's wrong or it isn't.' A thought struck her. 'Has Sarah had another nightmare?'

'No, not exactly.'

'What do you mean, not exactly?'

'I'll have to go in a minute. Fiona's in the bathroom and she's about to come back.'

'Don't you want her to know you're phoning me? If something's happened....'

'Nothing's happened. Ah—' He broke off, presumably at Fiona's reappearance. When he spoke again his voice had changed in a way Abbie couldn't define. A note of helplessness, perhaps? What was going on?

'I'm changing our flights,' Keith said. 'I'll try to get us back to Edinburgh this evening. I'll drive the girls straight up to Carleith.'

'But I'm down here till Monday. Down south, with my friend.'

'Abbie, please. I need you to come home. The twins want to see you.'

'But you're not due back for two days. Why are you changing the flights? Are *you* ill, or is something wrong with Fiona?'

He sounded grim now, with a coldness in his voice that frightened her. 'No, none of us is ill. But I want the twins to see you as soon as possible. I really can't say any more at the moment. I'll call you later.'

Then Keith was gone and Bill was fully awake beside her, his legs still curled around hers, the way they'd slept – cosied up together as though they'd been sharing a bed for years.

'Was that Keith?'

'Yes. Bill, I'm worried.' Her voice came out shaky and she realized she was shivering.

Bill's arms encircled her, trying to give comfort. 'Is everything all right with your girls?'

'No – I don't know. He wouldn't say. Just that he's coming home early, bringing the girls straight to my house. I'll have to leave this morning.'

'But Abbie—'

She almost shouted at him. 'Bill! You don't understand. Something's wrong, I know it is. With one or both of the girls. He wouldn't let me speak to them. I don't know what's going on.' She sat straight up in the bed, staring at her phone display as though it might be able to tell her.

'But if something was wrong, why didn't he say? Were the twins there with him?'

'No, he was in his bedroom. Fiona had gone to the bathroom. The twins were in their room asleep.'

'So if they were ill, either of them, he'd have told you.'

'Of course he would. Bill, I've just remembered. When I asked if Sarah had had a nightmare, he said, "Not exactly." So it must be something to do with that. Then he said he'd have to go, that Fiona was coming back.'

'So it's something he didn't want Fiona to hear.'

'I suppose so.'

'How about phoning the girls – they have their own mobiles, don't they?'

'Good idea.' She was pressing buttons while still replying. But after a few seconds she threw her phone down on the bed in frustration.

'I've got Sarah's answer phone. No doubt I'll get Lizzie's, too.'

'Try, you never know.'

'Bill, I'm frightened,' she said, picking up her phone and pressing the keys again.

'I know, my love. But try to keep calm.'

When Abbie got a similar answer phone message from Lizzie's phone, she began to sob. 'What if something really bad has happened and he daren't tell me? What if one of them is in hospital? Or both of them. Or even worse.'

'No, no, no. It can't be anything like that. He'd have said.'

'He wants to tell me in person. That must be it. He doesn't want to break bad news over the phone.'

'Have you got the number of the hotel? Perhaps we can phone and ask someone there.'

'I daren't.'

'Shall I do it?'

'I've got the number written down somewhere. My diary, in my handbag.'

'I think your bag is in the living room. Shall I get it?'

'Yes, please. No. I don't know....'

Bill was getting out of bed, making for the door, a little unsteady on his feet. Abbie threw back her side of the duvet and put her legs out, too, ready to follow. Then her phone rang again.

'It's him, it's Keith!' she cried.

Bill stopped in the doorway, then came back to sit beside her on the bed.

'Keith, for God's sake tell me properly this time, what's going on?'

'OK, Abbie. I'm outside now. I can talk to you.'

She drew a deep breath. 'So tell me what's happened. Quick, I want to know.'

'Abbie, the twins are not ill and they are not injured. They're safe, believe me. I just need to get them home as soon as possible.'

'Has there been an attack – has the hotel been bombed?'

'No, of course not. Nothing like that.'

'You said "not exactly" when I asked if Sarah had a nightmare. Is it something to do with that?'

'Yes. Something to do with it. But—'

She interrupted. 'Did she sleepwalk, out of her room? Out of the hotel?'

'No. Why, has she ever done that at home?'

'No, I just wondered. My imagination is going mad. Unless you tell me soon....'

'OK. Abbie. Listen, the twins are upset. There's been a big altercation with Fiona.'

'An altercation – you mean a row? Just a row? Then why the hell all this fuss? Can't you sort out an argument without bringing them home? Do you have to wake me at the crack of dawn and make me think there's been a terrible accident?'

'It was quite a bad altercation. Not exactly a row. More of a discovery. Leading to a conflict.'

'What kind of discovery?' She was calming down. Whatever kind of argument there'd been, it couldn't compete with the fears that had been raging inside her.

'Listen, Abbie, let me explain. I went for a walk on my own yesterday evening while Fiona read the twins a bedtime story. We've been doing that every day. She likes to have a bit of time with them on her own. I thought it was a good thing, to encourage bonding. No, don't interrupt. I know you don't like Fiona. Well, now's your chance to say, "I told you so". It started raining and I came back early. I found her reading to them from a book, a set of stories she'd written.'

'Stories she'd written herself? What kind of stories?'

'Well. As it turns out, unsuitable ones.'

'Unsuitable in what way?'

Bill, beside her, was looking puzzled again.

'Oh, Abbie. I'll explain better when I see you. I don't want to stay out here too long. The twins may wake up.'

'Keith, tell me.'

She heard Keith clear his throat. 'Very explicit. You know, sexual. Violent. Not the sort of thing you'd want eleven-year-olds to hear. That's why they're upset, it turns out. We had a long talk last night. They kept trying to tell me it was OK, that they hadn't minded. They were trying to protect Fiona, for some reason.'

'My God!'

'I got it out of them in the end. It must have been what was causing Sarah's nightmares. And the trouble at school.'

'But how long has it been going on, these stories?'

'Months, apparently. I think I told you that Fiona has been doing some writing of her own. She asked if she could try out her stories on the twins. There didn't seem any reason to refuse. The twins said they liked them so it continued.'

'You didn't read the stories yourself, first?'

'She wouldn't let me. Said she wanted to test them on her intended audience, children of the twins' age. She didn't want my criticism – she thought it might put her off.'

'But why didn't Sarah and Lizzie tell us?'

'I don't know. Some kind of loyalty to Fiona, I think. They didn't want to get her into trouble.'

'Right – I'm getting the next train home.'

'Good. I'm about to ring to change the flights. I'm bringing the twins back on my own. Fiona is staying on here.'

'I'm disgusted you're still speaking to her, sharing a bed. That you didn't throw her out.'

'I wanted to. Believe me. But she was upset. I'm not letting her near the twins, don't worry. As soon as they've woken and had breakfast, we're off.'

'Please let me speak to them.'

'Look, Abbie, I think it's best not. They're still fast asleep. I kept checking on them all night. If they hear you crying, it'll upset them. It's better you see them when we get home. As long as you're there in your bungalow when we arrive, it'll be fine.'

She saw the sense in what Keith said, much as she wanted to speak to Lizzie and Sarah.

'I've got to go,' she told Bill. 'Did you pick up the gist of that?'

'More or less,' he replied. 'Look, I'll drive you up to Dundee. If we set off now—'

'No, no, no. I need time to think. I'll get the first train. If I leave straightaway for the station, there might be an early one.'

'Better to phone and find out. But I'm happy to drive you, I really am. I won't get in your way, I'll stay in that guest house again, the Tay Prospect.'

'No, Bill. It's very kind of you, but I have to do this on my own.'

He sighed in a way that choked Abbie's throat with guilt. 'I don't see why. Is it because Keith and the girls don't know you're staying with me? If you don't want them to know, I can drop you some-where – I needn't be seen. Though I don't quite understand—'

'No, it's not that.' She wasn't sure why, but it felt important to get away, to be on her own, to try to get her head round what was going on. To wrestle with the fear that it was the joy she'd had with Bill last night that had somehow harmed her girls. Ridiculous and irrational, of course, but needing to be defeated, just the same. As though she had betrayed the twins by seeking her own pleasure, and now they must all be punished.

'Abbie, please let me help. I know you're upset, but I want to understand. You seem to have gone into a world of your own.'

She wanted to let him in on her nightmare, or part of her did. But a louder part insisted that there was no time. Bill had become a luxury to be left for later, when things returned, if they ever did, to normal.

'I'm sorry, Bill. I'm not trying to exclude you. I appreciate your concern and I know you want to help. But there isn't really anything you can do at the moment. I just have to get back to my twins as soon as possible.'

Bill sighed, picked up his bedside phone and dialled National Rail Enquiries, while Abbie pulled on her clothes and pushed her belongings into her travel bag. Her suitcase remained almost unpacked from her arrival yesterday.

'The first through train to Dundee is at 10.30,' Bill said as he put down the phone. 'There are earlier trains heading north, but you'd have to change. The 10.30 sounds like your best bet.'

'You sure?'

'Yep. But the offer's still open. I'll drive you up there if you like.'

'No. But thanks.'

'Will you be able to change your ticket?'

'I doubt it. I'll buy a new one.'

'Let me make you some breakfast, at least. There's no point setting off yet.'

'Just coffee, then.'

He moved close to her and took each of her hands in his, trying to make her look at him. She knew that if she let him hug her she would start to cry and that she couldn't afford tears, not just now. Perhaps when she was on the train, heading for home. Or perhaps the anger would come first, the bitter stuff she could feel welling up inside her, pure hatred for the woman who had dared to harm her daughters.

Keith's tone had suggested ignorance and carelessness on Fiona's part, rather than any desire to hurt the girls. Perhaps that was Keith wanting to protect his beloved, or perhaps he was right. But even if it were true, Abbie knew that when Fiona's behaviour had fully sunk in, she would want nothing less than to kill her.

The train was almost empty and Abbie found herself a window seat on her own. She spent the first half-hour of the journey gazing at the landscape, aware of flashes of sunlight reflecting off defunct industrial sites and power plants, but seeing almost nothing. Not even thinking or feeling, just focusing her mind on the train's progress, willing herself closer to her daughters, who were still in distant Venice.

After the first two or three stations the seats around her began to fill up and Abbie decided to phone Kate while she still had the chance to chat in private. It was after midday now, so Kate would presumably be awake. Not that she would object to being woken in circumstances like these.

Kate knew that Abbie was in Birmingham that weekend, and had raised her eyebrows slightly at the news, smiling when Abbie assured her that it was merely a friendly visit. Kate had suspected, of course, what Abbie had managed to deny to herself, that both she and Bill were interested in rather more than friendship. Abbie marvelled for a second or two at her own self-deception. But there was no point in thinking about that now.

'Hi, Abbie. How's it going in Brum? You having a good time?'

'No. At least, I was. I'll tell you sometime. But Keith rang me last night with awful news.'

'What, the twins? What's happened?'

'It's OK. They're not ill or hurt. But he's bringing them straight home. There's been a terrible upset with Fiona. I still can't believe what she's done.' Abbie told Kate as much of the story as she knew.

'I never trusted that woman,' said Kate.'

'You only met her once.'

'Twice. And I saw her on television, remember, that afternoon show. She was too good to be true. That slow, little-girly voice. And so smug. Abbie – you must want to kill her.'

'I do.'

'I'll help you.'

'Thanks.'

'How could she do that to your girls?'

'I feel so bad. I trusted her with them.'

'You trusted Keith. That's not so unreasonable.'

'I suppose not. But it turns out he didn't know her at all.'

'He was taken in by the evil bitch.'

'He thinks she didn't mean to hurt them. I could tell from his voice. He might even forgive her. It wouldn't surprise me.'

'Whether she meant to or not, she *has* hurt them,' said Kate. 'All those nightmares of Sarah's.'

'I know – and Lizzie's upsets at school. But what really makes me weep is the thought that they didn't tell me or Keith.'

'Why didn't they? I can see they might not have wanted to tell Keith, but why didn't they tell you what was going on?'

'I don't know and it worries me. I asked them so many times if anything was bothering them. I even asked if they were happy with Daddy and Fiona being together. All they said was that they didn't like it when they kissed. And that they wanted to see their father on his own sometimes – which seemed fair enough. And once they got the chance to do that, they seemed so much better.'

'I suppose it was when Fiona was away that they were better.'

'It was, looking back. Why didn't I put two and two together?'

'You mustn't blame yourself. No one saw it – it wasn't just you.'

'But I'm their mother. I'm supposed to see things like that.'

'Don't beat yourself up, Abbie. You'll see them soon. Perhaps they'll be in a better state than you expect. At least you know what's going on, now – you can start putting things right.'

'It might have damaged them for life. Oh God, Kate, they might be permanently traumatized by this.'

'No. They won't.'

'Kate....' Abbie was close to tears. They had stopped at another station and a woman with a baby and a toddler hesitated beside Abbie's table but then, to her relief, moved on.

'Hush, hush, now. It's going to be OK. Once that horrible woman's off the scene. I'll help if I can. Maybe we can take the twins away on a trip, you and me, for a few days. Help them forget.'

'Kate, you're a sweetie.' Abbie's tears were flooding now.

'We'll sort this out. They'll be OK, Sarah and Lizzie. Really they will. I know them. I love them.'

'I know you do. They love you, too.'

'Good.' Kate paused. 'Abbie, it may not be the best time, but could I just ask? Don't tell me if you don't want to. But you and Bill – did you?'

'Yes, we did. If it's any business of yours.' Abbie heard herself give a strange snort, almost like one of Kate's.

'Why doesn't that surprise me? Good. I'm happy for you. You and Bill have always been meant for each other.'

'Perhaps.'

'What's all this "perhaps"? I hope you're not having doubts already?'

'No, of course I'm not, not like that. But it seems unreal. It all happened so suddenly, last night. It feels like a dream. Then I woke up to this – Keith's phone call, reality. I feel as though I'm being punished for being happy.'

'Abbie, you don't need me to tell you that's bollocks.'

'I know it is. But I can't help feeling it. As though I took my eyes off my daughters for a few minutes, and look what happened.'

'But you didn't! Or if you did, you were entitled to – they were in Italy with Keith. There was nothing you could do for them. Even *you* deserve time off occasionally.'

'I know. It's not rational. Motherhood isn't.'

'Don't speak to me about motherhood.'

'Sorry. Oh – someone's coming to sit beside me now. I'll have to stop talking.'

'Sure? Well, you know where I am. I'll see you very soon. What time are Keith and the twins getting back?'

'I don't know yet. I expect he'll phone to tell me.'

'But you'll be home first?'

'I hope so. Unless this train breaks down.'

'If you want me to come round, while you're there on your own, just ring me.'

'Thanks, Kate. I'll see how it goes.'

Abbie tried very hard to compose her face as a young man with a briefcase took the seat opposite. He cast her a brief glance then opened up his laptop and began to type.

chapter fifteen

'They're both fast asleep.' Keith returned to Abbie's living room after checking on the twins in their bedroom.

Abbie noticed for the first time how grey-faced and haggard he looked. She had forgotten the way his eyebrows knitted together in what looked like a frown when he was exhausted. To her surprise, she felt a twinge of concern that was not so far from affection.

'Good. At last. Shall I make some coffee?'

Keith shook his head as he made himself comfortable in the armchair, one leg over the arm as he always used to on the chairs at home. It was almost midnight. Keith and the girls had been late, not arriving until after 9 p.m. because of a delay in take-off followed by a security alert at Edinburgh airport.

The twins had looked better than Abbie had feared, but they were not their usual selves. Both were pale and said little; both clung to her longer than usual when they hugged. Abbie had tried to behave as though nothing was wrong, to keep the worry out of her voice, but she wasn't sure whether she had succeeded. Neither twin made any mention of the fact that they were home two days early. Lizzie rushed into the bedroom to be reunited with some treasure she had forgotten to take with her, and Sarah asked for a bowl of cornflakes.

'Of course you can have cornflakes. When did you last eat? I can cook a meal for all of us if you like.'

Abbie had put out sausages and bacon to grill and a couple of cans of baked beans to heat up – the girls' favourite. But no one other than Sarah, it appeared, was hungry.

'It's good to get back to cornflakes,' Sarah said. 'I'm sick of bread rolls and croissants. They didn't have proper marmalade, either. But we got wicked clothes, Mum – wait till I show you.'

Lizzie appeared from her bedroom at this point. 'Daddy won't let us keep the things Fiona bought us,' she reminded her sister. 'Remember, he said we had to give them back.'

This was the first mention of Fiona by any of them since they'd got home. Abbie wondered whether she should follow it up in some way, but couldn't think how.

Sarah got in first, anyway. 'That's not fair. They were presents. If you fall out with someone, you don't have to give their presents back.'

'Yes, you do,' said Lizzie. 'Like if people get divorced they have to give their wedding presents back. It was on Coronation Street.'

'Did you and Daddy have to give your wedding presents back when you got divorced?' asked Sarah.

By the time Abbie had finished explaining that, no, too many years had passed, they were well away from the subject of Fiona.

Once they were all sitting down in the living-room with Abbie and the twins squashed together on the sofa and Keith opposite, Keith broached the subject.

'I think we three have some explaining to do to Mummy,' he said, looking at the girls with an expression of mild enquiry, as though they were about to tell Abbie why they hadn't got round to sending her a postcard. But she could see the tension underneath.

Sarah put one hand up to her face, while Lizzie said, 'I'll do the explaining if you like. Shall I, Daddy?'

'Er … well, if you'd like to.' He stared at her as though his small daughter had suddenly become an adult. He gave his head a shake as though to clear it.

'All right,' said Lizzie. 'It's very simple, really.' A form of words she had picked up, perhaps, from one of her teachers. 'Fiona forgot we were only eleven – nearly twelve – and she read us some stories she had written for older girls. Or boys. Or grown-ups. I'm not sure who they were for.' She looked up at her father, who nodded his head, encouraging her to go on.

'They were about two girls who were twins like us. They weren't meant to *be* us, Daddy said.'

'Yes, they were,' said Sarah.

'No, they weren't. Were they, Daddy? It was just ...' she paused, '... coincidence. That they were twins like us.' She looked at Keith again.

'Perhaps,' he said. 'We don't know. Anyway—'

'*I'm* telling it,' said Lizzie. 'These girls went into a wood and they met a man who was a sort of monster.'

'He was just a man,' said Sarah. 'Not a monster.'

'He was like a monster,' put in their father. 'Big and strong and cruel.'

'He *was* a monster,' said Lizzie. 'He had a blue face – don't you remember?'

'No, he didn't,' said Sarah.

'Yes, he did.'

'That's just how you imagined him.'

'Never mind about the colour of his face,' said Abbie – the first time she'd spoken since they began. 'Tell me what he did.'

Lizzie drew breath to preface another impressive word. 'He *raped* the twin girls. He had sex with them when they didn't want to.'

'It wasn't just that,' said Sarah. 'He hurt them. Remember, he pulled off their fingers one at a time. And he—'

'No, he didn't. You're mixing it up with that other story.'

'He *did* do that. Remember what he was going to do with the fingers?'

Lizzie shivered. 'No, I don't.'

'Mummy, it said the girls were bleeding where he raped them,' said Sarah. 'I asked Fiona why, but she wouldn't tell us. Will you tell us? Does that happen when you have sex?'

'Of course it doesn't.'

'Yes, it does,' said Lizzie. 'I saw that on TV as well. A girl had sex for the first time and there was blood on her bedclothes afterwards.'

'What have you been watching?' asked Abbie.

'Just a soap.'

'Mummy, *is* there blood when you've had sex?' asked Sarah.

'No, darling.' Abbie tried to reassure her frightened daughter. 'Perhaps the first time, just a little bit. Nothing to worry about.'

'But there was lots of blood when the monster raped the girls,' said Lizzie. 'Isabella and Katerina, they were called. They were princesses.'

'No, they weren't,' said Sarah.

'Girls, stop arguing about things that don't matter,' said Keith. 'Whether or not they were princesses is an unimportant detail.'

Lizzie glared at him, ready to argue, then bit her lip as Sarah said, 'The worst thing was how frightened they were. I used to go to sleep thinking about it. I could sort of taste how scared they were.'

Abbie shook her head and drew her arm more tightly round the girls' warm backs. 'You poor little things.'

'It's like you know it won't happen to you because it's all made up,' said Lizzie. 'But it's the scariness that gets to you. It made you feel you were one of them. I was always Isabella. She was the braver one.'

'No, she wasn't,' said Sarah. 'Anyway, why did *you* have to be her? I could be her if I wanted.'

'You were Katerina, the scared one. Fiona meant you to be her, I could tell.'

'I don't think so,' said Keith. 'I don't think Fiona was trying to pretend that those two girls were you two.'

'Daddy, she *was*.'

'Do you think she meant to frighten you?' asked Abbie.

Sarah frowned, uncertain and unhappy. 'I don't know. I don't think so. Fiona is nice to us, she's kind and she buys us things. Unless it was all pretend. Do you think it was all pretend, Lizzie, when she was being nice?'

Lizzie shook her head. 'No, it wasn't pretend. Fiona is some-times annoying when she takes up Daddy's attention, but she's not nasty. I think she just made a mistake.'

Keith's sigh of relief was audible, though he tried to turn it into a cough. 'I agree,' he said. 'I've known Fiona a good while now. We're well past the infatuation stage, she and I.'

'Are you?' asked Abbie.

'Of course. I can see her for the person she is. This has come as a shock, of course. All I knew was that she wanted to write books herself. She asked me if she could read some of her stuff to Lizzie and Sarah.'

'And you said yes,' said Sarah.

'I did. I regret it now. I feel so bad, girls, that I didn't read those stories myself first. But as I've already explained, she wouldn't let me. She thought I'd be like a teacher, criticizing them.'

'Giving you a bad mark,' said Sarah.

'Two out of ten,' added Lizzie.

'Exactly. She said she'd rather try them out first on the kind of people they were written for. Which, of course, is just what I did when I first wrote my stories – tried them out on you two.'

'When we were little,' said Lizzie.

'But the difference was,' said Sarah, 'that you knew what kind of stories to write for our age. And Fiona didn't.'

'It appears not.'

Abbie's head was beginning to ache. 'What do you girls think we should do now?' she asked. 'What would you like to happen?'

'Nothing,' said Sarah. 'It's been too much of a fuss already. I want it all to go away.'

'I just want to go back to school on Tuesday,' said Lizzie. 'Forget all about it.'

'But what about the nightmares?'

'I won't have any more of them now,' said Sarah. 'It's all finished. Can we stop talking about it?'

'In a minute,' said Keith. 'That's probably enough for tonight, anyway. You've been very honest and helpful, both of you. But can I just ask you how you'd feel about seeing Fiona again?'

'Don't ask them that!' Abbie cried, unable to stop herself. 'It's such an unfair question. Why should they have to see her again?'

'That's why I'm asking them.' A note of antagonism had crept into Keith's voice, the first that evening. 'Girls, what do you think?'

The twins looked from one parent to the other, unsure what to say.

'Let me say what I think, 'said Abbie. 'They should *never* see her again. Nor should you, Keith. She betrayed your trust and the twins have suffered. I don't know how you can even contemplate it. I'll take out a court order, if necessary, to prevent her seeing the girls.'

Sarah sniffed, beginning to cry. 'I don't care, Mummy,' she said, 'Just don't let it start you and Daddy off arguing again.'

Keith and Abbie exchanged glances and decided it was time for the twins to go to bed.

'Do you think Sarah will have any more nightmares?' Abbie asked Keith.

It was almost 2 a.m. She had made coffee for herself, as an excuse to escape for a few minutes. There was plenty more to say but she couldn't help wishing Keith would fall asleep. Her head was buzzing, her headache worse, and she longed for time to think it all through. She didn't feel at all sleepy – she was in an emergency mode where she felt she could go on for ever, as long as was needed.

'I've no idea,' Keith replied. 'Maybe not, now it's all sorted.'

This irritated her. 'You can't really think it's sorted, just because we've talked about it with the girls?'

'I didn't mean that. I just meant that maybe Sarah's nightmares will stop, now that she knows there won't be any more stories.'

'What did you say to Fiona when you left?'

'We were hardly speaking. I was furious with her, if that makes you feel any better. I told her I never wanted to see her again.'

'Good. But in that case, why all this nonsense about asking the twins if they want to see her?'

'I want them to be part of the decision.'

'But surely the decision's made? If you've told Fiona it's all over between you—'

'She may be expecting me to take back what I said, when I've calmed down. I don't know. She made a mistake, I know that. She would never have deliberately harmed Lizzie and Sarah.'

'Are you sure?'

'Of course I'm sure. Abbie, I know you couldn't stand her, and that's perhaps not surprising, but she was, I assure you – she is – a decent, reasonable person. Not someone who would hurt the kids. God, if I thought that—'

'But she *has* hurt them – look what she's done.'

'Not intentionally.'

'But if it wasn't deliberate, then she must be stupid. Or mad. Either way, she's not fit to be in charge of children or young people. I don't know how you can even think of seeing her again, after what she's done.'

'No. Well, perhaps I won't. But I can't make the decision just like that. Fiona and I are in love.'

She stared at him. 'You're still in love with her, after this?'

Keith looked almost ready to cry and once again Abbie felt a pang of sympathy that surprised her.

'It's all been so sudden,' he said. 'Such a shock. Fiona is in a bad state herself.'

'I'm glad to hear it.'

'She was very upset when I read the story myself and confronted her.'

'Hadn't it even occurred to her that her stories might be the cause of Sarah's nightmares?'

'I don't think so. We didn't talk about it much. She seemed to think Sarah's nightmares were connected to the divorce. Her own parents divorced when she was young. Ryan is not her natural father. She can remember being unhappy when her mother and father split up. She spent a lot of time with a weird old great-aunt or something. That's one reason she always tried so hard to be friendly to the girls. She does try. And I think she genuinely cares about them. They like her.'

'That's what makes it so tragic.'

'I *will* end the relationship, Abbie. I have to, don't I, whatever the twins say?'

'Of course you must. Poor girls, they're trying so hard to say the right thing. Not to upset anyone. They're even being protective towards Fiona, bless them.'

'I'll make sure, tomorrow, that Fiona knows it's all over. But I refuse to hate her. I can't do that. You can't go from love to hate in a single day.'

'Can't you?'

'No. I can't.'

'Well, that's up to you. I'm sure I hate her enough for us both.'

'I expect you do.'

They were silent for a few minutes. Abbie drank her coffee, thinking how strange it was to have Keith here in the house so late at night. She pictured them together in their old home in Edinburgh, relaxing in the living room once the twins were in bed. It was like another lifetime.

'I'll get you a sleeping bag,' she said.

'Thanks.'

'Just help yourself to anything you want. Make yourself at home.'

'That's good of you.'

'I'll leave you to it, in a minute.'

'OK. But first, should we start talking about how to try and repair some of the damage?'

'I'm taking the twins to the GP first thing Monday. I expect she'll give us a referral of some kind, to a psychologist or psychiatrist. And I'll speak to the school, explain what's been going on.'

'I'll come along with you, if you like,' said Keith. 'If you think it would help.'

'Would you do that?'

'Of course. They're my daughters, too. And I'm partly to blame for all this.' Keith paused. 'I brought one of Fiona's stories home. Do you want to see it?'

'Not now. I don't think I can stand it at the moment. I'll look at it tomorrow.'

'I had to smuggle it out. She would never have let me take it.'

'I expect the psychiatrist, or whoever we speak to, will want to see it.'

'I'll get hold of the other stories as soon as I can.'

'All right. Well, there's nothing more we can do for now. I'm going to bed.'

'One more thing, Abbie.'

'What is it?'

'I want to spend some weekends here with you and the twins, if that's OK with you. As many as I can. I think we should be together as a family. Or a sort-of family. Obviously not you and me—'

'Of course not.'

'But the four of us, for the girls' sake. We'll have to make a big effort, you and I, to get on. What do you think?'

'It's a good idea. I'm sure it will help.'

'Would you be happy if I came here most weekends?'

She thought of Bill. He would understand, surely – he would have to. These were emergency measures. 'Won't it affect your work? What about your trips abroad?'

'This is more important.'

'Well. Right. Let's try it then, and see how it goes.'

Early next morning while the twins were still asleep, Keith showed Abbie Fiona's story, the one he had managed to sneak into his suitcase.

Abbie, after lying awake for some time, had slept for three hours, buried in a black hole with no dreams, and then woken suddenly as though disturbed by something. She looked into the twins' room, but all was quiet. She stood for a few minutes beside their bunk beds, soothed by their breathing, willing them to recover from what had happened. There was a sense of peace in the room you could almost drink. She prayed as best she could, to a God she did not quite believe in, that they would be healed.

She lay in bed after that for an hour or so, unable to go back to sleep. At seven-thirty she got up and padded softly round the kitchen, trying not to wake Keith on the other side of the wall. But as she poured her coffee the door opened and there he was in his dressing gown, his hair rumpled in a way that made her heart stop, as though time really had gone backwards.

'Morning, Abbie. Any chance of coffee?'

'I was just making some. Sorry if I woke you.'

He looked out of the window to the brightening sky. 'You didn't. I've been awake most of the night. No, the sofa was fine; I was comfortable enough. But I couldn't stop thinking about Fiona and the girls.'

She handed him a mug of coffee. 'Any chance of seeing that story now, before the twins wake up?'

'OK. Let's sit in the living room and read it together, shall we?'

She opened the curtains, making the morning as ordinary as possible. Late October, damp outside after a heavy shower, the sky clearing as a wind got up. The sun might break through, later. She must phone Kate and, of course, Bill. She'd sent him a text to tell him she was home, but that was all she had managed so far.

They sat side by side on the sofa to read. The quality of the illustrations was, as Abbie had expected, high. The drawings were pen and ink with a subtle wash of colour that let the graininess of the paper show through. The fictional twins were dressed in fussy

Victorian clothes, with frilly pinafores and buckle shoes, but had a distinct look, in their faces at least, of Lizzie and Sarah.

There was a mystical element to the early pages that took Abbie by surprise. Something almost spiritual, that in other circumstances she might have found appealing.

'It's good stuff, in its way,' said Keith. 'Fiona can write as well as draw. I was surprised.'

There was nothing explicitly nasty in the first few pages, though there were hints of what was to come. The man-monster, who lived in a hut in the woods, was never fully drawn. His body writhed itself out of the twisted shapes of the trees and branches. Vague menace lurked among the brilliant green plant life and the exaggerated shapes of the flora in the undergrowth.

'So where's the bad stuff?' she asked.

It was further on, Keith told her. It started on page fourteen. She speeded up, both wanting and not wanting to read the scene that had so disturbed her children. She felt sick with tension as she approached the stated page. She remembered the poetry book she'd had as a child, with the excerpt from *Hiawatha* containing a line about ghosts and shadows. It had scared her so much that her mother had stuck the pages together with glue. She had forgotten, since that time, how frightening the printed word could be.

Of course she had been younger than the twins, only just reading for herself – perhaps about six. But what had so terrified her was a simple mention of ghosts – nothing like the description of a rape by a monster-man who had caused young girls to bleed.

'I don't want to read it,' she said, her voice shaky.

Keith edged up closer. 'It's really not so bad,' he said. 'I mean, not for adults.'

'I'm seeing it through the twins' eyes.'

'Even so, after all this build-up it'll probably seem tamer than you were expecting.' He paused. 'Would you rather I read it aloud?'

They were touching, she registered – his thigh against hers. He didn't seem to be aware of it. Even if he was, she was sure he was offering no more than comfort. Nevertheless, she moved away as gently as she could.

'No, it's OK. I'd rather read it myself.'

She read it at great speed the first time, checking for key words.

There would be time to go back and reread it more carefully later.

'Why, Keith? Why would anyone write such stuff? Fiona's not stupid – she must realize what this is like.'

'There'd be no problem if it was aimed at adults.'

'But it's a fairy tale. It's meant for kids.'

'There are plenty of adult fairy tales.'

'But why, then, read it to eleven-year-olds? And it's worse than that, isn't it? She based this story on our twins, on their characters as well as their appearance. She's got Isabella being the leader and Katerina being more timid, and she's put in all the squabbling they do. She's observed Lizzie and Sarah and put them in a book, where she makes unspeakably horrible things happen to them. Then she reads it to them as a bedtime story.'

'I'm as baffled as you.'

'That woman is never going near our girls again. As I said yesterday, I'll take out a court order.'

'It won't be necessary. I'll talk to her. I'll make sure she fully understands what she's done.'

A new fear struck Abbie. 'Keith, you don't think she'll try and get revenge? Go to the press or something?'

'What can she go to the press about? She'll only get herself into trouble. I've done nothing wrong. I could probably wreck her career if I wanted, by going public, but I don't think she's worth the trouble.'

'But Keith, don't you see, if the story got in the papers it would be awful publicity for the twins. They'd be so humiliated. It might damage them more than ever.'

'She can't name the girls. There are privacy laws for minors.'

'You might be able to take her to court, but it could be too late then. Imagine Sarah and Lizzie in the tabloids.'

'Fiona wouldn't do that.'

'You don't know what she's capable of. Anyway, it might leak out accidentally. The papers would love it, now you're so well known.'

'Fame has its down side, I'm discovering.'

'I can't believe we're sitting here quivering, frightened of what Fiona might do.'

Keith extended an arm across her shoulder and immediately withdrew it. 'Abbie, don't worry. We'll get through this. I've a feeling Fiona will just want to lie low. If she causes trouble, we'll think of something. Trust me.'

'Abbie, how are you? What's happening?'

'Bill! I was going to phone you earlier on. Sorry.'

A voice came from the living room. 'Mummy, who's that on the phone?'

'Shhh, Lizzie. It's Bill from Birmingham.'

It was Sunday evening and the four of them had just finished dinner.

'I've been worrying about you,' said Bill. 'And the twins. I sent you a text.'

'Did you? I haven't checked my phone all day, sorry. Hang on, I'll get it.'

'It doesn't matter. Have you a minute, now, to talk?'

'Er, yes. Let me take this into the bedroom. It's rather noisy in the hall.'

She shut the bedroom door and sat down on the bed. Bill's voice seemed to come from another world. It was almost impossible to believe she'd been with him in Birmingham only yesterday morning.

'Take it easy, Abbie, you sound on edge. I can phone back later if you like.'

'No, it's OK. It's a good time. Keith's in the kitchen and the girls are watching TV.'

'Keith is still with you?'

'Yes. He offered to stay for a few days, so we can both, you know, be with the girls.'

'Yes, I see. How are they?'

'They seem all right, so far. No nightmares last night. They keep saying they want to forget it all, to get back to normal. They want to go back to school on Tuesday, but I'm waiting to see what the doctor says. Neither of us has any idea how badly this has affected them.'

'Perhaps they'll be fine, now it's out in the open and they know they won't see Fiona again.'

'I wish I could believe that.' Her voice came out more snappy than she had intended.

'Sorry. I didn't mean to make light of it.'

'No, I'm sorry. I'm exhausted.'

'I'm not surprised.'

'How are you, Bill? Have you spoken to Jon?'

'I tried to apologize to him on the phone. He gave a grunt which I can only hope meant he accepted it. But I don't know where we go from here.'

'I hope you can work things out. Bill, I'm going to have to go. Sarah's calling me for something.'

'How long is Keith staying?'

'A few more days, I think. He's coming with us tomorrow to the doctor's and the school. It'll be good to have him there.'

'You two are getting on all right, then?'

'I suppose we are. Better than we have for years, funnily enough. Lizzie said this afternoon it was like it used to be. Of course it isn't, but I know what she means. We were walking along Carleith beach and we could have been on one of our old beach trips in the Edinburgh days. Bill, are you still there?'

'Of course I am.'

Her sensitivity was at half-mast. She had a vague sense that something was not quite right, but she felt disconnected from whatever it was.

She heard him take a deep breath. 'Abbie, it was good, wasn't it? You and me, Friday night?'

'It was great, Bill. It was wonderful. I can't believe it was only two days ago. It feels like another lifetime.'

'I know you're preoccupied with all that's happened since. I understand, of course, but I hope that what we discovered between us won't evaporate.'

'Of course it won't evaporate.' Just give me a few weeks, she wanted to say, just give me months or years if necessary, to deal with all this, to see the twins restored to normal. Then I'll be back.

'OK.' His tone was flat, but once again it seemed to have nothing to do with her, as though he was a character on TV, a book put down to be resumed later when life wasn't so pressing.

'Shall I call you again tomorrow?' he asked.

'Please do. Hang on, that's Sarah again, she's lost something. I'll speak to you soon, Bill.'

Returning to the kitchen, to Keith's clatter and the thumping of cupboard doors as he tried to work out where things were kept, a small portion of her mind idled over whether she could have said anything to upset Bill. It didn't seem likely, but she was left with the memory of that hollow, flat sound in his voice, as though she had disappointed or hurt him. Perhaps she should phone him back and check?

But Keith asked where she kept the glass tumblers and the moment passed.

chapter sixteen

'Abbie, what a nice surprise. Come in.'

It was Tuesday evening and Keith and the twins were at home in Carleith, eating fish and chips from the local shop on the seafront. Abbie, who had lost her appetite, had decided to give this meal a miss and take the opportunity to call on Kate.

Kate was lying on her sofa, surrounded by soft drink cans and empty biscuit wrappers, watching a reality TV show. The air was sour, as though she had been there with the windows shut all day.

'Pam said you'd phoned in sick so I thought I'd drop by.'

'It's good to see you. I'm worn out. I started the day with a stomachache and feeling dizzy, but I felt so bored and fed up I wished I'd gone to work. My mother's been on the phone all day, trying to persuade me to go up to Aberdeen. "At least come for a wee break," she says. Silly woman – she thinks I can take time off whenever I like.'

'How's your dad?'

'According to Mum, his angina's bad again. Here, take a seat. Move those magazines off the chair. Have a fig roll.'

'No, thanks. Is he really worse, do you think, or is it one of your mother's ploys?'

'I wish I knew. They've taken him in for more tests so I suppose there's something in it. But the way she goes on you'd think he was at death's door.'

'Angina's a serious condition.'

'I know, but he's had it for years. As long as he takes his medication he's fine. She's just playing on my sense of guilt. "Wouldn't you feel bad if you never saw him again?" she says in her voice of doom. But that's enough of my troubles. Sure you won't have a biscuit? There are some Jaffa cakes around somewhere.'

'I can't face eating.'

'Abbie, you're a silly girl. You need your food. But tell me, how are the twins?'

'Surprisingly well. We took them to the doctor's yesterday.'

'And how did that go?'

'Well, the GP was a new one and she recognized Keith from his photos in the paper so we seemed to spend half the time talking about that. But once she'd got over her flurry of admiration she was quite good. Asked us all lots of questions. The twins didn't seem to mind too much. She made an appointment for us all to see some kind of therapist early next week.'

'What, Keith too? Is he staying on, then?'

'No, he's going back to Edinburgh tomorrow for a few days. He's coming back up here on Friday. But he wants me to phone him if there's any trouble – he says he'll drive straight up.'

'Quite a change of attitude.'

'Yes. He feels responsible. Which, of course, he is, at least in part. He's trying to make it up to the girls. He's in danger of spoiling them.'

'That won't hurt, will it, for a little while?'

'Probably not. It's doing them good, I must say, having him around. They love it. I heard Lizzie ask him this morning if he'd like to come to live with us for good.'

Kate's eyes widened. 'Really? What did he say to that?'

'He just laughed it off. Said that he and Mummy were good friends but we weren't going back to being husband and wife. She seemed to accept that.'

Kate gave Abbie a long look. 'Do you think there's any chance? I mean, would you want to?'

'No way! It's good having him around just now, but once things were back to normal we'd start to drive each other mad. No, Kate, the marriage is not about to be resurrected.'

'Just as well, for Bill's sake.'

'Oh. Yes.' Abbie realized with a guilty start how little she had thought about Bill since arriving home.

'Have you spoken to him much since you got back?'

'He phoned me yesterday evening. It's difficult, though, now Keith's around. It's a small bungalow for four people. Not easy to make a private phone call.'

'Especially a romantic one.'

'Yes. Not that I feel very romantic, after all this.'

Kate bit into a biscuit. 'Have you explained it to Bill? Does he understand what's going on?'

'He knows what happened, why they came home early. I was with him when I got Keith's phone call, remember.'

'Yes, but does he understand how you feel? Why you need Keith around at the moment?'

'I think so. What is there to understand?'

'You're being a bit dense. He's going to start feeling left out if you're not careful.'

'Oh, I don't think so. No, I explained to him that I needed to give all my attention to the twins for the time being. He understands that – he's got kids of his own.'

'Well, if you're sure. Imagine if it was the other way round. All that romance one night and then you're left high and dry next day because of a problem with your partner's children. And then the ex moves back in.'

'Keith hasn't moved back in.'

'I'm only trying to see it from Bill's point of view.'

'I'm sure it's all right. Bill knows me well enough. After Friday night, he knows I love him and I'd never go back to Keith. And he understands how much I worry about the twins and how serious this is.'

'Don't forget to tell him you love him.'

'Of course I won't.'

'In fact, why don't you phone him from here? Use the phone in the hall, then you've got as much privacy as you like.'

'That's great idea, thanks. I'll do it a bit later.'

'Why not now?'

'He may still be working.'

'What, at ten to eight?'

'If he's got a deadline, he might be. Oh, all right. I'll try in five minutes.'

'Hello, Bill.'

Bill hadn't been there when she'd tried to phone him from Kate's, so she had left it until Wednesday evening. Keith had now gone home.

'Abbie.' There was no interrogative inflection and no energy in his voice, which was flat – little more than a growl in his throat.

Her own voice came out toneless in response. She had a sensation of tightness, like the beginning of a cold, at the back of her throat.

'Is this a bad time?' she asked. 'I can call back later.'

'No, not especially. I mean, it's fine.'

'Are your boys with you?'

'Some hopes! No, I was doing a bit of work on a script. But it can wait. It was crap, anyway. We can't all be brilliant writers.'

'I'm sure it wasn't crap. Perhaps I should go away and let you get on with it.'

'Don't go. How did you get on at the doctor's with the twins?'

'It was good, quite helpful. She was very understanding. We're going to have a kind of family counselling. The twins may have some on their own, too, depending how it goes.'

'That sounds good. Is Keith still with you?'

'No, he left earlier today.'

'Is he going to be part of the counselling sessions?'

'Yes. At least for a while. They want to see the four of us together.'

'A real family affair, then.'

'Except that we're not a family.'

'No?'

'Of course not. Keith and I are well and truly divorced. Nothing's going to change that. He's just trying to help the girls.'

'I know.' After a pause, which seemed to last for ever, he said, 'Abbie, I was wondering....'

'Yes?'

'Can I come and see you, this weekend? It feels so strange, as I told you before. We got so close, and now—'

'I know. I'm sorry. It was bad timing.'

'I don't want to sound selfish. Maybe I *am* being selfish, but I really miss you. I know your twins have had a terrible time. But perhaps I can help, if I come and stay. What do you think?'

'Oh, Bill....'

'What? Do you want me to come or not?'

'I'd love to see you, you know I would. There's nothing I'd like better.'

'But....'

'What?'

'You were going to add a "but".'

'Was I? Yes, I suppose I was. The thing is, Keith is coming back here at the weekend, the plan being that we spend as much time with the twins, both of us, as we can. The GP and the teachers all thought that was a good idea.'

'Of course. I understand.'

'And the house is so small. If there was a bit more room—'

'But you wouldn't want me there, anyway. Not while the four of you are together, being a family.'

'It's not like that.'

'Isn't it?'

'Bill, you know I could never love Keith again, don't you?'

'If you say so.'

'Now you're being silly. *Please* don't misunderstand. This is hard enough for me as it is. Don't you think I'd love to be able to drop everything and come back down to Birmingham? But I can't. We've got to put the twins first at the moment.'

'Of course you have.'

'As soon as things get back to normal you can come and stay. And I'll come down to see you again. We'll resume where we left off.'

Silence.

'What is it? Bill, say something.'

'Abbie, I'm sorry. I don't know if I can.'

'Can what?'

'If I *can* resume where we left off, at some unknown time in the future. I don't know if I can convince myself.'

'Convince yourself of what?'

'That you love me. It's happened before. You and I start to get close and then something gets in the way. I know you can't help it. I know this is a serious thing. But it seems it's always something to do with your family. They always get between us.'

She was stunned. 'That's a horrible thing to say. I suppose by "my family" you mean the twins. As if they can help what's happened....'

'I know, and I'm sorry. I'm not blaming the twins or you. But you said yourself a while back that you didn't think you were ready for a new relationship. I'm beginning to see what you mean. I don't think you are. I don't think you will be, until those girls are a lot older.'

'"Those girls" – what an expression! Those girls are my daughters, and they've just been through the most awful experience—'

'I know they have and I'm very sorry. I just have to say this. I don't think it's right, you and me. Or I can't do it, anyway, the thing you seem to be asking. The way you want to break off and then resume whenever you feel ready. Either we have a proper relationship or we don't. I can't hang round waiting for Keith to move out again, if he ever does.'

'Bill! There is nothing going on between me and Keith.'

'Did I say there was? Look, Abbie, I have to go. I'm worried about Jon and up to my eyes in work. We had a proposal for a new series turned down today. My career is going down the plughole. As I said before, we can't all be successful like your Keith.'

'He's not my Keith. And he had to wait a long time for his success.'

'Well, I'm having to wait even longer for mine. Abbie, I've said it all now. I'd better go. Please don't cry—'

'I'm not crying – I'm furious. I can't believe you'd do this. Just when I need you most....'

'But you don't need me, do you? That's the point. You just want me to fill in the gaps in your life, the times when your family aren't being demanding. The rest of the time you're absorbed with them. Perhaps that's how it should be. Perhaps I'd be a better father if I was like that with Jon and Sam. I don't know. I don't know anything any more. I'm going, Abbie. 'Bye.'

Kate was back at work on Thursday, and she and Abbie sat outside at lunchtime, eating their sandwiches in a patch of unusually warm late October sun. Abbie found herself unexpectedly hungry, despite her distress, and realized she had eaten very little for days. But her ham salad was tasteless and she kept reaching over to pinch one of Kate's salt-and-vinegar crisps.

She had not dared examine her feelings since her conversation with Bill the night before. A cold mass had lodged in her chest where her heart should be and her fingers had lost their grip – she had broken two plates at breakfast time – but at work she seemed, to her surprise, to be functioning more or less as normal.

'You were right, Kate,' she said. 'I spoke to Bill last night and he didn't understand about Keith coming here for weekends. He seems to think there's something going on.'

Kate stopped chewing and looked at her with alarm. 'Abbie, you must *make* him understand. Keep telling him. Reassure him that he's the one you love.'

'I tried to. He wouldn't listen. He started by asking if he could come and stay this weekend.'

'Sounds like a good idea. He'll feel better when he's seen you in person.'

'But I can't cope with him coming up here. It's enough having to worry about the twins.'

'How are they?'

'They came home from school yesterday quite happy. They're both missing Keith and they're busy making plans for the weekend, when he comes back.'

'Hmm.'

'They love the idea of doing things as a family again. They want to go to Lunan Bay, the four of us.'

'But you're not a family.'

'We have to be, just now, for the girls.'

Kate took another bite of her sandwich. 'You don't want to get their hopes up, let them start thinking you're getting back together.'

'They don't think that.'

'Are you sure?'

'I'll talk to them again, I'll make sure they understand how it is.'

'But you must talk to Bill, too. Make him see. Maybe he could come for the weekend but not stay with you. I can see it would be weird, having him and Keith under the same roof. Bill could stay here with me. No, perhaps not. At the guest house again, then. You two could at least get together for a few hours here and there.'

Abbie pushed the remains of her salad away. 'It's hardly worth him coming all the way from Birmingham for that. Anyway, he wouldn't. He's not speaking to me. I tried phoning him from work this morning and he didn't answer.'

'He was probably out.'

'He works at home. And I called his mobile. He saw my name and switched off, I'm sure he did.'

Kate shook her head. 'Oh, Abbie. Just when it was going so well.'

'It was never meant to be.' Abbie reached for another of Kate's crisps.

'Here – take the bag if you want them.'

'No thanks.'

'Abbie, don't give up on Bill. You know you love him.'

'I thought I did. It all seems a million years ago. I'm a different person since all this stuff about Fiona came out. The part of me that loves Bill has gone into hibernation.'

'It'll come out again when you've got over the shock. You've had a terrible few days.'

'But that's not going to go away. I've got to give all my time and energy now to looking after the twins.'

'Not at the expense of your own sanity. That's no good for anyone. And you won't do the twins any favours by being over-protective.'

'I'm not going to be over-protective. It's more a case of putting them at the centre of things. Perhaps Bill's right, perhaps there *isn't* room for him in all that.'

'But he loves you – you love each other.'

'I can never love him as much as I love my daughters. The last few days have helped me see that. And it's not fair on him, is it, to pretend that I can?'

'Don't pretend, tell him. He's got children of his own. Surely he can understand?'

'It's too much to ask, to expect him to wait in the background until I'm ready for him again. To hover around waiting for me to call. He deserves someone better. He's having a bad time with his work and his boys and he doesn't need me to make things worse.'

'No, he needs you to make them better.'

'I'll phone him later on. I'll have one last try. If it doesn't work, that's it. I'll accept that God has decreed I'm not to have a lover.'

'You're not thinking straight, Abbie.'

'I feel as though I've got flu. My legs are shaky and I'm dropping things.'

'You're exhausted. And you're hardly eating. Let me get you a Mars bar.'

'Nothing has any taste.'

'You still need energy. And you need some sleep. Perhaps you should take some time off work.'

'No, Kate. I can't sleep, anyway. Only for an hour or so at a time, then I wake up, my heart pounding, as though there's an emergency.'

'Abbie! Try to calm down. Your girls are going to be fine. I know they are.'

'I hope so. Sometimes it all feels like nothing, as though it may blow over in a few days. At other times it feels as though they've both been in a terrible accident and we don't know how bad the injuries are or even whether they'll survive.'

'They'll survive and they'll recover. It sounds as though they've already started. You and Keith love them and they're getting professional help. They'll be fine, but it may take a while and in the meantime you need to look after yourself. And speak to Bill. Tell him all you've just told me.'

'OK, I'll try. Now we'd better get back to work – it's nearly two o'clock.'

Kate looked at her watch. 'I'd better hurry – I'm supposed to be meeting up with Steve to discuss my new monitor.'

Abbie tried phoning Bill at ten to eleven that night. The twins were asleep and she was nodding off herself, the television on, an unread book beside her on the sofa. Perhaps if she managed to speak to Bill, to sort things out with him, she would be able to have a proper sleep.

There was no answer on his landline, which rang and rang without going on to the answering machine. She pictured Bill's flat with the window looking over the canal, the beige carpet where they had made love and the bed where they had made love again. She remembered the string of lights twinkling along the edge of the canal.

She tried his mobile, which rang eight or nine times and then stopped. He was avoiding her, that was certain. She was about to give up when he picked up and said, 'Hello?' as though she was a stranger.

'Bill, it's me.'

'Yes, I know. Hello, Abbie.'

'I wondered if we could talk?'

She heard him sigh. 'Is there much to say? How are the twins?'

'They seem to be OK. They went to school today.'

'No problems?'

'No. They seemed to enjoy it.'

'Good. Well....'

'How are your boys?'

'Same as ever. As far as I know.'

'Can we talk about us?'

'Is there an us?'

'Bill, that's cruel. You're hurting me.'

'I'm sorry. But I did try to explain. Is Keith still coming back at the weekend?'

'Yes. I told you why. It's for the twins, not me. Keith and I are never going to get back together. You don't need to worry about that.'

'I'm not worried. I'm just fed up with being put on hold every time you have family trouble. Yes, I know it's a major problem and I know you think I'm heartless. Perhaps I am. You're best away from me.'

'But I love you.'

He sighed again, and there was a pause so long she thought he had switched off. Then he said, 'Those words carry a lot of weight. You shouldn't say them lightly.'

'I'm not. I *do* love you, Bill. Please try to understand. Eventually, perhaps even in a few weeks' time, if the twins are OK, we should be able to get back to normal. Keith is not going to spend his weekends in Carleith for ever. He's got his career to get on with, apart from anything else.'

'Lucky him.'

'I'm sorry your work's not going well. I know how much it means to you.'

'Comedy shows on Radio 4 are hardly *The Great Green Wizard*.'

'Your day will come. And even if it doesn't.... Sorry, that came out wrong. Of course your day will come. You'll have your break-through. You'll get your TV series. And even if you don't, the radio gives pleasure to a lot of people....' She stopped, detecting the patronizing note in her voice. Where had that come from?

'It's OK, Abbie, you don't need to counsel me. I've been in the depths before where my work's concerned. I'll deal with it.'

'Right. Sorry.'

'And I'll deal with my love-life, too. I got over Deb and I'll no doubt get over you.' He paused, and his voice gave a little crack as he said, 'But it might help if I didn't have to hear your voice.'

'Bill!'

'Sorry. I didn't quite mean it like that.'

'How about if we planned for me to come and stay with you in a month's time? All being well with the girls....'

'No. Abbie, it's over between us – please accept that. *I'm* trying to. No, don't start crying, I can't bear it. And don't shout at me. Please. Good luck with everything. I hope your girls are OK. I hope things work out for you. Now I really do have to go.'

The ice inside Abbie melted all at once, flooding her chest as though her heart had burst. Anger was everywhere, in every recess of her brain and body. Anger and hurt, humiliation, guilt and shame. Bill was back in his own world, with Jon and Sam, Deb and Curtis. Looking out on his ducks and geese and his occasional pair of swans.

They were finished.

chapter seventeen

'Department of Physics.'

'Could I speak to Abbie Brinnett, please?' The voice was weak, hesitant and vaguely familiar.

'Speaking.'

Abbie still held out a hope every time she answered the phone that it might be Bill. Why he would call her at work she didn't know – except that it seemed no less likely than his calling her at all. It was almost six weeks now since he had told her they were finished. Below her ever-present concerns about the twins there flowed a cold, steady undercurrent of sadness. She tried not to examine it but it was always there, whatever she did. Work had become something of a solace and she welcomed its routines and minor crises as distractions from her real life.

'Abbie – this is Fiona.'

Of course – the girlish voice, tinny in tone. Abbie took a deep breath and held the phone further away from her face. She didn't put it down but she didn't speak either. No words would come.

'Fiona Claremont. Keith's partner.'

This was enough to stir Abbie into speech. 'You mean his *ex*-partner. Fiona – how dare you phone me?'

'I have a lot of things to say. Please listen.'

'If you think I'm going to listen to you, you are sadly mistaken. After what you did to my girls you can count yourself lucky I've not been to the police. Yet.'

'I'm sorry about all that.'

'You're *what*?' Abbie banged the phone down hard on the desk. It made a faint whirring sound, but as she picked it up to replace it she could still hear Fiona's voice. She clicked it off, grasping the slim white receiver between her fingers and picturing Fiona's throat.

She breathed fiercely for a few seconds, studying the words of the document on her computer screen, noticing a grammatical error that somehow became part of the nightmare, like a sickeningly persistent detail in a feverish dream.

'Abbie – calm down.' Kate was beside her, gripping her shoulder. 'I take it that was Fiona.'

'How did she find me here? How did she get my number?'

'Not too difficult, when you think about it. She knows where you work, doesn't she? It's easy enough to phone the university switchboard – or to look on the department web page for that matter.'

Abbie was still breathing quickly and her head felt light. 'She had the nerve to try and apologize.'

'I'll take all incoming calls from now on.'

'You can't do that. You're not here all the time.'

'I'll make sure I am. I'll get to work earlier in the mornings.'

'Don't be silly. Anyway – who's to say she won't phone me at home?'

'You're ex-directory, aren't you?'

'Yes, but I'm sure she could get hold of my number if she wanted. She knows my address – she's been to the house. And she could easily have copied the number from Keith's diary, come to that.'

'Perhaps she won't bother you again. You were pretty sharp with her. She may have got the message.'

'She wants to stir up more trouble, I'm sure of it. What if she turns up at the house when the twins are home? Just when they're beginning to settle down a bit – she could throw them right back to square one.'

'Wish I could get my hands on the evil bitch.'

And what would you do? thought Abbie. You've no more power over her than I have. Then her eyes went back to the phone and her fingers tightened around something invisible – a smooth column that offered resistance at first but gave way slowly as the pressure increased. She had never imagined killing anyone before. In the moments before she vanquished the image, a desire that shocked her with its strength flooded her body.

She turned to Kate, aware of her face flushing crimson, fearing that her thoughts were visible.

'Abbie – I have to speak to you. There are things you need to know.'

It was Saturday – three days after Fiona's phone call at work. Keith had taken the twins away first thing to spend a weekend with his parents, celebrating his mother's birthday in Livingston. It would be the first time Abbie had been apart from them for longer than a working day for over seven weeks. Fred had given her permission to work shorter hours on a temporary basis, so that she could pick them up from school each day and take them straight home. Keith was still coming to stay every weekend.

She had picked up the phone beside her bed, heart thudding, in her half-asleep state, with the usual hope that it might be Bill. It was just after 10 a.m. and she had been enjoying the lie-in.

'Go away, Fiona. I don't want to speak to you.'

'Abbie – you must listen. It's important stuff – about your girls.'

'What stuff?' It was a mistake, she knew. She should have clicked Fiona off and unplugged the phone. Keith could always reach her on her mobile if he needed to.

Fiona's high-pitched voice reminded her of scratchy old radio recordings. It grated, like the sound she remembered from her schooldays – the squeal of chalk across a board. A shudder ran through her body, but she kept the receiver to her ear.

'I never meant to hurt them,' said Fiona. 'You must believe me. It was all a terrible mistake, reading them the stories. I thought they would like them.'

'You must be even more stupid than I thought.'

'I used to like that kind of thing when I was their age.'

'Then you must have been a very strange child. Not only precocious but perverted. That stuff you wrote was horrible. And the drawings. Vile, nasty – have you any idea what damage you've done? I don't understand how you could possibly have thought—'

'That's why I want to explain. Please give me the chance.'

'Why should I?'

'Because it might help.'

'All right – say it quickly, then. Two sentences. Then go away and leave us in peace.'

'It will take a bit longer than that. I was hoping we could meet, just you and I. Have a proper talk. You don't really know me at all. If you did, it might help you understand.'

'I've no desire to understand.'

'If you agree to meet with me, I'll go away and you'll never see or hear from me again.'

Did Fiona know she was on her own that weekend, and if so, how? Was it possible that Keith had told her – that he had lied about breaking off all contact? She needed to know.

Fiona continued. 'How about this evening? Can I come to your house?'

'No, you can't.'

'OK – how about we meet in a pub, then? That one down on the sea front – what's it called?'

'The Red Fox?' Why hadn't she just said no?

'Why don't we meet up there? Eight this evening?'

'Just a quick drink, then. You say whatever you have to say and then you go.'

'Of course. That's the plan.'

I must be mad, thought Abbie, putting bread in the toaster and gulping orange juice.

'You've agreed to meet her?' Kate's mouth opened so wide she almost lost her piece of jam doughnut.

It was afternoon and Kate had driven over to Abbie's in her father's car, carrying a large bag of assorted cakes. It was a hastily arranged visit: Kate had phoned Abbie to say that her parents had turned up that morning on a surprise visit which turned out to have a hidden agenda. Kate's mother had brought the details of another job she'd seen advertised in the local paper that was 'right up Kate's street'. When Kate told her she wasn't interested, her mother went, in Kate's words, into one of her hissy fits.

Kate had said, 'I've managed to get rid of them for a bit – she's dragging my dad round the shops to look for new shoes. Can I come over and see you while I've got their car?'

'Of course.' Abbie wondered whether she should tell Kate about Fiona's phone call and their prospective meeting. She had decided not to, but Kate on her arrival, inquisitive as always, took a look at the engagement calendar where Abbie had scribbled beside today's date: 'Fiona – Red Fox – 8 p.m'.

Kate shook her head. 'You must be mad.'

'Maybe I am.'

'Don't go, Abbie. You'll only get upset. What good can it do?'

'It may help me stop going over and over it my mind. If I can understand her – even a bit – I might be able to let it go. The therapist seems to think I'm the main problem at the moment, holding everyone else up by not being able to move on. If I meet Fiona and hear her side of things, it could be just what I need.'

'But she's a madwoman. You're not going to get any sense from her.'

'She sounded quite normal, in a way, when we spoke. No, Kate – I'm going to do this. I need to do it – for the twins' sake.'

'You're not planning to tell them you met her?'

'Of course not. I may not even tell Keith. It'll be interesting, actually, to see if he already knows about it. He tells me he's had no contact with Fiona but I'm suspicious about her call. How did she know I'd be on my own this weekend?'

'I think it's a stupid idea. She's crazy – she could even be dangerous.'

'No. She never tried to hurt the girls – not physically. It's not as though she's violent or anything.'

'You don't know that. I still think you should have gone to the police.'

'Keith doesn't want to. He thinks it would make things worse for the girls.'

'Who knows what other kids she may be harming?'

'Come on, Kate – she read them stories, she didn't molest them. I know what she did is dreadful, but she's not some kind of pervert. She made a bad error of judgement. She's hardly going to get the chance to do that to anyone else's kids.'

'Why not? She could get a job in a playgroup or a school. She should be on the sex offenders' register.'

'She's not intending to get a job with kids. She's an artist – a good one. And if she tries to get any of that stuff published, she won't get far. Not with kids in mind.'

Kate shook her head. 'I think you're making a bad mistake. I can see why you're doing it, but I don't think you should.' She brushed crumbs from her lap on to Abbie's carpet. 'Tell you what. Why don't I come with you?'

'It's good of you to offer, but no – I want to do this on my own. She'd probably clam up, anyway, if you were there – refuse to say a word.'

'That might be just as well.'

'No, Kate. Don't worry about me. I can look after myself. And we'll be in the pub, remember – there'll be other people around.'

'If there's any trouble, promise you'll give me a ring.'

'OK. Though you'll be back home by then, won't you? It's a long way to drive to rescue me, even if your dad lets you use his car again.'

'It'd make more sense if I could stay here. But I'll have to be home by about six to make my parents something to eat.'

'Don't worry about me.' Abbie passed the paper bag to Kate. 'Here, have another doughnut – there's a couple left.'

Abbie took another sip of lemonade and glanced at her watch for the fifth time. It was almost half-past eight and there was still no sign of Fiona.

The Red Fox was a drab place, livened only a little by the Christmas streamers draped across the bar. The maroon curtains, stained and greasy, were drawn against the December evening. Peering behind them, she could see a couple of street lamps casting shadows on the promenade. The sea was an invisible black mass beyond – the tide close to high, she had noticed on arrival, with an occasional wave lapping over.

It was not a pleasant night to be out. Perhaps Fiona had changed her mind? Abbie's relief was tempered with disappointment. Had she really been hoping to meet Fiona, after all? Perhaps an unconscious part of her mind had planned some kind of attack.

The pub had four other occupants, all male. The barman was engaged in a passionate discussion with two of them about the relative merits and fortunes of Dundee's two football clubs. The fourth man sat alone, a couple of tables away from Abbie, and caught her eye every time she looked up. Last time she'd glanced towards the door he had offered the beginnings of a smile. She wanted to move further away but it seemed too obvious.

Her memory shot back to that evening in May in the Mouse and Man, when she was celebrating her divorce. That was just before meeting Bill. Kate had spent much of the time trying to persuade her to join a dating agency. Well, she had – and look where she was now. No better off with regard to her love life and with something that, try as she might to resist the cliché, she could only describe as a broken heart.

Thinking of Bill as the door opened, she found herself somehow expecting the newcomer to be him. But it wasn't, of course – it was Fiona, dwarfed by an enormous bottle-green woollen coat that looked like something worn by a general in World War II. Fiona's face was pasty in the stark overhead lighting and she appeared insubstantial and vulnerable. Abbie realized she had never before seen her without Keith.

She forced her lips to return Fiona's hesitant smile. Then she remembered that she owed this woman nothing.

Fiona mumbled a greeting and Abbie returned it, keeping all expression from her voice.

'Thanks for agreeing to this,' Fiona said.

Abbie looked into her eyes for a moment, then raised her own to one of the beams above her head, which was painted to look like oak and was beginning to peel.

'I'll get myself a drink,' said Fiona. 'Can I get anything for you?'

Abbie's hand covered the top of her nearly empty glass. 'No, I'm fine.'

'Sure? A refill?'

'No, thanks.'

Fiona removed the huge overcoat and revealed a lemon mohair jumper and a long grey skirt. She appeared to have lost some weight. The dress she'd worn for the TV interview would look better on her now, Abbie reflected.

If she hadn't hated the woman so much she would have felt concern. Fiona's face, at close quarters, was not so much pasty as patchy. Her cheeks and nose were red and sore-looking, her forehead and chin almost white. Part of that could be put down to the December wind, but not the whole of it. The lemon jumper didn't help – in the harsh lighting it had taken on a green tinge which was reflected in her face.

The man opposite, whom Abbie had seen giving Fiona the once-over as she removed her coat, now turned back to his drink.

'Back in a minute,' said Fiona.

'Take your time.'

Fiona returned with a half-pint glass of lager, from which she took a long swig. Then she looked up as though waiting for Abbie to speak. Her irises were the palest grey Abbie had ever seen – barely distinguishable from the whites. This, combined with her green-tinted complexion, gave her a ghostly, ethereal look and Abbie's shoulders gave a little shudder. Ridiculous, she told herself, that I should be afraid of her. She's the one who should fear me.

'Go on then,' Abbie said. 'You wanted to meet me. Let's hear what you have to say.'

'Not a bad place, this.'

'We haven't come here to talk about the pub.'

'No, of course not. Just trying to—'

'There's no point trying to break the ice where I'm concerned. There's ice a mile thick between us, after what you've done.'

'Nicely put,' said Fiona. 'Perhaps you should be the writer?'

'Get on with it, Fiona. I haven't got all evening.' The longer Abbie stared at Fiona, the bigger and stronger she was starting to feel – like a tough-talking woman from an American movie. Someone who would stand for nothing – who would not flinch from wringing the neck of this frail, washed-out woman who had harmed her daughters.

Fiona's voice was tinny, but her enunciation, as always, was perfect. 'I'm truly sorry for what I did.' She could have been a small girl apologizing to her mother for breaking a vase.

'Have you *any idea* what you did?' Abbie spoke slowly, her voice coming out unusually deep and resonant compared with Fiona's. She was aware of the man opposite listening in and discovered she didn't mind, that she felt empowered, if anything, by having an audience.

'I know I did wrong. I should never have read my work to your twins.' Fiona's voice was little more than a whisper.

Speak up, Abbie wanted to say, so everyone can hear you. 'Your *work*, as you call it – was a piece of vile, nasty, violent, porno-graphic—'

'No, it wasn't. There was nothing remotely pornographic about it. They were drawings, not photos, and there was nothing explic-itly sexual about them.'

Abbie's heart was beginning to thud. She was hot under her thick woollen jacket and her skin felt itchy and sore. She longed to be out in the cold air. 'Fiona – you forget that I have actually seen your story.'

'Only one of them.'

'The two main characters were female twins. The same age as Lizzie and Sarah – with faces exactly like theirs.'

'They were never meant to be your girls. They were much older.'

'Lizzie and Sarah identified with them. They even decided which one was which.'

'They weren't meant to do that. It was just a story.'

'Do you really expect me to believe you?' Abbie heard her own words come out so slowly it seemed she would never draw breath again. Everything around her seemed to be slowly freezing up – Fiona's blinking, the man with his drink, the thumping background music someone had just turned on.

'The thing about the faces – they just came out that way. It sometimes happens when you don't mean it to. You base your char-acters on real people without realizing it. Keith says it happens in his books. He told me that once—'

'Fiona, I am not interested in Keith's books. Nor in your draw-ings – except that you used my children as models and then read them the stuff. Showed them pictures of – God, I can hardly say it – of a monster *raping* them – making them *bleed*. Sarah is terrified now at the thought of sex. Says she never wants to have it, ever in her life.' Abbie looked away from Fiona's eyes, which seemed to have stopped blinking. She caught the gaze of the man opposite, who was listening with interest. She blushed and looked down, no longer wanting an audience.

'The pictures did not show them being raped.'

'They very nearly did. It didn't take much imagination.'

'That's the whole point. It's what the reader brings to it. You're an adult and you seem to have rather an unpleasant mind, if you don't mind my saying so. That's why you saw it as rape. Children are so much more innocent – they would only see a monster attacking them.'

'He made them bleed. You could see it in the pictures.'

'That's because he bit them.'

'Sarah and Lizzie said it was rape.'

'I think if you look again, Abbie, you'll find it a good deal less explicit than you seem to think. Your girls, for whatever reason, may have read something more into it. Perhaps they've been reading other adult stuff or watching clips on the internet. Children are very sophisticated nowadays.'

'Lizzie and Sarah have never watched anything like that.'

'How can you be so sure? You don't know what they see, at friends' houses and so on. You can't control them all the time.'

'Fiona – that stuff you showed them was sickening. My daughters are seeing a psychologist twice a week. All four of us are having a family session on Saturdays. Sarah has had nightmares. Lizzie has been behaving badly at school. Both of them have trouble paying attention in class.'

'I've already said I'm sorry.'

'You've spent the last ten minutes trying to defend yourself.'

'Only because you exaggerate it all so much.'

Abbie shook her head, removed her hand from over her glass and took another sip. Her mouth was dry and she wished she had more lemonade.

'Like another drink now?' Fiona asked.

'No.' Abbie glared at the man opposite, who looked away. 'What possessed you to write and draw such stuff in the first place?'

Fiona took a slow drink of lager. 'As Keith always says, you don't choose what you write about – it chooses you.'

'That doesn't give you licence to—'

'You asked me a question, Abbie. Give me a chance to explain.'

'Go on then, if you must.'

'Dark, mysterious stories interest me. Ones with an element of danger. They always have. When I was young I spent my holidays with a great-aunt. She could have been a writer if she'd had the chance. She had a fantastic imagination – she created elves and princes, werewolves and nymphs. A mixture of ancient myth and modern culture. In some ways her stories were terrifying – but they enthralled me. She encouraged me to draw and write my own. That's what got me interested in art.' She paused. 'I've done well. My great-aunt would be proud of me.'

'Yes, you have done well. I'm not questioning your ability. But that makes it even worse, that you're using your gifts for such horrible—'

'I haven't finished. Let me go on, Abbie. Please.'

Abbie gave a grunt.

Fiona continued. 'I was a lonely child, without brothers and sisters or friends. I created whole worlds to entertain myself.'

'Lots of children do that.'

'And ever since, I've wanted to share those worlds with other children. Is that so bad?'

'It wouldn't be, if the stuff wasn't so vile.'

'I accept I misjudged the age group. I should have shown those stories to Keith first.'

'I still can't understand why you didn't.'

'I didn't want his critical comments. I wanted to try out my work on the kind of people it was written for.'

'I find it difficult to believe you could have got it so wrong.'

'I can only apologize. Please forgive me, Abbie.' The flash had gone from Fiona's eyes and she looked weak and tired again, child-like and timid.

'I can't forgive you, Fiona. It's not up to me to forgive. I'm not the one you harmed. The only people who can ever forgive you are my daughters, in years to come. Whether they'll be able to, I don't know. But it's up to them.'

'Is there any chance I could meet them? Just briefly, to say I'm sorry?'

'Fiona – are you completely mad? No, no and no. I'm not letting you near Sarah and Lizzie ever again. Ever! Got that?'

Fiona raised a hand and brushed back her hair from her face. 'Yes. I get it.'

Abbie's mobile phone gave a beep from within her handbag. It was probably Kate checking up on her.

'It's so hot in here. I think I might faint,' said Fiona.

'You've said your piece – we should probably leave. In fact, why don't you go now? I need to visit the loo, then I'm going home.'

'I'm feeling claustrophobic. I need air. Let's walk outside. There's one more thing I need to say.'

'Is your car nearby?'

'The other end of the promenade. Where's yours?'

'I didn't bring my car. I walked down.'

'In the rain?'

'It wasn't raining then – just foggy.'

'Will you walk along with me, Abbie, to my car? Then I'll give you a lift home, if you like.'

'No, thanks. I'd prefer to walk.'

Fiona stood up and started to work her arms into the sleeves of her enormous coat. Abbie headed for the bathroom, hoping that Fiona would have gone when she emerged. In the cubicle, she read Kate's text, which said simply, 'How's it going?'

She rang the number, and Kate answered within seconds. 'Are you OK? Did she turn up? What's happening?'

'I'm fine. Yes, she turned up. She started by apologizing and ended up trying to justify herself.'

'So has she gone now?'

'I hope so – but I've a feeling she's waiting outside for me. She said she had something else to tell me. We may walk along the promenade for a bit.'

'Are you mad?'

'Fiona's feeling a bit dizzy. She needs some fresh air.'

'Abbie, you will never cease to amaze me. You actually sound sorry for her.'

'Of course I'm not. I just want to get rid of her, stop her pestering me. If I let her say this one last thing....'

'Then there'll be another and another and—'

'No there won't. I've told her in no uncertain terms not to bother me again. Listen – I'll call you from home in half an hour and tell you all about it.'

'Half an hour?'

'I haven't got the car – I walked down to the pub.'

'In this weather?'

'I needed to clear my head. Look, I must go. With a bit of luck she'll have got fed up with waiting and left.'

'I'll keep my phone beside me – call if you need help.'

As Abbie emerged from the toilets she saw Fiona, who had struck up a conversation with the man sitting nearby. She showed no further signs of claustrophobia or dizziness and her face had taken on a little colour.

The man made a parting comment Abbie didn't catch but which made Fiona laugh. Abbie zipped her jacket and pulled on her gloves. The rain was heavier, the uneven promenade filling up with deep black puddles that looked like oil. The sea, barely visible in the light from the street lamps, heaved up to the sea wall, still occasionally spilling over. It was an unusually high tide for December. The air was cold and Abbie pulled her scarf more tightly round her neck. She began to wish she had brought her own car after all and that she hadn't allowed herself to be talked into hearing Fiona's 'one more thing'.

'I still feel a bit unsteady. May I take your arm?'

Abbie held out her arm without thinking, and then wished she hadn't. Having Fiona clinging to her like an old woman or small child was an odd and unnerving sensation. She remembered walking with the twins a few years ago, when they had appeared to compete over who could pull harder on her arms.

'So, you and Keith – what's the story?' Fiona asked.

'I thought you were going to tell me one final thing, not ask questions?'

They passed under a street lamp and Fiona's face glowed in the diffuse orange light. Their pace was slow and Abbie was very cold.

'It's all part of it. You'll see in a minute. Just tell me about Keith – he's living with you again, isn't he?'

'What makes you think that?'

'What you said earlier, about going to see a counsellor together.'

Abbie was about to assure her that, no, Keith was not living with her. But something stopped her. She didn't owe Fiona any explanations. If Fiona wanted to think she and Keith were back together, let her.

'It's none of your business what Keith and I do.'

Abbie felt, rather than heard, Fiona's growl. It seemed to travel in a wave from Fiona's thickly coated arm to hers, sending a shiver through her body that left her colder than ever.

'So you are back together. I thought so.'

'We're spending time together. It's partly to help the girls.' Keep Fiona guessing – that was a good tactic. Make her suffer.

'That's a good one.'

'It's true.'

'And do you like the things I taught him?'

'What?'

'The poor guy was stuck in adolescence where sex was concerned.'

'I've no idea what you mean.' A wave surged over the wall and emptied part of itself into the top of Abbie's boots. It was shockingly cold.

'I felt so sorry for him.'

Fiona's arm was pulling down with increasing weight on hers – it was as though she was pleading to be picked up and carried. Abbie wrenched her shoulder, trying to release the grip, but Fiona clung even harder.

'What are you talking about?'

'Your pathetic sex life.'

'Keith and I always had a good sex life. Not that it's any of your business.'

'Oh, I made it my business to educate him. You'll be feeling the benefits now, now doubt. Don't worry – I haven't got HIV. I haven't contaminated your precious ex.'

Abbie yanked harder this time and managed to release her arm from Fiona's grip. 'Right – that's enough. I'm going.'

'Just tell me, Abbie. Satisfy my curiosity. *Are* you sleeping together again? Keith told me so much about you – your frigidity, your prudishness, your total inability to have fun. I felt sorry for him and for the twins, too – having you for a mother. Maybe I taught them some useful things after all. That sex can be dangerous and exciting – that fear is part of pleasure. Don't think for a minute they didn't enjoy those stories, Abbie. They may have been frightened, but I saw their little faces light up. I saw—'

Abbie saw only a blur as her hand, apparently of its own accord, slapped Fiona on the cheek. 'How dare you? How dare you say those things about my girls?'

Fiona made no sound but jumped back from the blow and began to rummage in her pocket – searching, Abbie supposed, for a tissue. She was about to offer one of her own when the ludicrousness of doing so struck her. Instead her hand, now relieved of its glove, followed up the slap with several more. 'Now get out of our lives for ever. Go away!'

Fiona flinched with each blow but stood her ground, face aglow, as though this was what she had been waiting for. When Abbie stopped, she said, 'You want to use violence, do you? That's fine with me. You just keep on slapping me while I stab you with this.' She turned the hand that had emerged from her pocket, revealing not a tissue but a small knife that caught the streetlight on its blade. 'I'm warning you – stay away from Keith. I love him in a way you could never dream of. I want him back and I'll do anything to get him.'

The fear that gripped Abbie was like nothing she had ever known. An icy hand inside her chest gripped and squeezed, the way she imagined a heart attack would feel. It seemed impossible her heart could beat any faster. She opened her mouth to scream but no sound came out. Fiona had grabbed Abbie's scarf and was tugging on it as though to strangle her. In Fiona's white hand, which struck Abbie for the first time as ridiculously small, like a child's, was the knife – an inch or so from Abbie's right eye. Too close to focus properly, but clear enough to trigger a new burst of adrenalin, to bring vomit to her throat and dissolve the muscles in her legs.

Then, somehow, she found words. 'Fiona – stop! This is stupid.'

Fiona didn't speak. Her eyes had glazed over in a way that frightened Abbie almost as much as the knife. It was as though the iris had merged with the cornea – all was that same dead-fish-like greyish-white.

'Fiona – if you kill me, you'll go to jail.'

Fiona's voice was all the more menacing for its tinkling, girlish tone. 'Keith is part of me. We belong together. Nothing can stop that.'

'I lied about me and Keith. We're not together. Fiona – let me go!'

'You're vile and ugly and you don't deserve him.'

Abbie struggled to break free but the scarf held her. As Fiona's cold hand closed over her mouth, she managed to produce a scream.

Fiona's other hand slipped down and touched the knife to Abbie's throat.

chapter eighteen

Abbie didn't know how long they stayed like that. After the scream, her eyes snapped shut and her body froze. She tried to tell herself that if she didn't struggle, Fiona wouldn't harm her. Yet she didn't really believe it. That knife might at any moment pierce her skin and find its way to the carotid artery. How long would she go on living after the artery was punctured? One second, five, half a minute or more? Would she see her own blood pumping out of her, hot and frothing?

The thumping of her heart turned into pounding footsteps and a shrill voice. 'Let her go! I've got a knife.'

Abbie opened her eyes and saw Kate with something in her hand – something cylindrical and solid Abbie could swear was a cucumber – which she waved in Fiona's face.

'I said let her go, you lunatic!'

It wasn't Abbie's story any more – she was as detached from it now as from a film on TV – a disappointing film you felt no compulsion to watch. Fiona, seeing the cucumber, gave a little snort. She was still holding the knife to Abbie's throat and her eyes were glazed over, gleaming in the light from Kate's torch. The hand had gone from Abbie's mouth but the grip on her scarf did not slacken and her head was beginning to spin from lack of oxygen.

Then came a flash of metal in the torchlight and the cucumber became a knife – ah, now she understood: the cucumber had *held* a knife, concealed in its watery flesh. There was a squelching sound as it emerged, followed by a thud and a splash as the cucumber fell into one of the puddles around Abbie's feet.

Kate, she saw, was holding a knife to Fiona's throat. Abbie reflected that the scene had a curious symmetry about it. Perhaps this film was better than she'd thought.

Fiona squealed and let go of Abbie's scarf. Abbie took in sweet cold air and almost fell over with the shock of it. Fiona dropped her knife and set off at a run with Kate in close pursuit.

'Kate, leave her – let her go!' Abbie bent over to pick up Fiona's knife and the cucumber. It seemed important to be tidy. Blood rushed to her head and she found herself sitting in icy water. Then Kate's arm was there, clad in a soft tracksuit material, encircling Abbie and pulling her to her feet.

Kate's face was flushed and she was out of breath. 'It's OK. She's gone.'

Abbie looked in turn at the cucumber in her left hand and the knife in her right. Then she gazed into Kate's face. 'How did you know? Why did you have these with you?'

'You're shaking. And you're wet through.' Kate led Abbie to the sea wall, where they sat down, ignoring the fact that it was drenched by the high tide. Abbie couldn't get much wetter, anyway, and Kate didn't seem to care.

Kate took a Mars bar from her pocket, tore it open and broke off a chunk. 'Here – eat this. You need blood sugar.'

Abbie took it without objection. It tasted wonderful. 'I don't understand,' she mumbled. 'How did you know to come? How did you know Fiona had a knife?'

'I heard you scream.'

'What, all the way from Dundee?'

'Of course not, you loony. I was just along the promenade. Parked my car at the other end. Next to what I assume is Fiona's Clio. Bright yellow. I was already heading your way – then I heard you and started to run.'

'But why were you there in the first place?'

'Here – have another piece. When you told me you were meeting Fiona in the Red Fox I thought I'd drive along to Carleith, just in case. You know I never trusted her. Seems I was right.'

'So – when you texted me...?'

'I was already parked here. My dad took a bit of persuading to let me use his car again. Especially as I managed to give it a little scrape this afternoon. But I told him I'd get some beer for him while I was out – that clinched it. I've been waiting in the car all the time you were chatting. Bloody long time, too. I was frozen.'

'And the knife...?'

'Again – just in case. Be prepared and all that.'

'The cucumber?'

'Happened to be lying on the work surface in the kitchen. Mum got me to make her a salad. Seemed a good way to carry the knife – I just shoved the blade in.'

'You came rushing up with that knife when you saw Fiona holding me?'

'Not much else I could do, really.'

'You were very brave. And possibly very stupid.'

'There wasn't time to think. If I'd called the police instead – how long would it have taken them to get here?'

'We should call them now. She might come back.' Abbie peered into the darkness. The rain had eased off to a misty drizzle.

'She won't come back. I scared her off for good with my cucumber.'

Abbie found herself giggling, unable to stop. Kate's arm went round her shoulder. 'Come on – let's get you home. We'll think about phoning the police after that. First thing is to get you tucked up with a mug of cocoa and a hot-water bottle.'

'That does sound nice.'

Less than ten minutes later, Kate pulled up outside Abbie's bungalow. Another car was parked across the entrance to her drive – a police car with its lights on.

Two uniformed policemen got out and announced rather unnecessarily that they were from Tayside Police.

After a short interchange in which Kate and Abbie's identities were checked and confirmed, one of the policemen said, 'Mrs Brinnett, you are under arrest for possession of an offensive weapon in a public place. Ms Anderson, you are under arrest for assault. You do not have to say anything....'

The words, familiar from TV police dramas, washed over Abbie. 'But ... we didn't. It was her, it was Fiona....'

'Could you show me what you have in your hands, Mrs Brinnett?'

In one hand, Abbie was clutching Fiona's knife. In the other, for some reason, was the cucumber.

'Would you get in the car, please? We need to take you to the station for questioning.'

'You've got it all wrong. It was Fiona – she held the knife at me. This is *her* knife.'

As they got in the car, Abbie noticed Kate pushing her own knife down to the bottom of her bag.

'Bill – is that you? Something awful's happened. I'm at the police station – I've been arrested for having a knife.' Abbie, who had felt unexpectedly calm during the ride in the police car and a preliminary interview at the station, was surprised to hear the shake in her voice.

'Abbie, what the hell—?'

'I'm under arrest. I can't stay on the phone for long. Fiona tried to kill me. Kate ran up with a knife in a cucumber. She—'

'Abbie, are you feeling all right?'

'Yes, I'm fine. No, of course I'm not. I have to go for another interview. Fiona held a knife to my throat. The police don't seem to believe us. Please, please come....'

Bill mumbled something inaudible and then the phone went dead.

A car rumbled past the house and Abbie peered behind the curtain and watched it go on its way. Not Bill. It had been a stupid idea to ring him from the police station at ten to midnight. He hadn't seemed to understand a word she said. Not surprising, perhaps, since he'd been half-asleep and she hadn't told her story well. Perhaps he had assumed she was drunk.

Kate was in the twins' room, presumably fast asleep. They'd got back at 3.15 a.m., having finally convinced the police of their story. Kate had been issued with a caution for carrying an offensive weapon.

Unable to sleep, Abbie had spent the last three hours kneeling on the kitchen floor digging out ingrained dirt from between the tiles. It was the only way she could think of to pass the time. Every time a car drove by, she jumped up to see if it was Bill. Now, at 6.30 a.m., she had begun to give up hope.

She should have done the sensible thing and phoned Keith. Not that he could have driven up to see her, since he had the twins – but he would have listened while she told the gruesome tale.

But the person she had most wanted during that panicky, unreal time at the station was Bill.

Even if he had understood her story, it was too much to ask him to drive all the way to Dundee. Six at best, on a dark, stormy night, when he probably had meetings next day. It was more than could be expected of anyone – especially of a man she hadn't spoken to for more than three weeks – a man who believed she was back together with Keith.

The curiously satisfying task of digging out the dirt from her floor tiles finished, she wandered into the living-room and sat down on the sofa, pulling a blanket over her legs.

The doorbell disturbed her from the deep sleep that had unexpectedly overtaken her. She scrabbled with the key in the lock, her fingers clumsy and stiff.

On the drive stood Bill, looking grey, cold and exhausted. Without thinking, she held out her arms and he stepped into them.

Minutes later as they sat side by side on the sofa, Abbie began her story. She had got no further than Fiona's second phone call when Bill shook his head. 'Abbie – I'm sorry. You'll have to start again. You told me on the phone you'd been arrested – I don't understand.'

'Sorry. That bit comes later. Shall I make some coffee?'

'That would be wonderful.'

Abbie headed for the kitchen, where she filled the kettle. Bill followed her.

'I'm so glad you're here. I didn't think you'd come.'

'I had to come, after all that stuff you said.' A shadow crossed his brow. 'It is true, is it? You didn't spin me some fairy tale?'

'Of course it's true. As if I'd get you to come all this way on false pretences....'

'No. Of course you wouldn't. I'm sorry.'

'Would you like some food?'

'No. What I really need is to lie down. My back's killing me.'

'You can have my bed. I'm sleeping on the sofa.'

'So where's Keith?'

'Keith? He's in Edinburgh with the twins.'

'Why?'

'He's taken them to his flat for the weekend. For a change. To give me a bit of a rest.'

'He's kept his flat, then?'

'Of course he's kept his flat.'

'I thought that maybe now you were back together, he'd have sold it. But I suppose he can afford to keep it on.'

Abbie stopped in the middle of pouring hot water into a mug. 'Bill – I told you. Keith and I are *not* back together. Neither of us wants that. Keith has been coming for weekends so we can spend time with the girls and go to therapy sessions together.'

Bill said nothing so she put milk in his coffee before resuming. 'Our marriage is well and truly over. We are only getting together for the sake of the twins. Please believe me.'

Bill looked as though it was all too much to take in. 'Sorry. I've just driven for nearly seven hours with only one stop. I'm completely knackered.'

'You have some sleep, then. Would you rather stay on the sofa? I'll leave you in peace. I can explain everything later, when you feel rested.'

Bill, sitting now, took a swig of scalding coffee and winced. 'That's better. No, I'll be all right in a minute. I want to know what happened. Are you sure you're OK? Not hurt?'

'No, not hurt. Suffering from a bit of shock. I've never been held at knifepoint before.'

'At knifepoint?'

'It's all true, Bill. I didn't lie to you. Fiona attacked me. If it wasn't for Kate—'

'But why the hell...?'

'Because, it appears, Fiona is a nutter. She threatened me with a knife. When Kate frightened her off, she called the police and told them *we* attacked *her*. That's why they arrested us. The police caught up with her car halfway to Aberdeen – she was driving like a maniac. I should never have agreed to meet her. Kate didn't want me to. When I think what she might have done to the twins....' Abbie's eyes filled with tears.

Bill's arm was round her. 'It's OK. They've got her now. She won't do any more harm.'

'I should have reported her, after the stuff with the stories. I wanted to, but Keith didn't. I should never have listened to him.'

'I still don't understand why the police arrested you and Kate.'

'They believed Fiona's story. I'll tell you the rest in the morning. I'm feeling very sleepy now.'

Bill adjusted the cushion for Abbie's head and within a few seconds she was in a deep sleep.

Abbie woke to hear pans clattering in the kitchen. Kate must be cooking breakfast. Bill was asleep beside her, making faint and melodious snores. She pulled herself upright as gently as she could to avoid disturbing him.

After a few moments, his eyes opened. 'Abbie – I love you.'

'What?'

'I love you. Will you marry me?'

She felt obliged to remind him. 'But you broke things off. You thought I was back with Keith. You wanted nothing more to do with me.'

'Tell me, Abbie – why did you phone me from the station? Wasn't there anyone closer than three hundred and sixty miles away you could have called?'

'I'm sorry. I should have called Keith. Or my neighbours.'

'You don't need to apologize. I just want to know why you chose me.'

'You were the person I wanted.'

'That's all I need to hear.' He drew his finger lightly across her forehead. The sensation was delightful.

He continued, 'Now, will you answer my question?'

'Is "yes" a good answer?'

'It's the answer I was hoping for.'

Kate opened the living door ten minutes later, carrying a plate of bacon, eggs and sausages, and found them kissing.

Bill devoured his breakfast while Abbie and Kate between them told the full story of the night's events.

'So if Kate hadn't come along, I might be dead,' Abbie concluded.

'She'd never have killed you,' said Kate, not sounding fully convinced.

'She looked as though she meant to.'

'You're a brave woman, Kate,' said Bill. 'Though an alternative would have been to call the police and tell them you feared for Abbie's safety.'

'They'd never have believed me. All I had to go on was a vague feeling of distrust. I didn't know Fiona was going to bring a knife.'

'But you brought one of your own, just in case?'

'And a cucumber,' said Abbie.

'It was lying on the kitchen table beside the knife. I thought it would make a good – what's that thing cowboys keep their knives in?'

'Holster,' said Abbie.

'No – scabbard,' said Bill.

'Well, whatever. Fiona laughed when she saw the cucumber. But when I pulled the knife out, she changed her tune.'

'It sounds like some crazy comedy sketch,' said Bill.

'It didn't feel like it, I can tell you,' said Abbie. 'I was petrified. Never been anywhere near as scared as that in my life.'

'I'm not surprised. Fiona must be unhinged, to threaten you like that.'

'We told the police everything – the way she read her stories to the twins, the whole lot. They told us she'll be given tests. If she's not sent to prison for assault, she'll be made to have psychiatric treatment.'

'More bacon, Bill? Abbie? There's plenty left in the pan,' said Kate.

'No, I'm fine, thanks,' Abbie replied. 'What about you – you've hardly eaten a thing?'

Kate had been toying with the solitary sausage on her plate. 'I'm not hungry. Made me feel a bit sick, to be honest, the smell of cooking.'

'That's not like you,' said Abbie. 'Maybe it's the shock. Would you like some cereal instead?'

Kate shuddered. 'No thanks. I'm not hungry at all. In fact, if you don't mind, I think I'll go back to bed for a while.'

Bill tackled the washing up and Abbie restored the kitchen to order, since Kate had removed all the pans from the cupboards in order to find the right one and had somehow managed to splash bacon fat on every surface.

The phone rang and Abbie pushed the saucepan she was holding into the cupboard. She hadn't told Keith, yet, what had happened. Could he somehow have heard?

But the voice on the line was shrill, female and angry. The words were difficult to make out and for a few horrible seconds Abbie thought it was Fiona. But no – this was an older woman.

'I'm sorry – could you speak more slowly? Who did you say you were?'

'Molly Anderson. Kate's mother. Is she with you?'

'Kate? Yes, she's here. Didn't you know?' Abbie had assumed Kate had phoned her parents from the station to tell them where she was and let them know she was going home with Abbie.

'Last thing I knew, she was setting off last night to meet someone in a pub. In our car! I suppose she went home with them. Came crawling to you, did she, in the early hours?'

'No she did not. Mrs Anderson, Kate's been with me all the time. She was very brave – I got attacked and she came to my rescue with a knife.'

'She's got you involved in her low-life ways, has she? And I thought you were a nice woman.'

'I am a nice – Kate's a nice – look, she's here, would you like to speak to her?'

Kate appeared in the hall, eyes bleary and hair in disarray. She snatched the phone from Abbie. 'Let me deal with her.'

Abbie left them to it and returned to the kitchen.

'Now you see why I don't want to live with them,' said Kate.

Two hours later, Bill, Abbie and Kate were walking across the sands at Lunan Bay. The weather had cleared up and a faint sun was playing on the water. Bill had suggested the trip, saying he fancied some fresh air and it might do them all good to get out of the house.

'I always did understand,' said Abbie. 'Especially after meeting them at your flat that time. It was completely unreasonable, expecting you to drop your life in Dundee and move up there to look after them.'

'Yes, but it's more than that. If they were pleasant to me I might at least have considered it. Moving to Aberdeen, anyway, if not actually into their house. But I could never live with Mum. Once she heard I'd been at the police station – did you hear what she said?'

'No.'

'Well, first of all she assumed I was guilty. Before she knew anything about what happened. As though it was no more than she expected of me. Ever since – well, when I was young and had some trouble with the police – she thinks of me as a criminal. And a prostitute. And God knows what else. Not only that – but just because I forgot to tell them I was at your house, she and Dad assumed I'd gone off with their car – smashed it up or something or sold it and run off with the money. Neither of them trusts me. Yet they expect me to live with them and be their servant and kowtow to all their plans for me. I hate them!'

'Your mother did sound very worked up,' said Abbie.

'Just say "no" to them, once and for all,' suggested Bill.

'I've been telling her to do that for months,' said Abbie.

'OK, well I haven't been able to, up to now – but this is the last straw. I'll drive back there later on, deposit their car and say my goodbyes. Tell them I won't darken their doors again. That I'm staying in Dundee whatever happens.'

'That's the spirit,' said Abbie.

'Good for you,' said Bill. 'We've got a bit of news, too, as it happens.'

'Let me guess. You two are getting married?'

Abbie gasped. 'How did you work that out?'

'Well, it's pretty obvious you're back together. I'm so thrilled.' As Kate hugged Abbie and Bill in turn the sun emerged fully from a cloud and the pale, empty shoreline took on a look of summer.

'It's going to take a while to work things out,' said Abbie. 'Bill has to find a job up here.'

'Either that or go freelance. And I want to sort things out with my sons before I move.'

'Yes, and the twins will need some time to get to know Bill,' said Abbie.

'So you'll still be in Dundee?'

'That's the plan,' said Abbie. 'I don't want to take Sarah and Lizzie too far from Keith. It's a bit easier for Bill as his boys are older, though of course it's complicated with Jon.'

'Well, I'm glad you're staying here,' said Kate. 'Very glad. I'd miss you.'

'I'd miss you, too,' said Abbie.

Kate stopped beside a pool of water and dabbled the toes of her trainers in it, looking down. 'I've got a bit more news of my own, as it happens.'

'What's that?' asked Bill.

Something in Kate's voice made Abbie peer into her face. 'I thought you seemed different. You're not...?'

'Pregnant? Not that I know of.' Kate's face took on a thoughtful look, followed by one of concentration, as though she was doing mental arithmetic.

'Sorry,' said Abbie. 'I don't know what made me think of that.'

'It's not as unlikely as it was. Steve and I have been out a couple of times.'

'I did wonder if there was something going on,' said Abbie.

'It's early days and I don't know what will happen. So don't start saying, "I told you so." But anyway, that's not the thing I was going to tell you.'

'Tell us, then.'

'I've been accepted by the Computing Department to do a part-time degree. As long as I pass some exams first. I've already put my name down for evening classes.'

'That's wonderful, Kate! Well done!'

Abbie and Bill hugged Kate in turn.

'I always knew you could do it,' said Abbie.

'Well, I finally plucked up the courage, after all that business with my parents. Time I took charge of my own life.'

The three of them continued their walk across the sands. After a few minutes, Kate clutched her throat and crouched down over a pool of water. 'Just walk on, please. I'll be with you very soon.'